THE TREASURE OF TEPATAMWA

The Seventh Book of Dubious Magic

by RENOIR

Raising a glass to Randy.

Thank you, Maurie.

And, as ever,

for my darling Muse Meredith.

Table of Contents

1 ME AND MY MAN

I want to write all of this down before I forget any detail. It seems unlikely that I ever would, there's so much strangeness about it. But so much strangeness seems to attend the man I've chosen to spend my life with that perhaps some of these details will eventually get 'crowded out'. There's already been so much that's happened in the time we've been together, this story is another part of it. I suspect there'll be more to come.

A big part of what I'm writing down I can vouch for, because I was there. Sometimes I've had to rely on second-hand information, but most of that has come from reliable sources, one of whom I'd trust with my life (and have).

My name is Elizabeth McKew. Most people call me Elizabeth. People who I don't like get to call me Ms. McKew, or "Yes, ma'am". Some of the people I don't like apparently call me, "Oh. Her."

One person gets to call me Q. It comes from McKew, obviously, but it's also short for QE2, as in Queen Elizabeth. I had a husband who used to call me Queenie. I don't like to be reminded of him, which is why only one person gets to call me Q. More about that one later.

I used to be a Public Servant. I was a good one, too. Before that I was a secretary for a private consulting firm. Good at that, too. I've had a few administrative jobs over the years, and everyone I've ever worked for has told me they didn't want me to leave. That's always a nice thing to hear, but for various reasons I moved on anyway.

Now though, I'm an author. Well, I aspire to be. Let me rephrase that – I *am* an author and I aspire to be a *published* author. When my first novel is finished, which will be soon, I hope.

I've left the Aussie capital Canberra (my last place of paid employment) and now I'm travelling the world. I *was* chasing my family history, but now I'm chasing stories attached to it.

You see, I'm descended from Vikings who settled in the islands to the north and west of Scotland and I'd decided I want to write about their culture and their history. While I was researching that, I stumbled onto one particularly interesting ancestor.

'Prince Henry' of Orkney, who wasn't really a prince at all, but had ambitions of establishing his own kingdom. This was way back in the late 1300s and early 1400s. That's where it gets interesting. We're talking about the best part of a century before Columbus took off from Spain.

Henry, it seems, was inspired by *his* Viking ancestors. He set sail to parts unknown, and ended up on the east coast of what we now call America. I've come looking for evidence of that. There are bits and pieces that I've read, and I want to find out more.

Not long ago we were in Norway, where someone shot me and I nearly died. What saved me apparently was a combination of luck (I fell into a snowdrift that slowed down all my vital signs and preserved me) and the efforts of my boyfriend.

I promised before I'd tell you more about him. He's the one who came up with the nickname Q. That's him over there, in the purple t-shirt. John B. Stewart. He's another ex-Public Servant out of Canberra. Well, that's where we met. Not where he's originally from. As near as I can tell he's not quite sure where he's originally from.

He spent part of his childhood in Brisbane, but doesn't know, or at least remember, anything of the first ten years of his life. Or if he does, he hasn't told anyone, including me.

I call him my 'boyfriend', but that seems an inadequate word. As I explore being a writer I'm finding that's a recurring problem with the English language. JB isn't just my boyfriend. He's my best friend, and my lover – neither of which quite convey the depth of what I feel for him. I like the French term 'beau' – perhaps that's what I'll call him.

He'll tell anyone who'll listen that he's "just an ordinary bloke." He's not. You wouldn't think it to look at him. He's got nothing particularly special about him. He could be a bit tidier. Trim his hair? Either grow a real beard or stand closer to the razor? To be fair, at one point the beard was starting to develop nicely, but part of it got burned off in a fire when we were in Scotland and it's never looked quite right since.

He could dress better more often. Most of the time you'll only see him in jeans and a purple t-shirt. He has other purple shirts. I've seen a Hawaiian one, and I know he has a purple silk dress shirt, because I bought it for him. He's not unusually tall or especially handsome.

What *is* remarkable about John B. is – well, there are two things really, to my mind.

One is our relationship. He loves me. He doesn't just say that he loves me. I've heard that before. To have faith in the truth of those words is a new and pretty fabulous experience for me.

The other special thing about my beau is that he's a wizard. Yes, I know that sounds odd, and I struggled to come to terms with it too. But clearly he can do magic. It started a while ago, back in Canberra. He hit his head on a poker machine. I wasn't there. It was before we were together, but I gather there was rather a lot of single malt whisky involved. That was commonplace for John B. at the time, although he's cut down quite a bit. He doesn't live on the stuff the way he reckons he used to. He thanks me for that, which is nice.

I admit I don't understand this magic of his. It puzzles me. Frankly, there are times when it scares me, but it seems to work. He wishes for things, and they happen, although not always in a way you'd predict. Strange ways sometimes, but happen they do. It's saved my life, and other people's, including his own.

As I said, we were in Norway. After the incident in which I was shot, apparently all of the people who were somehow responsible for that are now dead. JB says he never laid a hand on any of them, and I believe him. But a series of… unfortunate incidents befell all of them. It seems that's how his magic works. Our friend Wilko calls John B. a 'walking improbability field' – peculiar coincidences happen around him a lot.

 Much as I liked Norway, and the friends we made there, once I'd properly recovered I really wanted to move on. The story of Prince Henry of Orkney had me intrigued, and that's what led us to where this adventure took place.

.o0o.

2 TRAVEL, BUGGED

That 'where' was the coast of Maine in the northern USA. I was searching for evidence of the colony Henry established six hundred years ago.

They say that 'getting there is half the fun'. Not this time it wasn't.

We were flying in to Chicago. The plan was to get a train across from there to Boston, and then head up to Maine. It was a long flight. I'd slept, on and off, but never really got comfortable. Instead, I'd settled in to enjoying some decent wine and some movies.

In hindsight I should have agreed with JB's suggestion that we fly first class. But no, I didn't want to feel like we were being "posh". I suppose I could hear my mother's voice in my head. She despised "posh" – what mattered to her was "proper". I spent far too much of my life trying to live up to that before I realised they were her rules not mine, but for all that I'm trying to beat that mindset, sometimes my subconscious betrays me. I think this was one of them. I was all for flying economy, out of habit I suppose, but JB pointed out that we didn't need to.

John B. isn't short of money, not that you'd know by looking at him. He's not ostentatious – I think perhaps he feels a little awkward about how he came by his wealth. It is, admittedly, a strange story. Another one. I was there. He'd been abducted by a Russian scientist and held prisoner on a little island in Bass Strait – I did tell you strangeness and JB are regular companions. I don't know quite why that Doctor Solovyev wanted him or what he was doing to him in his strange experiments, but somehow JB gained access to a Swiss bank account the Russian had been building up into a very substantial amount for years.

The scientist and his two equally unpleasant assistants came to a messy end. I don't lament the passing of any of them, I must admit. Especially the big ugly bruiser who'd made no secret of his desire to kick in my rib cage. The bugger had made a start on the job too, before he died. No loss.

But out of all of that came what John B. describes as his 'endowment', which he uses to keep a credit card topped up.

Did you ever read Norman Lindsay's *The Magic Pudding*? As much as you eat, the pudding never runs out? That's what this credit card is like.

So my beau was right, we didn't *have* to fly economy. He insisted it wasn't about the 'showing off' of first class, rather that he was concerned about my comfort, while I was still recovering from being shot in the back. It was a fair point, I had to concede, and so we settled on the compromise of business class.

I know that some people who've only ever flown economy have the idea that the folks who fly further forward are somehow better behaved. Let me tell you, like the song says, 'it ain't necessarily so'. Just because someone pays more money for their seat doesn't mean they treat it, or anyone around them, with any respect.

Unfortunately I was stuck behind just such a ratbag.

John B was oblivious. He might even have been asleep, although I could hear the Beatles' '*Don't Pass Me By*' playing very loudly in his headset.

I was sitting behind a portly youngish man with a buzz-cut hairstyle. He might have thought he looked like a US Marine, but he more resembled the Three Stooges' Curly Joe.

The pudgy passenger suddenly decided to turn his seat into a day bed, and threw his weight into reclining the seat back as far as it would go. The idea of checking with the person sitting behind him never entered the nubbin of his head.

My tray table bucked and bounced, sending my cup flying. Luckily there hadn't been much wine left in it, and most of the spillage hit the wall and floor rather than my clothes. Nonetheless, I was mightily peeved, and swatted the back of the man's headrest with the palm of my hand.

"Hey! Quit that! I'm trying to sleep!" he protested angrily.

"And I'm trying to enjoy a quiet drink and a movie!" I snapped back. "I'd rather do that without your head in my lap."

"I can put my seat back if I want to! That's why they make them this way."

The heated exchange turned out to have filtered through the guitar solo John B. had been trying to enjoy. He removed his headset and laid what he probably hoped was a soothing hand on my leg as he leaned forward and quietly said to the pudgy man, "Do you have to lie the seat as far back as it will go?"

"It's how I'm comfortable!" said Buzz-cut defensively.

"It's not comfortable for the young lady behind you," John B. pointed out.

"That's not my problem," said the passenger in front.

 With great effort I bit my tongue, recognizing that John B. was trying to be diplomatic on my behalf, and that it was rather a new role for him.

"You might at least look back and see if there's anyone behind you first," JB continued patiently.

"I don't have to!"

"I can't see that it'll be very comfortable for you trying to sleep with her knees in your back," the wizard said.

"I don't care. It's my seat, I paid for it, and I want to sleep. Stop trying to disturb me!" The man was as petulant as a small child.

 John B. shook his head and said, "I wish you'd get how downright painful your sort of behavior can be."

Buzz-cut snorted, jammed plugs into his ears and pulled a sleeping mask over his eyes. He started making loud snoring noises that may or may not have been genuine.

I sat for a few moments, waiting for something to happen. All that happened was the snoring sounds got louder.

"Your magic didn't work," I said to John B., probably not hiding the disappointment in my voice.

He shrugged and said, "Just because you don't see it, doesn't mean it doesn't happen. Have a little faith. He'll get his."

I grumbled and tried to get comfortable. My beau, bless him, saw how well that wasn't working and swapped seats with me. It's only as I write this that it occurs to me just what that meant. Oh, I knew it meant he'd be sliding under Buzz-cut's bulk, but JB was quite casual about that.

"I'm not trying to watch a movie, sweetheart. Just listen to music and enjoy a decent red. I'd prefer a good single malt but the Scotch they're offering just doesn't do it for me."

So I got to sit up just as much as I wanted, drink my chardonnay and watch classic old movies until my temper cooled. Relaxed in the aisle seat, while my lovely man did everything he could to avoid looking out the window. I'd forgotten he doesn't like heights.

I think that's a fairly recent development. I've heard about him being thrown off a cliff in Hawaii – not so much from him, but from Wilko who was on the island with him. I suspect that's made him more *aware* of high places. So yeah, swapping seats was a bigger deal than it seems at first glance, and all the more reason for that slob in the seat in front to get some comeuppance.

A couple of days later John B. handed me a newspaper and pointed to a small article. It was a little curiosity piece about a freak accident on a flight from Chicago to Miami.

Alongside the article was a photo of a frowning, jowly young man with very short hair. It took a moment, but as I read the story I realized that I recognised the unattractive face.

I was thus very pleased to learn that on his connecting flight, Buzz-cut was seated behind another passenger who slammed *her* seat back into *his* lap. It was just as he was about to take his first mouthful of a fresh black coffee.

The story explained that the cup was knocked from his hand and the hot liquid splashed into his lap and poured down his right leg. He'd been rushed to hospital on landing apparently. It caused nasty scalds on his thigh and scrotum and, er, elsewhere, although the left side was remarkably untouched. I thought back to exactly what John B. had said to him on our flight. Down right painful indeed. I don't understand his magic, but sometimes I do love how it works.

I'd have liked to spend some more time in Chicago. I arrived knowing little and expecting less, but what I saw in the day and evening we spent waiting for our train was impressive. We took a lovely sunset cruise around the bay and up and down the river. It was a wonderful way to admire the architecture, and the commentary about the city's history was excellent. It wasn't a bad bottle of bubbles that John B. bought, either.

Our train was called the Lake Shore Limited. It left around 9:30 that night, and I must admit, after the plane trip and a day of being a tourist I was weary. John B. didn't have us in seats for the whole trip though. He'd booked a bedroom. Sofa and shower, and two bunks. Nice.

I got the bottom bunk – it's a foot wider than the top one, we worked out. I was in bed and trying to sleep by a quarter to ten, I reckon. JB was lying there above me reading a book about the history of Native American languages that he'd bought at a second hand bookstore. He seems to absorb history, and bits of it come out at all sorts of times. Same with various languages. He's an interesting man in a lot of ways, when I consider it.

Riding on a train is one thing. But trying to sleep on one is altogether another, certainly for me. I can see how some people find the rhythm and rattle restful, but not me, I'm afraid.

After a while I called up, "You awake, babe?"

"Yep. Are you?"

I was too tired to appreciate the joke, and just replied, "Yeah. Can't sleep either. Hey babe – wanna come on down and share a bunk for a while?"

"It'll be a bit squeezy. Are you okay with that tonight?"

"We've shared smaller, and yes, I'm *very* okay with it."

I wasn't kidding. The very first night that we slept together had been in a little guesthouse on Islay, off the Scottish coast, in a room with two single beds that I'll swear were narrower than this metre-wide bunk.

And I *was* very okay with John B. joining me. You know what? The rhythm and rattling of a train may not put me to sleep, but they do add even more interest to the art of love. Eventually I did fall asleep. Smiling, so I'm told, and I believe it. I love afterglow.

.o0o.

3 BOARDERS REPELLENT, NOT REPELLED

Extract from the diary of Mrs. Harriet Ridgeway:

Dear diary,

A most extraordinary event today. We took Brian's new boat out on its maiden voyage. That would have made the day special in any case, but as it turned out, well! Let me explain.

Brian has named the boat after me, dear thing that he is, and he's very proud of it. Sorry, that should be 'her', he keeps reminding me.

We'd set off quite early this morning, to motor around some of the islands in Casco Bay. I believe there are colonies of puffins nesting on some of the smaller ones, and I did so want to see some of the dear little things. Apparently they avoid the more inhabited islands, so in order to see them, we must go to their little hideaways.

We'd hoped to spend time enjoying the views but we ran into some annoyingly heavy banks of fog. It was typically lovely in the clear stretches of course and we were frankly enjoying the simple plea-sure of being on the water. The *Harriet* was chugging along quite merrily, and I think we'd gotten ourselves quite off the main thor-oughfares of the Bay. Is that the right term? I must ask Brian, but you know what I mean, diary.

We were back in another fog patch. Suddenly from around the headland of one of the small islands came the most extraordinary sight. A pirate ship! Well, I say ship but really it was smaller than a proper ship, more a boat really. But quite a substantial one.

I'm not making this up, diary. It looked like something out of one of those movies with Errol Flynn or that Johnny Sparrow fellow, but on a smaller scale.

I wasn't quite sure whether to believe my eyes at first, but it not only approached us, it sailed right alongside us. Well, not 'sailed'. It had three masts but no sails. It moved at a good speed though – certainly matched the *Harriet*.

Brian said later that he knew there was something wrong when he saw the skull and crossbones flag at the top of the strange boat's mast, above the basket with the curly-haired fellow in it. But I'm getting ahead of myself.

As the odd boat approached, Brian slowed down the *Harriet*, out of surprise, or even shock I suspect. Next I knew, the wooden planks on the side of the strange boat were scuffing up against *Harriet*'s lovely clean hull, and there were lines being thrown onto our deck. The fellow throwing the ropes was a remarkably good shot I must say. (Is one a 'shot' with a rope? Perhaps he was a good 'throw'?) His three ropes lassoed three quite solid fittings on our boat, then we were pulled tight in – all three lines drawn at once by, I'm sure, the biggest man I've ever seen!

Before Brian could do anything about the situation, not that I've any notion of what he might have done, a group of extraordinary figures leapt from the extraordinary boat onto our *Harriet*. They were dressed as pirates!

I confess, I thought that either I was dreaming, or we were part of some elaborate prank. The two men who were apparently the leaders were both big fellows with red hair and beards that poked out from the spotted handkerchiefs they wore as masks. I thought it was cowboys who did that?

The one with a very bushy beard brandished a cutlass, just like in the movies! The other had a much more modern-looking handgun.

He was the one that demanded that we hand over any valuables that we had on board. Of course, I told him not to be silly. Why would we have valuables out on the boat with us?

"His wallet for a start," said the taller, less overweight of the pair. Even as he said that, the bird on his shoulder… Did I mention the bird? It was a parrot (of course, I suppose). A strange green colour, with peculiar white eyes.

The appalling parrot fluttered from his shoulder onto mine, and before I realised what was happening it had snapped the chain of my necklace with its beak, and flown back to the pirate with it! I'd worn Aunt Georgia's silver and pearl piece in honour of the *Harriet*'s maiden voyage. Dear Auntie was always so fond of the water.

Another of the strangely garbed men then grasped my arm and tore off my silver bracelet. The fellow with the parrot did admonish him that there was "no need for roughness" but made no move to return my jewellery! Although when the same rough man tried to remove my wedding ring, the bearded chap did order him to "cease and desist". Yes, those were the very words he used!

He actually bowed, and explained to me that he appreciated the difference between monetary value and sentimental value! That was quite a shock! Well, the whole experience was a shock, obviously.

While my jewellery was being taken, another of the – well, pirates I suppose I must call them – accosted Brian and demanded his wallet. Brian of course objected strenuously, until confronted by another of the pirates who was quite the largest man I have ever seen in my life. Whilst the two bearded men were big, one of them quite portly, this fellow was perhaps a head taller, broad-shouldered and very solidly constructed.

My dear Brian is by no means a small man, but alongside this fellow he looked like a schoolboy. Any thoughts Brian may have had of reaching for the gun he keeps in the cabin – we always feel safer with a gun nearby – were put aside when the giant dropped a hand on his shoulder. I'm sure I have a frying pan smaller than that hand!

The giant had what I thought was a surprisingly kind voice. He held Brian's shoulder quite firmly and suggested that he shouldn't struggle. Intimidated as he was, Brian stood quietly for a moment while the fatter of the two bearded men 'frisked' him.

The pirate seemed to have no interest in Brian's cards, but was very quick to remove the quantity of notes. I'm afraid that distressed Brian, for he reacted quite badly. He couldn't move much in the big fellow's grip, but he did flail about quite violently and caught the portly chap in the face with his hand. He may even have dislodged the spotted cloth mask. I couldn't see from my position. I did notice an odd look on Brian's face for a moment – I must ask him about it when we've both calmed down.

The bearded fellow slapped Brian's hand down and said, "That was a very foolish thing to do."

Then the big one transferred his grip to pin Brian's arms to his sides – I think he actually sighed as he did so.

While all this was going on, two others of the raiding party had gone below and evidently been pilfering like common burglars! They emerged with their arms full of all our electrical equipment. I remember one of them saying, "We can get a bit for this, cap'n. This is top of the range stuff," – well, of course it is. Was. As if Brian and I would have anything else!

To which the chap with the parrot replied, "Aar, more pieces of eight – well done, me hearties!" Yes, he really did speak like this.

Apparently satisfied that they'd removed everything they wanted, the rogues went back to their ship. The man with the parrot and the giant were first to go. The other red-bearded man stood over us while the rest were leaving, undoing most of their lines as they went. He'd exchanged a few quiet words with one of the two men who'd been rummaging below, then said to Brian something like, "You're a very foolish fellow. You were asked politely not to struggle."

Brian sputtered something in outrage. I'm afraid he was somewhat incoherent. The portly bearded man shook his head and cast off the last of their lines as he climbed back onto their strange boat.

Unlikely as the craft looked, it sped away at a remarkable pace and disappeared around the headland of one of the small islands. I did worry that Brian might do something impulsive like try to pursue them, but he just sat in his captain's chair. I think the poor dear was in a state of shock.

I offered him a drink, but he said he wanted to pull himself together. I understand his distress of course. The whole experience has been utterly nerve-wracking!

I've thought it best to record my impressions in you, dear diary, while they're still fresh in my mind.

Must go – Brian is calling me. He says he's found something odd in a locker.

This was the last line that Mrs. Ridgeway wrote.

Her somewhat charred journal was recovered from debris identified as being from the Harriet. This had washed ashore on a beach in a quiet section of Casco Bay. Forensic examination suggests that the vessel had been destroyed in a violent explosion. No trace of survivors was found.

.o0o.

4 NEW ENGLAND, OLD STORIES

It was eight o'clock at night when we pulled into Boston. Again, in hindsight it's a city I'd like to spend more time in. But I felt like I was on a mission. Determined to track down all I could about 'Prince' Henry, as quickly as I could. Don't ask me what prompted the urgency. I told myself, and John B., that having made the decision to write the book I wanted to pull information together while I felt I had momentum.

The daylight part of the rail journey had been relaxing. So much so that I don't remember a great deal of it. I know we didn't leave our bedroom until after nine, and we spent a fair proportion of the day in a comfortable seat looking out the window. It's a mode of travel that suits JB. Good views, little effort, and no heights except for the occasional bridge. I've a hunch we'll be on more trains as time goes by.

I dozed rather a lot. John B. read, and we took turns fetching drinks from the snack bar two carriages along. When I was awake I was spending time immersed in my notebooks, and reading bits from John B.'s book that he thought might be relevant to me.

Did you know that there are two tribes in Nova Scotia and the north of Maine called the Micmaq and the Penikuk? *Micmac* is Gaelic for 'beloved sons', and Penicuik was the district in Scotland where Prince Henry's land was. I'm starting to really get John B.'s fascination for history!

When we got to Boston we spent the night in the sort of motel you'd find near a traffic hub – airport, big railway station, major bus interchange – anywhere in the Western world. It's like all these motel chains buy from a big factory that churns out the rooms, the furniture and the fittings. Even the artwork on the walls seems to all come from the same catalogue.

Next morning we went looking for wheels. John B. was all for finding a van or car we liked, buying it, and then selling it when we were finished. After all, he could afford it.

I had another idea. "Babe, we'd be better off renting. If there's a problem, then it's someone else's job to fix it, and let us have another vehicle. If there's a really big problem that's – God forbid – our fault, *then* we can be very glad of your reserves."

"I think you're becoming my manager, as well as my beloved," he replied.

"Is that a problem, babe?" I asked, unsure of the tone of his voice.

He laughed. "Far from it!" Then his face turned serious again. "Just so long as you're first and foremost my friend, and my love."

"Deal." We kissed. Then went looking to rent a vehicle.

I won't go into a lot of detail about how we decided on which vehicle to hire. We talked about distance, fuel economy, the likelihood of going off-road depending on where my search might take us, and of course, comfort. The weather in New England wasn't as cold as what we'd just left in Norway, but I did want a decent heating system! We settled for a silver SUV four-wheel drive - a BMW X3. John B. could probably go into some detail about it. Wilko could doubtless tell you a lot more. I'll just say she was comfortable and did everything we asked of her. For no obvious reason that I can remember we christened her Yvette.

It turned out that Yvette had a built-in navigation system. We didn't spot it at first – too busy playing with the music system that shared the same touchscreen, I must admit. It led to a funny little exchange as we tried to get out of Boston based solely on the directions the girl in the car rental office had told us.

I said to John B., "Turn left on Watt Street."

"Which one?" he replied.

"Watt."

"That's what I said."

"Watt Street, coming up on the left," I explained.

"What street coming up on the left?"

"Yes."

"What?"

"Right."

 JB looked at me, clearly puzzled. "I thought you said left?"

"Pardon?"

"You said turn left."

"That's right," I said.

"Ah."

"On Watt Street," I explained.

 I think his teeth were clenched as John B. said, "That's what I was asking. I think I've gone through the twilight zone into an Abbott and Costello routine…"

 Suddenly I saw the street sign we needed and shouted, "Turn left here!"

 JB must have seen the sign too, though I didn't realise that for a moment. "Oh, right..." he said.

"No, left!" I instinctively answered.

 "Got it."

We did finally make it out of Boston with our sanity intact (I think).

And somewhere on the highway through New Hampshire I stumbled on the navigation system. Of course, it was of limited help at first, since we didn't have a clear idea of our destination. 'Somewhere on the coast of Maine' wasn't really something I could put into the system.

It was a nice, easy day's driving. We made a couple of little stops along the way, but got to Portland in the early evening. After checking out a couple of options we took a room in a lovely small motel. I doubt that the furniture and décor were really antiques, but they were good reproductions and the effect was beautiful. Just the right side of too cutesy.

As excited as I was to be on Prince Henry's trail, I also knew that it had been a long few days' travel. We had an early night, and took our time the next morning before setting off into town. The Information Centre, the library, bookshops – anywhere that we could try to discover any history. And wow – was there history to be explored. Sadly, none of what we found seemed to be specifically about my family connection.

By the end of the day we both needed a drink. We found a pub we liked the look of - the *Salty Dog Tavern*. We were having a quiet conversation about the day's successes or otherwise. I thought we were being quiet, but evidently loud enough for inquisitive ears, because a local fellow unexpectedly joined us.

Standing no higher than my nose, and deeply tanned, if his hair had been long and white instead of short and dark he'd have resembled a slightly oversized but skinny gnome. His attempt at a beard was worse than JB's, though better trimmed.

He was an odd little man, who introduced himself as Sam McFerris. He seemed quite friendly. Charming, really, and extremely chatty. We were tired. John B. will chat with almost anybody in a bar with good Scotch, and this was a bar with a very good array of single malts. At one point I did notice Sam surreptitiously slip one of the shot glasses into the rather worn cruise-line tote bag he carried over his shoulder, but as I said, we were tired and he was charming enough for it to seem like a 'lovable rogue' thing to do. He may even have winked at me.

 A lot of time was spent chatting about where in the world we'd all been, and the odd or funny experiences we'd had travelling. John B. especially gave a heavily expurgated version of his travelogue. Some of the experiences he's told me about, and many that I've shared with him, aren't the stuff of friendly bar room conversation.

 I did notice that any experience we'd describe, Sam would match or try to trump. Some people are just like that, aren't they? Compensating for something inside their own head. Anyway, the company was entertaining enough for us to agree to catch up again the following evening at another bar that Sam recommended.

 JB and I had another day of exploring Portland. We spent quite a bit of time in Henry Wadsworth Longfellow's old house. The poet had no particular relevance to me, but it was a beautifully restored and maintained 'time capsule'.

 We spent some of the afternoon on a harbour cruise that actually covered disappointingly little of Casco Bay, where Portland sits. We learned mostly modern history, and saw enough to realise that the bay is quite extensive, and littered with small islands. Some of them are large enough to have thriving communities, others permanently inhabited by one or two families, others are tourist spots and some, we were told by the guide, 'weren't worth the trouble of trying to get to'.

 By the time we got to the *Aye Noah Place* – a waterfront bar that turned into a nightclub later in the evening – we were both again very ready for a drink.

 The limited range of whiskys wasn't to JB's taste. Either McFerris had exaggerated the place, or he knew less about good Scotch than he'd indicated. My beau and I picked out a quiet table and settled in to enjoying a bottle of good Californian white zinfandel while we talked about our day, and what to do next.

We'd just been discussing Prince Henry when our new friend arrived, with more company. His companion was introduced as Dean Parsons. Curly haired, and a similar size and build to JB, he was less chatty than Sam. He seemed more inclined to listen to the conversation than add to it. I admit, I really didn't warm to him. He was introduced as Sam's house-mate, but their body language made it clear that there was more to the relationship. (I found out later that the *Aye Noah Place*'s nighttime incar-nation was a popular gay hangout, which is evidently what prompted him to suggest it as a meeting place.)

With idle curiosity I noted that the unsuccessful McFerris beard had been shaved off. I wondered if the sight of John B.'s scruffy chin had given him a moment of self-realization and put him off.

Our previous experience told us that Sam seemed to be one of those fellows who knew something about anything you happened to talk about. A mine of information – some of it even turned out to be true. They'd arrived in time to hear some of our conversation about "where we should look next", and McFerris suggested that he could help.

When I explained a little of what I was searching for, (without going into too much detail) he'd replied, "Oh yes, I know about that. Where you want is the Popham colony." He proceeded to give us directions to a place called Popham Beach. He also talked about an "old stone tower that we really *had* to see", at which point he tapped the side of his nose, nodded in a way that I'm sure was meant to be mysterious, and changed the subject.

Over the course of a longer evening than JB or I had intended, McFerris explained in snippets that this Popham was the site of the first English colonial settlement in North America, and that the location had only been identified in 1994. Dean didn't add much beyond an occasional, "That's right," which may or may not have indicated that he actually knew any-thing about it.

Sam said that while he'd visited the site several times, he hadn't been directly involved in the archaeology. He implied that he had some sort of family connection to the colony, without actually saying that much. When

I tried to probe a bit, he went off on a tangent about his present-day family.

Over a few glasses of wine (that JB was paying for, trying to 'facilitate my research' he later said) McFerris told several stories about his "truly horrible" sister. If even half of them are true she really must be awful. He tells a story well, but now the drinking is done I do wonder.

He seemed a good listener, but thinking back I realise that a lot of the time his interest was in gleaning bits that he could somehow relate to himself. Dean's attitude seemed similar, for all his reticence.

Narcissism aside, the colony at Popham Beach was a good clue. It seemed to me a promising place to start.

The *Aye Noah Place* clientele was showing a distinct change in character by the time John B. and I took our leave. Neither of us mind being in a gay bar – we both socialized at a couple back in Canberra in our working days (JB especially, I didn't get out much) – but there was a vaguely unpleasant atmosphere coming over the place. Not quite predatory, I don't think, but not welcoming of a straight couple, either.

We thanked Sam McFerris for his advice and company, exchanged final obviously shallow pleasantries with Dean Parsons, and finished the third bottle of wine. Having paid for all of them, JB wasn't prepared to leave any for the two 'boys' to finish after watching them pour themselves generous serves while we talked.

So the next morning – not early – JB and I drove from Portland up to Popham Beach. The beach itself is six miles long, and most if not all of it is 'State Park'. Near one end of it though, tucked around the corner from the expanse of white sand, we found a little tree-lined bay that fitted our new acquaintance's description pretty well. While Popham Beach itself still had a good sprinkling of visitors, despite the chill in the air, this bit was deserted. Coming around the headland was like going through a dimensional warp in a science-fiction TV show.

The first thing that struck me was the complete absence of the tower that

McFerris had told me about. Given his description, I expected it to be pretty bloody obvious, frankly. What we saw was trees, in a mass stretching up a slope. They didn't seem tall enough to hide a tower of any importance.

Nonetheless, we were having a good little explore of the small bay that McFerris had said was significant to the colony. The little beach at the bay yielded nothing. There was an area that looked like it had been cleared, and the sandy soil turned over. John B. suggested it at least looked like some archaeological survey work had been done there, though not recently. I'll take his word for it.

Soon we followed a track up into what in Australia we'd call 'the bush'. Here it's 'the woods'. Lots of trees and scrubby undergrowth.

We didn't find anything obviously 600 years old. What we did find was some rather more recent history that had been abandoned. World War Two vintage buildings – gun emplacements and small barracks and blockhouses.

Military history certainly isn't a matter of great interest to me. Not that period of history anyway. Nor to JB really, although he does have a great fondness for history in general I've found. He studied it when he was younger, and still reads a lot. The Second World War's more of a specialty of our friend Wilko – he'd have appreciated this little site we found.

I suppose it was out of some consideration for Wilko's interest that we spent a bit of time poking around the abandoned buildings, figuring we'd share the story of anything interesting we found. It was while we were engrossed in exploring that we became aware of being watched.

We were in a tumbledown concrete blockhouse – I think it may have been a kitchen, there might have been the remains of a sink or something if I remember right. There was a noise from outside. A branch snapped. It was only because we chanced to not be talking at that precise moment that we even heard it.

"Animal?" I asked.

"I guess so," John B. replied.

 But he did go quietly to the doorway and look out into the woods. I joined him there. Nothing to be seen, as far as I could tell. We walked out of that building and started up the path to the next one, further up a small hill. This time though we walked without talking, and there was rustling in leaf litter, somewhere off to our right.

 I still suspected it was some kind of animal – a small harmless one, preferably. My hearing is a little sharper than my beau's, I think. (Too much loud rock'n'roll through headphones in his youth, he's suggested.) But I was pretty sure I heard a couple more little sounds, now that I was actually listening for them.

 There was a big concrete slab at the side of the path. Standing in the middle of that gave us both a chance to look around, trying not to be too obvious about it. There were several huge bolts poking up from the slab, rusty but still impressively solid. According to John B. there would once have been a big gun on the spot.

 Whoever or whatever was out there stayed still while we were on the old gun emplacement. JB gave my hand a squeeze and we started to amble uphill towards yet another concrete building.

 As we walked my beau the wizard quietly said, "I wish you'd reveal yourself."

 I couldn't help myself. I replied, "Mah goodness sir! Surely y'all do not expect me to disrobe out here in the woods?"

 Long before we became a couple, when we were workmates becoming friends, John B. and I started doing this funny little thing where we'd talk to each other in terrible Deep South accents. I think we both got them from old Warner Brothers cartoons. I know I did.

JB laughed and put an arm around me. "Not what I had in mind, pretty lady, but the idea certainly has a lot of appeal!" he teased.

We were snuggling in together as we walked into the blockhouse. Maybe that caused a bit of distraction behind us, as there was a sudden grunt and a choked-off "Oh damn!" from outside.

We rushed back out, and saw a man on his knees at the edge of the old gun emplacement. He'd obviously stubbed a toe and tripped on one of the big securing bolts.

He wasn't a young man, and instinctively I went to help him to his feet. He was about average height, lean and wiry. His beard was more silver than grey, and more neatly trimmed than his hair, which looked like he'd cut it himself in front of a cloudy mirror.

It's funny – I could almost imagine John B. looking rather like him in years to come.

After I'd helped him up he held out a hand and introduced himself as Lanny French. I never did find out what 'Lanny' was short for. I'm guessing Lancelot – that would be old-fashioned enough to suit this charming gentleman.

It was as if by the simple act of helping him to his feet I'd convinced him we were somehow 'safe'.

He did ask what brought us to the area. Lanny turned out to be a sort of unofficial 'caretaker'. I don't think it gets a lot of visitors, and it's remarkably unspoiled by graffiti. Not completely untouched, but better than I'd have expected. Maybe Lanny and others like him, who take some pride in their local history, are the reason.

Self-appointed 'watchman' or not, I didn't feel threatened by him at all. There was something dynamic about him. An energy that impressed me. John B. was a little more reserved. I don't think he mistrusted him. Perhaps I'm flattering myself, but I suspect he was just a little jealous – Lanny took such an interest in me (or in my story really, I think, once I explained why we were there) and I may have played up to him a little. Not deliberately, just a natural response.

Lanny led us from the abandoned buildings back down out of the woods to another spot around a little headland from where we'd been exploring earlier. There more company joined us. Just as Lanny had startled us by apparently stalking us, it happened again when an imposing figure stepped silently out from behind a tree.

It was a substantial tree, because the man who'd suddenly emerged was a much bigger man than Lanny.

"So ya found them," he said.

"Yes, and they're harmless," replied Lanny.

"Ya sure about that?"

Lanny looked at me, then John B. Looked hard. I can still remember how intense his gaze was. Then he shrugged and said in his soft voice, "As sure as I can be."

"We-e-ll, if I haven't learned to trust ya by now, I never will, will I?"

The large man thrust out his hand and introduced himself as Cowley Honeywell.

"No offence, folks," he said. "But I like to keep a quiet eye on Lanny. Make sure he doesn't get himself into trouble."

"And we like to keep a quiet eye on this place, to make sure no trouble comes to it," added Lanny.

"So it is a special place?" I asked.

"Ye-e-es," said Cowley cautiously.

I realised there was nothing to be gained from being secretive. I like to think I'm a fair judge of character, and there was something about these two men I immediately took to. The way they stood together – not quite hand in hand but close enough to be in each other's 'personal space' – the bond, the affection between them was obvious. Trusting them was easy. Quite unlike Sam McFerris and, especially, Dean Parsons.

I explained how we came to be there, and what it was we were looking for.

They laughed.

"There was no colony here? That man in the bar – McFerris – led us astray?" I asked.

"We-e-ll, yes and no."

There was a twinkle in Lanny's eye as he said, "You have to be a bit care-ful, dealing with Saxa. That's what Sam gets called by some folks. Some people you talk to, you take what they say with a grain of salt. With him, it's sacks of the stuff."

"But he mostly means well," defended the big man. "There was a colony established here many years ago. Gets called the Popham Colony now, but more correctly, it was the Sagadahoc Colony. Just not the one ya are looking for."

I must have looked skeptical, because he went on to explain. "It was in 1607. The Virginia Company of Plymouth established a place here. The plan was to use the trees here for ship building – natural masts."

"Same as Norfolk Island down in our part of the world," remarked JB, the history student. "Only that was a government enterprise, using convict labour."

Cowley nodded. "Whereas here, it was a private enterprise. Folks here built the first ship made in the New World – a pinnace called *Virginia of*

Sagadahoc. Sailed over to England, then actually made it back as a supply vessel in 1609. Even survived a big hurricane off Bermuda that sank the company's flagship. Damned fine piece of boatbuilding. Lasted longer than the colony."

"Disease or disaster?" I asked.

"Neither," replied Lanny with a smile. "More like a kind of… well, something between local politics and family squabbles, as near as anyone knows. Certainly the loss of life here was a lot less than at the colony over at Jamestown in Virginia who were their supposed rivals."

"Well, if Saxa McFerris' family *were* heavily involved in the colony, and they were anything like the present-day relatives as he described them, no wonder the place didn't last," John B. wryly observed.

I noticed Cowley looked slightly uncomfortable at that remark, but the mention of our helpful friend's chatter prompted my memory. I was just about to speak when my beau got in ahead of me.

"McFerris – Saxa as you called him, said something about a stone tower that we should look at. If it's here, it's bloody well disguised," said John B.

Cowley nodded. "I'd guess he means the tower at Mt. Battie. That's a little ways northeast of here in West Penobscot Bay."

That rang a bell for me. "I've read about that. It's a reconstruction, isn't it? Of the original tower in Scotland?"

"No," said Lanny. "It's a reconstruction of the reconstruction. The one in Rhode Island, called the Newport Tower, is supposed to look a lot like a very ancient one in the Orkney Islands, north of Scotland."

"The Orkneys – Prince Henry's original home. Hardly seems a coincidence," I observed.

"I reckon you're right, pretty lady," agreed John B. (I do love it when he calls me that!) "If I remember rightly from looking at some of the books you've been researching, it'd be the round tower of Saint Magnus in Egilsay. Supposedly built where Magnus the monk died in 1117, when it was an 'ecclesiastic island' as they were called."

I probably stared at him for a moment. I know I'd read that – I remembered it after he said it – but I've no idea how he just conjures up these pieces of history, seemingly on demand. Especially when he's so damned vague about his own history! He just drops them into a conversation so casually, it's like he's just mentioning something he happened to see.

"We could go down to Rhode Island, I guess, and go looking for the tower there," mused John B. "I didn't think that was the area you were particularly interested in, though. I thought the St. Clair settlement was further north."

Lanny shook his head apologetically. "I'm afraid there's not much more we can tell you. We know a bit about what's hereabouts, the old Sagadahoc colony, but I don't think it's especially relevant to you. It's two centuries too late. I don't really know where's the best place for you to start looking."

"But I can tell ya who ya should talk to," said Cowley. "She's a writer, not from these parts originally, but she's got a place way back up in the hills a few miles from here. She goes by the name of Texas Dorothy."

.o0o.

5 TWO MEN AND A BOAT

Extract from statement to Sgt. B. J. Haynes, Portland Police, by Mr. Juan Roca:

I am visiting Maine from San Diego. It is my ambition to fish off coast of every state of the US that faces sea. I was out on Casco Bay in little runabout that I had hired for a day of fishing.

As I travelled north there was big fog. I tried to keep out of worst of it as it was very hard to see. Out of fog came ship. I rubbed my eyes, not believing at first. It was pirate ship, like in old movies or books. Even had skull and bones flag on one mast. I was too shocked to go fast enough to get away.

Pirate ship came alongside me, threw rope with hook to snag my little boat, then dropped rope ladder. Two men climbed down into my boat.

They were both dressed like pirates. Long boots, bandanas, cloth tied around faces. One man had red beard I think. That man had green parrot on his shoulder and carried big sword. Other man had no weapons, but was very, very big, more than seven feet tall I think.

Big man held me by my arms while other one frisked me. Took my wallet, took only cash from it. $200, maybe a little more. Took my cell phone and threw it overboard.

Horrible green bird flew onto my shoulder and started snapping at chains on my neck. I wear four very valuable gold chains I inherited from my grandfather, rich man in Mexico. I do not like to leave them in hotel. I have always felt them safer with me. Until this day.

Man with beard said something like, "Arr, they be fine pieces, me hearty," and took all four chains off me. Bird then flew back onto his shoulder.

Big man slapped me on chest so I fell down. Other man held sword to my chest and nodded.

Then big man lifted my outboard motor out of water and bent propeller blades. With bare hand he bent them! "You can fix that later," he said. Deep voice.

"Aar, when ye've paddled home," said other man as he kicked oar lying in bottom of my little boat.

They climbed back up ladder while I still was lying down. I saw one other man, maybe two, on pirate ship looking down at me.

Pirate ship moved off, quick but quiet, back into fog. Ship had no sails up on mast but I remember realising she sailed into wind.

I rowed away as fast as I could. Took many hours, and helpful current, to get home.

Boat hire company has penalized me for damage to outboard motor, but more important is loss of my grandfather's gold chains. Very old and valuable. Also loss of money from wallet.

I am sorry I cannot identify men better. Both white. One maybe six feet tall. Solid build, some red beard stuck out from behind cloth on his face.

Other man very big. Maybe seven feet tall, and heavy build. I could see no hair under bandana, so maybe bald, or very short hair.

This happened northern part of Casco Bay on open water.

Note appended by Sgt. Haynes:

Mr. Roca attended the station clearly under the influence of alcohol. He admitted to consuming "several tequilas" which he claimed had been to "settle his nerves".   He was unable to offer any evidence of his having owned any "valuable gold jewellery". While the claim to have been wearing such jewellery while fishing is not the most implausible part of his outlandish story, it nonetheless seems ridic- ulous. I suspect that Mr. Roca intends to make an insurance claim and has reported to this station only to further that claim. No further action by this department is recommended.

.o0o.

6 THE WRITER IN THE WOODS

Lanny and Cowley weren't able to give us an address for Texas Dorothy that we could usefully put into Yvette's navigation system. 'Somewhere out along Sheepscot River' was about as useful as 'somewhere on the Maine coast' had been. But they did explain how to get to a town called Windsor, and were positive that someone there would know how to find this supposedly helpful woman.

We headed inland the next morning. Along the way we stopped in Windsor at a nice little diner and tried out the 'traditional local delicacies' that Cowley had been particularly insistent that we would enjoy: lobster roll, whoopee pie and Moxie. The first one is pretty obvious, shredded lobster meat and a tangy sauce in a fresh bread roll. JB had been pleased to learn that his 'seafood allergy' extended only to prawns, and he's develped a taste for lobster. The local version was good. A whoopee pie is two round slabs of chocolate cake with a thick layer of some creamy white filling (marshmallow fluff, I'm told) in between. Outrageously sweet, which seems to be the American taste. And Moxie is a soft drink that doesn't taste quite like anything else I've had. Somehow it manages to be sweet with a bitter aftertaste – something herbal, I think. Not a combination I'd like to live on, but altogether rather tasty, and certainly filling. I don't know about 'traditional'. How many generations does it take to make a tradition?

The suggestion that someone in Windsor would know where to find Texas Dorothy was right on the money. The waitress in the diner was the first person we asked. She knew who we meant, and got the guy out in the kitchen to give us directions. Apparently he delivered supplies up to her once in a while. It seems to me that everybody in Maine knows somebody who they say can help. Sometimes they even can.

The road out to the writer's place was winding but sealed. It took us through some thickly timbered forest . We passed a few driveways that disappeared off into the gloom between tall trees – evidently people around here value their privacy. But in a cul-de-sac at the end of this road we found a mailbox, cleverly crafted from a big old television, with the mail slot cut into the control panel above the knobs and dials. I presumed the owner must now have a set with a remote control. Across the screen, lettered neatly in white paint, was the name 'Duncum'.

The property itself seemed quite big, but the house was modest. A two storey wooden place that somehow just said 'faded glory'. Not ramshackle, but you could compile a lengthy list of repairs required just by standing, looking at it. John B. stepped onto the small porch and knocked on the peeling brown paint of a front door that didn't quite hang straight.

I freely admit I didn't expect the door to be opened by a tall Native American man. He cut an impressive figure, with long glossy black hair, weathered but unlined skin and finely chiseled features that made his age hard to guess.

"G'day. I'm John B. Stewart, this is Elizabeth McKew, and I'm willing to bet you're not Texas Dorothy."

Sometimes even I don't know how to react to my beau. This time I had to bite down on breaking out laughing – not because of what JB said but because of the tall dark man's response. He raised one eyebrow *exactly* like Mr. Spock in 'Star Trek', and replied, in a voice eerily like Leonard Nimoy's, "Indeed."

To recover myself I stepped forward and asked, "Is this the writer's house, or have we gotten ourselves lost?"

A piping voice came from somewhere inside. "Y'all have got the right place, hon. Bring 'em in, Big Heart."

The stern dark face split into a smile and we were ushered in.

The first door off the little entrance hall opened onto a cluttered kitchen that looked well used. The door adjoining that led into a small comfortable lounge that already seemed crowded. There were two old armchairs occupied by men who could have been relatives of Big Heart, with a third relative sitting cross-legged on the floor. All three were looking respectfully at a white woman in a wheelchair, seated at the far end of the room.

I'm old-fashioned enough to have been delighted when all three men stood up as I entered the room. He was behind me, but I'm sure JB smiled in appreciation of the gesture too. He often laments that "chivalry isn't dead, but it's an endangered species".

"Welcome. Ain't it funny? I go weeks without seein' a soul, an' here's two sets of visitors in one day. Find yourselves a seat youngsters, an' tell me what brings ya out here," said the woman.

The 'youngsters' comment struck me as funny, because I was sure she could have been no more than late-thirties herself. But then, like Big Heart, she had one of those faces that the more you looked at it, the less certain you were of age.

One of the Native Americans (it's a clumsy term, but it seems like everything else is politically incorrect at present, even something I'd have thought flattering or positive like 'braves') gallantly insisted I take his chair, while he joined Big Heart and John B. in sitting on the floor. It's a naturally comfortable posture for my wizard, I've learned, having seen him slip straight into it in Scotland and Norway in recent times.

Introductions were made around the little circle. Big Heart's companions were Rain Chaser, Sings Like Frog, and Hair Stands Up. The latter's name seemed totally inappropriate, as, like the others, his glossy black locks hung down on his shoulders.
"Call me Harry," he said with a grin.

I later found that these names were coined in childhood, and it had taken years of regular application of animal fat and soot to plaster Harry's recalcitrant follicles into the desired style.

John B. and I introduced each other, and last was our hostess. Well, next to last. What I thought was a basket of knitting yarn on the floor beside the wheelchair suddenly barked, and the most beautiful pair of dark brown eyes opened amongst the tangle of pale caramel fur that I'd mistaken for wool.

The writer reached down and stroked the dog's head. "This is mah boy Mac. He's what they call a cavoodle – part poodle, part Cavalier spaniel."

At thc sound of his name, Mac barked again and wagged a scruffy tail. He sort of bounced up and down a bit in the basket.

"Poor little thang'd love ta be runnin' 'bout, fussin' over y'all, but his back legs don't even work so well as mine." At which point the introductions were completed. "Dorothy Duncum. Story teller. Well, collector and re-teller of stories if Ah'm bein' accurate."

You hear the expression often – looking into a person's eyes. Well she really looked into mine. I felt at first like a sparrow being considered by a cat. Was there enough to me to be worth the energy of capturing and consuming? Then she smiled and it was like a switch had been thrown and a light had come on.

"So you're from Texas?" I asked, wanting to establish a bit of a rapport before I jumped in to asking for her help.

"Well, that's mah most recent port o' call before fetchin' up here. Ah done travelled around a lot," she said with a smile.

It was a pretty smile. As I said, it was impossible to pick her age. She had pale skin, and hair so blonde it was almost white. Clearly she favoured pale colours – her cardigan, blouse and long skirt were in tones of white and pale blue, but rather than wash out her complexion they actually seemed to enhance it.

"Now, y'all were goin' ta tell me what brings ya here. Somethin' Ah can do for ya?"

"Oh, no," I replied, "I can wait. You've already got company."

The four native men smiled and nodded in acknowledgement, the movement in perfect unison as if guided by a single mind.

"Right gracious of ya, but it's alright. These fellas and Ah get together every so often to swap stories. You go ahead an' tell us yours," said Dorothy.

So I explained about my ancestor Prince Henry, and how we'd come looking for evidence of his settlement. As I spoke Dorothy never took her eyes off me, but I noticed her four guests exchanging thoughtful looks.

Once I'd finished I leaned back in my chair, took a deep breath, and asked, "Well, can you help?"

Dorothy sat looking thoughtful, her hands clasped in her lap. She tilted her head slightly to one side and said, "Ah gotta tell ya up front, Ah keep stories, hon, an' make sure they get passed on. Ah'm not a historian. That's someone else's job."

John B. had been very quiet, leaving me to explain for myself what I already knew, and what I hoped to learn. Just for a moment now I spotted what I thought was a troubled look cross his face. He told me later that his mind flicked back for a moment to Old Black Guy – the healer he'd met in Central Australia. And a few other people he'd encountered recently. People for whom the word "job" seemed to carry far more weight and depth than normal usage.

My wizard looked a little quizzically at Texas Dorothy. She met his gaze and gave him a bright smile.

"Let me think on it a while," Dorothy continued. "Why don' we all take a stroll round outside while Ah ponder?"

The three men on the floor got up to make way for the wheelchair, Rain Chaser picking up Mac's basket and placing it carefully on Dorothy's lap. The writer wheeled the chair herself out into a corridor that ran the length of the back of the house. Following her, we passed a bathroom, a small

tidy bedroom, and a flight of stairs leading up, before going out through
the back door onto a path created from a jumble of pavers and bricks.

The path apparently wrapped around the house, but Dorothy led us down
a gravel path that led off the pavers and into the adjoining woods. As soon
as we went under the shade of the trees I wished I hadn't left my jacket in
Yvette. The weather was brisk anyway, but out of the sun it was dead set
chilly. JB, bless him, kept an arm around my shoulders for warmth – but
that might have been more effective if he'd been wearing more than the
usual jeans and t-shirt.

Dorothy's white cardigan must have been warmer than it looked, as she
showed no sign of feeling cold. Her four visitors were dressed in a mix
of traditional and modern – jeans and checked shirts teamed with deerskin
mantles. Two wore moccasins and the others wore beautiful leather boots.

Suddenly we emerged back into sunlight. It was a little cleared strip on
a bend of the Sheepscot River. Some big rocks in a rough semicircle did
service as seats. Abruptly Mac started to bark, bouncing up in his basket,
with only Dorothy's firm hand restraining him from launching himself out.

I realised that a little bank dropped away where the clearing met the river
when a furry head poked up over it. It was about the size of Mac's head,
mostly covered in dark brown fur, with a muzzle like a bear and a pair of
round pink ears sticking up.

Big Heart and Hair Stands Up made odd gestures with their hands, while
Sings Like Frog and Rain Chaser gave respectful nods and the dog continued to bark madly.

The critter down on the bank looked wild eyed. Clearly it felt trapped,
with the group of us all between it and the woods. Then John B. strolled
towards it, muttering something very softly.

He stood by the river's edge, then next thing this animal jumped up,
caught onto his jeans' leg, and clambered up to sit on his shoulder. My

beau just smiled and casually stroked the dark fur of the animal's back, then ambled over to the edge of the forest.

At first I thought the little creature – it was about the size of Mac, was going to stay perched on John B.'s shoulder, but then it stood up, stretched and leapt off, disappearing into thick undergrowth in less time than it took me to write this sentence. And I type quickly.

"Was that some sort of wildcat?" I asked. I know John B. has a peculiar affinity for wild creatures. I remember something similar happened with a wildcat on Islay, and Wilko explained in a great deal of puzzled detail how JB and a native hawk adopted each other while in Hawaii.

"It's called a fisher cat," explained Dorothy, "Which is kinda funny cos it ain't a cat and it don't eat fish. Best think of it as a big weasel, or a small wolverine. Name comes from the way they run, sorta bound along with their tail stuck out jus' like a cat does. One o' the only critters that can hunt and kill a porcupine, cos they can move round an' strike so fast the prey can't protect itself prop'ly. Don't usually come near folks, but. "

Big Heart walked over to John B. and laid a large hand on my beau's shoulder.
"It is also the totem of my family, and of Hair Stands Up," he said. "It is clear that we are meant to trust you. We will talk."

I had to smile. I don't know how he does it.

We settled down, sitting on the rocks, with Texas Dorothy at one end of the arc. To my surprise, it was Harry who spoke first. I'd assumed Big Heart was somehow senior, if not in years.

"This isn't our story. Our tribe is Abnaki, but over the years we've lived with and alongside others. One such tribe is the Micmaq," he began.

"The one with the Gaelic name," I said, remembering John B.'s book.

"The Micmaq have old stories of the arrival centuries ago of fire-haired, green-eyed men on a 'bird with a broken wing'. I reckon that had some-thing to do with a sail flapping on a broken mast. They say that the leader of these men built himself an island, planted trees on it, and sailed away in his stone canoe," Harry continued, a faraway look on his face.

 Perhaps I looked puzzled, because Big Heart interjected, "This must sure-ly refer to the visitors building a new boat. Masts, a covered deck and a hull of dressed timber, all would be strange to a people whose own water-craft were dugout pine logs and birch bark canoes."

"That makes sense," I agreed. "So these Micmaq had some interaction with what sounds like Prince Henry's immigrants."

"Do we have any clues as to where?" asked John B.

"Both the Micmaq and the Abnaki used to live further north, up New-foundland way. If your ancestor came from the direction you suggest, it'd make sense for any contact to have happened up there somewhere," suggested Rain Chaser.

"Another long drive coming up, babe," I said apologetically.

"Hey, that's fine with me sweetheart, as long as it gets us what you need," replied my gallant beau.

"Um, driving to Newfoundland is perhaps not necessary," said Sings Like Frog hesitantly. "There is a small community of Micmaq families who live up along one of the old forest trails on the Kennebec River."

"Given a parcel of land once the valuable forest timber had been cleared," observed Harry. Nobody disagreed with his cynicism, I noticed.

"Ah know of 'em," agreed Dorothy. "Reckon some o' them might still recall a story to help y'all."

"Should we tell them you sent us?" I asked with a smile.

There was a smile in return as the authoress replied, "Cain't hurt none."

I did wonder aloud if someone might be available to navigate for us. A "forest trail on the Kennebec River" did seem yet another inadequate description to put into a satnav.

All of the Abnaki men had family commitments to attend to, although Big Heart did offer to come back in a few days if we didn't mind waiting that long. Call me impulsive (Lord knows, my mother often did) but I wasn't keen to delay. Sings Like Frog said he'd give us the clearest directions he could, and I was grateful to settle for that.

We all strolled back through the woods to Dorothy's house. A few times as we walked I wondered if I heard the sound of the fisher cat somewhere nearby but out of sight, but when I concentrated I thought the noises might have been made by something bigger. The local men exchanged worried glances.

"*Wintikowa*?" breathed Harry, softly.

Dorothy's nose wrinkled as she sniffed the air, then she laughed and replied, "*Miskwa.*"

Harry didn't look much cheered by that answer, although Rain Chaser relaxed visibly.

When we got back to the house a steaming pot of coffee was quickly prepared. As we sat around the lounge sipping I just had to ask, "What did you think we heard out there?"

Harry still seemed a bit shaken. "*Wintikowa*," he repeated. "The Great Beast of the forest. Have you heard of the wendigo?"

I shook my head. It was John B. who answered. "Think Bigfoot, or Sasquatch. Or down our way, the Yowie."

Now I understood.

"Weren't him," Dorothy said with her usual smile. "Not the smell. More likely a bear."

"Is that the word you used? Miskwa?" I asked.

Rain Chaser nodded. "The *miskwa* is totem to my family. She would not trouble us."

"Hey – that was the name of that action hero type fellow that we met on Shetland," I said. "Miskwa Burns. Said he was 'ex-Special Forces' as I recall."

Dorothy looked at me and blinked. "You knew Teddy?"

"Teddy?"

"Theodore. He grew up around these parts," explained the woman in the wheelchair. "Well, Ah say 'grew up'… Don't know he ever quite did that. He was a nice boy, Ah suppose, but he were, well, strange. Ah'm afraid the only 'special forces' in his life were his imagination and mebbe his sense of self-importance."

JB & I exchanged looks and nodded.

"Still," said Dorothy, with a tight little version of her smile, "Shouldn't speak ill of the dead."

John B. said quietly, "We were there when he was killed. Nearby, at least."

Texas Dorothy looked at him, her head slightly tilted. I had a momentary impression of him being watched by a great snowy owl.

"Ya know, that doesn't surprise me," the authoress said.

"And this wendigo," I said, suddenly wanting to shift the focus of conversation. "Is it anyone's totem?"

"Not nowadays," replied Dorothy. "If'n there was any families who ever claimed him as their own, they's long since died out now."

Big Heart looked grim. "There are too many of the people who have died out now."

"All too true, and not just here," agreed my wizard.

Again I thought it was diplomatic to shift the topic of conversation. I pointed to a shelf full of beads, mostly purple and white, strung onto belts and bands of varying widths and lengths, all seeming to be heaped randomly.

"Those are pretty – no, striking," I said.

"Wampum," said Sings Like Frog.

"Oh. That was used as a type of currency, wasn't it?" I asked, intrigued.

"Legal tender in the early days of Massachusetts trading. The purple ones were higher value than the white. A bit like dollars and cents," said my beau, the avid reader.

Texas Dorothy chuckled. At a gesture from her Big Heart held up one of the belts as she spoke. "They had an older value too. They was used in story tellin'. Each pattern woven into one of them there belts, y'see it? Each line an' each pattern was like a marker, ta help the memory of those what passed that particular story down the generations. Some of them there sets of beads is right old, an' prob'ly valuable one way or another." She grinned broadly. "Some of 'em are just right pretty."

From the proud looks on their faces I knew that some of the collection had been given by her Abnaki visitors, or their kin. "Valuable or not, they're lovely," I said.

Dorothy kindly offered us a bed for the night. She had a spare room upstairs, she said. But I decided against it. We had a room paid for, and

I wanted to be able to change clothes (and do some more research of my own) before we went on our next excursion, chasing yet another lead.

"We'll take you up on it soon I hope, if that's alright?" I said.

"Y'all are welcome to come back an' tell me what ya find. Ah reckon there's a fine story in ya, an' Ah'm interested in hearin' it. Ah've got thet spare room if'n you'd like to stay the night."

 She wrote her phone number on a piece of embossed notepaper. Big Heart's raised eyebrow suggested to me that it was an uncommon thing for this number to be given out, so I was appropriately honoured to take it and put it in my shirt pocket.

 We spent another half hour or so chatting. There was fun stuff – I learned that the soft drink 'Moxie' is a 'sound-alike' for an old Abnaki word meaning dark water. And there was sombre stuff. In 1724 an Abnaki village in the vicinity of where we were going next day suffered a midnight raid by 200 colonial troops that saw perhaps a hundred men, women and children slaughtered (a hundred pound bounty paid on each of their scalps!) and the survivors flee north to see out their days in what's now Quebec.

 It was well into the afternoon when we finally shook hands all round. Mac wagged his tail enthusiastically and licked any hands offered to him. Texas Dorothy and her Abnaki friends seemed genuine in wishing us well, and I did truly hope to see them again.

JB drove us back through the woods, Yvette's headlights on as the setting sun didn't penetrate the canopy of foliage above us. He and I chatted as we drove, particularly about the massacre at that poor village. History is littered with such events, all over the world. As my beau pointed out though, it's not just white men killing natives. Humans of all races have killed other humans en masse for a variety of reasons – religion, skin colour, greed for land or resources.

"I read a long while ago about someone's fear that one day the last right-handed man would kill the last left-handed man for the final scrap of food on a devastated planet," John B. said grimly.

"That's an unhappy vision of the future, and of the human spirit," I replied.

"Mm. I'm not always sure of it, but I'd like to think we're better than that."

I reached over and squeezed his leg. "I know you and I are."

.o0o.

7 THE LITTLE PEOPLE

Extract from Dorothy Duncum's book "The People Of Sunrise – Tribal Stories From Early New England":

Many tribes in this region, and across the continental US, indeed, across the world, have legends of a race of Little People.

Many of these stories share the notion that the Little People were there before the people of the storyteller's race or tribe. In almost all instances, magical powers are ascribed to this older race. They may be benevolent or malign. Sometimes this is not a constant, but is dependent on the mood of the individual. Either way, the legends suggest that when encountered, the Little People should be treated with courtesy, and caution.

In the New England region they are said to be few in number, living in the hills "way back in the woods". This is an unhelpfully vague term that may mean anywhere in higher country further inland than the speaker.

The Mohegan word for these Little People is *muhkeahweesug.* It is told that they had a miraculous power to make themselves disappear from sight.

"If they point their fingers at you, you cannot see them," is the story. Whether they become invisible, or vanish completely, is not always clear and perhaps not relevant.

What was important was that if one of the muhkeahweesug came to you and asked for something,
you must give it to them. If you failed to do
so, they would point at you. Not only would they
vanish, but so too would the thing that had been
asked for.

'What then was the point of being asked?' you may
wonder.

It seems that the muhkeahweesug took it upon themselves to test the character of people they came
in contact with, few as they were. If something
were not given willingly it would be taken anyway,
but if the thing were given courteously, the action would be rewarded. Generosity begat generosity.

Another characteristic of the muhkeahweesug is
that they are a very private people, to the point
of being secretive. Their homes are extremely
well hidden. Folk who have mysteriously disappeared are sometimes thought to have inadvertently stumbled across a muhkeahweesug home, and then
been bewitched or killed to prevent them revealing
the location.

There is a story of a squaw who was a healer in
her own tribe. One stormy night a muhkeahweesug
man came to her wigwam in the darkness and asked
for medicinal herbs and help for his sick wife.

The squaw readily agreed, and after gathering up
the medicines she was led out into the night. The
little man led her by the hand, for she could not
see her way in the conditions.

A long and difficult walk later she was brought
into a small hut constructed of bark and saplings,
but so cunningly wrought it seemed to fade into
the surrounding woods.

The squaw stayed at the side of the little woman
for several days, nursing her and applying salves
and medicines until the fever broke and her patient could again sleep peacefully, speak lucidly,
and move without discomfort.

At that point, the medicine woman submitted to being blindfolded with a length of hide. The muhkeahweesug man again led her by the hand over difficult terrain for a goodly while.

When he finally let go of her hand, she was invited
to remove the blindfold. Upon doing so she found
herself only a short distance from her own village. There was no sign of the little man, but at
her feet was a deerskin bag full of beautiful or-
naments and some fine practical tools such as needles and cutting blades.

She never saw nor heard from the muhkeahweesug
again. Her patient had not been a young woman,
and the squaw thought that the little people must
have died out.

This story was told to me by the granddaughter of
the squaw, who swore that the events occurred in
1903.

.o0o.

8 IT'S A GIFT

It turned into another interesting drive as we sought the Micmaq settlement next day. For the most part it was straightforward enough, along
good sealed roads up into the north of Maine. We passed through Augus-
ta, the second smallest State capital in the US, apparently. We stopped for
coffee in Skowhegan, then following Sings Like Frog's directions, travelled north for a bit before taking a frankly bewildering series of left and
right turns onto increasingly poor roads.

I was glad I'd written down our Abnaki friend's directions meticulously.
I doubted that even JB's talent for coincidence could have led us to where
we wanted to go!

We'd been travelling for hours, and estimated perhaps another half-
hour until our destination. Yvette was bouncing along a rutted trail that
I couldn't imagine had ever seen a logging truck. It dawned on me as I
stared out the window that this was natural pine forest, not the neatly laid
out plantation trees I've seen in Australia. Who knew what lived in the
darkness among those trunks? Moose certainly. Bears. Maybe even the
wendigo?

Suddenly John B. slammed on the brakes and Yvette juddered and
swerved to a halt.

"What…?" I began.

"Corner of my eye. Saw a hand waving, down low."

He backed the car up along the track.
"There!" he said, turned off the engine and jumped from the car.

As he headed in between the pine trees I jumped down from the passenger
seat and followed. I only just managed to avoid going flying when he
stopped suddenly and dropped to his knees right in front of me.

I'd had my eyes on John B.'s back. Now I realized what he was kneeling beside. A substantial branch had fallen from one of the great pine trees, and someone was pinned under it.

She was a youngish woman, early thirties at most. She lay on her back, her face and one arm all that were visible under the pine foliage. Although a lot of blood had drained from her face, I could see that her skin was a few shades darker than that of Big Heart and his kin.

"Sweetheart, how is your back?" JB asked me.

It took me a moment to realise he was talking about the wound where the bullet had been removed. "Fine," I replied truthfully.

"Okay. When I get this lump of wood raised, can you please slide her out, as gently as you can?"

I nodded and knelt beside the woman. She looked up at me and smiled, as though she recognised me. John B. was on his belly, and wriggled under the fallen branch as near to the trapped woman as he could manage. It was a big piece of wood – long, and with a diameter bigger than my thigh (and my legs aren't as thin as I might want, however much JB flatters me). Then he braced himself and did something like a push-up, with the timber across his shoulders and upper back.

A grunt was all he could manage, but I didn't need to be told that this was my moment. I gripped the woman under the arms and slid her towards me, as carefully but as quickly as I could. I knew there was a risk of spinal damage, but I really didn't see an option. Fortunately the carpet of pine needles under her made the movement easier.

"Clear," I called.

Another grunt, and my beau lowered his torso back to the ground. A few deep breaths, and then he wriggled back towards me. The woman was lying quite still, with her head resting in my lap, and it was only now that I realised that she was scarcely three feet tall. John B. rolled and hauled himself up to sit cross-legged beside me, groaning softly as he flexed his shoulders and back.

"Thank you, Wetassawametewa, and thank you, Child of the Sea," said the dark woman softly.

"Umm, you're welcome." I replied, immediately assuming concussion. "Are you hurt?"

"Ribs," she said, holding a hand to her right side. "I will live."

She said that with a tone of absolute finality.

"How about your back? Can you move, feel, properly?" asked John B.

 In reply she moved each limb in turn, slowly flexing joints and wiggling fingers and toes, the latter movement visible through the light moccasins she wore.

 She was dressed in a tunic that on me would have been a longish t-shirt, made from a soft hide and decorated with ornate stitching and beading on the hem. The pattern was strangely familiar. It was almost but not quite Viking, or Celtic.

"Please, call me Wehmisemawa," she said. Her voice was soft and deep. Her English was good, but there was an accent unlike any I'd ever heard. John B. looked intrigued by it too, but his focus was on her condition.

 He was very gently pressing at her sides, mentally noting the points at which she winced. Unbidden, she lifted her tunic, untroubled by being naked underneath it. Even on her dark skin, the blackness of a massive bruise across her body was clearly visible. Remarkably I thought, the skin itself was barely broken. There were only grazes and a few small areas where it had split and a little blood had welled and already dried.

"How long have you been pinned under there, Wehma… Wehmi…?" I asked.

"Wehmisemawa," she repeated, and smiled. "I'm not sure. Some hours. It was a little past dawn when the branch fell."

"Then it's been quite a few hours, Wehmisemawa," I replied, taking care to pronounce the name as she'd said it.

"Can you take a deep breath, please, Wehmisemawa?" asked John B., a palm laid gently across her right side.

She did so, and flinched momentarily. Without being asked to, she coughed into the palm of her hand. She looked at the hand and held it out for John B.'s inspection.

"No blood," they both said together.

"None that can be seen, anyway," continued John B. "I think you need an x-ray to be sure. You're breathing *sounds* clear, but there's clearly a broken rib or two, and they're near a lung…"

"I shall be fine. The bones will heal, and I will be a little short of breath for a time. But I'll recover. Don't fuss."

"Mm. At least let me get the first aid kit from Yvette, clean the grazes and patch you up a bit."

At Wehmisemawa's nod he got up and went to the car to fetch the kit that was standard issue on all such hire vehicles. As a matter of caution I'd already checked it and knew it was well provisioned.

"You seem to be very much in tune with your body," I observed to the small woman still using my lap as a pillow.

"I knew I wasn't badly hurt," she said. "Bad enough, but it was not life-threatening. The real danger was in being trapped as I was. There are bears around here."

"Oh good," I said. "And other marauders too?"

I must have looked around nervously, for our patient laughed lightly. "Perhaps. But I know I am safe with you two."

I thought that maybe it was a delayed reaction to shock when she sighed quite deeply, causing a wince, then closed her eyes. "Tell me a little of your story please, Child of the Sea."

"That's the second time you've called me that. What does it mean?"

"Your eyes. I know by your eyes. Tell me your story. Please."

Her breathing was getting shallower, and I was truly afraid she was slipping into unconsciousness. To keep her awake I told the story of how John B. and I had come to look for evidence of my ancestor's colony, and how we'd been directed from one place to another following the leads of the various 'informants' we'd encountered, and how we'd been on our way to seek the Micmaq community when we'd found her.

John B. had returned and was silently mopping clean her grazes and cuts while I still spoke. Both he and Wehmisemawa nodded occasionally as I talked. Then suddenly and to my surprise she opened her eyes and looked into mine, alert and intense.

"It is as foretold. I wasn't afraid as I lay there – I expected you both."

My beau and I looked at each other, neither of us knowing what to say. Had she struck her head? Or was this another of the weirdnesses that seem to follow JB?

Wehmisemawa continued. "My grand-daughter told me you'd be coming. A long time ago, when she was an old woman. But she told me you'd be here and that I'd be safe."

"Your grandmother, you mean?" I said, confused.

"I know what I mean. Don't tell me what I mean. I mean my grand-daughter. The third daughter of my first son. Oh, I should have gone with them, he said, but I knew someone had to be here for you. John Dimond said so, and I knew someone had to take the responsibility.”

 I looked at John B. again, and was quietly relieved to see that he looked as confused as I felt. His voice was gentle as he spoke.
“I realise *you* know what you mean, Wehmisemawa, but you’ve lost both of us, sorry.”

 The little woman looked over at him, as if puzzled by his remark. She groped among the folds of her tunic, still scrunched up around her neck, and withdrew a small deerskin bag on a hemp string that had evidently been around her neck. Her fingers delved into the bag and pulled some-thing out. She extended her hand to me and dropped the object into my palm.

 It was a locket. Small, round, and gold. It was very worn, but I recog-nized from my research the carved relief that adorned it. It was the family crest of the old St. Clairs of Orkney.

“My people have known for generations that one day a descendant of the White Prince would return. When he set off for his homeland it was to fetch more of his family. His sea people, to join those who still remained, and the people of this land who’d chosen to live alongside them.”

“Your people?” I asked.

“Some of them, too – a few. In time the community dispersed, absorbed back into the tribe that became known as the Micmaq. The White Prince slipped into legend, and eventually it was my family who took on the task of protecting the Prince’s treasure until he or his family returned to re-claim it.”

 I was, I admit, left speechless. John B. jumped in with a question that was *not* the first that sprang to my mind.
“He was killed by the forces of the King of England when he was back in the Orkneys. I believe it was always his intention to return here. But why your family, Wehmisemawa? Were they especially close to Henry?”

"I don't believe so, Wetassawametewa. It's just that those of my race are especially good at stealth and keeping things hidden. And we have better developed memories than most others."

 She said that in such a cryptic, almost conspiratorial way that for a moment I felt like she and John B. were sharing a secret.   She continued. "We have known this for many years. The treasure is rightfully owned by the Prince's descendant, but it will be earned by one of John Dimond's line, and those two together shall be worthy."

"And now you've completely lost me," said JB. "I'm confident that my darling here is descended from Henry St. Clair, but I've no idea who or what a John Dimond is."

 She seemed to ignore his comment. I jumped in with the question that was at the forefront of my thoughts.
"You said 'treasure' – what treasure?"

"When the White Prince departed, he left behind two boxes full of things he had originally brought with him. Family treasures, and other valuables acquired on the journey. That locket is an example, but I believe there are much more extravagant things."

"You've not seen them?" I asked, surprised again.

"They haven't been seen for many years. Only the locket was kept aside, and passed through the generations. The boxes were hidden in a cave that only my people remember the location of. By finding me and rescuing me you've proved you two are worthy, just as foretold."

"By your grand-daughter," said John B. cautiously.

"Yes, and older stories, Wetassawametewa."

"That's not the first time you've called me that. I understand that *metewa* means wizard, or something like it, but I don't know the extended version."

John B. was ahead of me with the little he knew, which I assumed he'd learned from the book he'd been reading on the train. Our new friend looked thoughtful, as if she was grappling to find the right words in English.

"Perhaps… mystic warrior? One who uses magic in a just cause."

"I'm flattered, but what can I say?" He grinned as he said, "You hardly know me."

"You found me, as foretold. You came here with the child of the sea. You have the eyes of John Dimond. Who can you be *but* Wetassawametewa?"

There were a few moments silence as my beau and I tried to digest this. I confess I should have been more interested in the mystery of John Dimond, but frankly I had another mystery calling for my attention.

"So, where is this cave that only your people know about? Somewhere near here?"

Wehmisemawa shook her head as she smoothed her tunic back down over her body, her ribs now wrapped in a bandage, and medicated dressings applied to her wounds.

"The cave is on the northern side of Tepatamwa – the island of love. But its entrance is under the water. There is a rock face that extends some way along that edge of the island. To find the cave you must dive at the point where a crack in the rock is the cleft in the heart."

"Pardon?"

"I'm sorry, child of the sea. I've never actually seen it – that's the description that's been part of the history for years."

"History, not legend," I said, staring again at the locket in my hand.

With careful help from John B., Wehmisemawa was getting to her feet.

She was even less tall than I'd estimated, standing barely more than waist high to me.

"Indeed," she said.

"And does history, or legend, foretell that we'll actually find this treasure?" I asked.

She smiled and took my hand, the one holding the locket, in both of hers. "No. Our knowledge ends at this point. Other than that I will live to tell the story of my rescuers to my son when he is old enough to understand, and he will tell his daughter, and that in time, she will tell me. Your destiny is your own, child of the sea. But you and your beloved are strong, and both of you carry much of the power of the past. The Wetassawametewa has survived much, and his love for you is clear."

My other hand reached for my wizard at that point, and I turned to smile into his face as Wehmisemawa mentioned our love. I felt the small woman let go of my hand as I turned away.

I looked back and she was gone. I hadn't heard a sound – not so much as a twig snapping or a branch rustling. The first aid kit lay beside a depression in the pine needles that was the only evidence that she'd ever been there. The only evidence beside our memories, and the golden locket that dangled from my hand.

.o0o.

9 SOME GIRLS

It didn't occur to either of us to continue on to the Micmaq community. I
didn't see a need. We had the information that we – *I*, had wanted. Well,
perhaps not exactly, but we had something dramatically more than expected.

A family treasure? I hadn't seen *that* coming. I'll admit it – I was bubbling with excitement all the way back to Portland. Even over dinner (in a
wonderful little French-inspired restaurant we'd happened onto) I was still
more fascinated by the prospect of two boxes of… what? Gold? Jewels?
Certainly something more tangible than a vanished community that had
apparently just intermarried and devolved into the local indigenous tribes.
There's just something magical about the word 'treasure'.

I suppose it's a little unusual for us that it was John B. who started thinking practically. It was at the end of dinner, lingering over liqueurs, when
he raised the question of legal ownership. Assuming there *was* a treasure,
and that we *could* find it, would I actually be the legal owner? And if necessary, how could I prove it?

Neither of us knew how Australian law would handle such a situation,
far less American law. But John B. knew someone who might, and that
someone was local.

After dinner when we got back to our room he went rummaging through
the old duffel bag that seems to hold all he owns in a jumble. It would
drive me insane, but it works for him. I know better than to try to change
him, not least because I know how I'd respond if he tried it on me – it took
me too long to realise that was one of the major problems in my marriage
to Sonny.

Anyway, from somewhere in the depths of the khaki bag he pulled out a
business card for 'Drake Professional Services' in Ogunquit, Maine. The
name on the card was Ariane Cook.

"We met while I was in Hawaii, on that golf trip with Wilko," he explained.

"I think I remember the name."

"She gave me the beanie I was wearing in Norway."

"The black one? Yes, I remember now."

 I remembered that it had crossed my mind to buy him a new one, probably purple. It's hard not to be at least a bit jealous of another woman's keepsake that your sweetheart wears.

"Ariane did legal stuff, Glexie was the accountant. They live together. I'll give her a call in the morning, find out if she can help, shall I?" he offered.

"Glexie was the golfer, wasn't she? The one that Wilko took a bit of an interest in?"

"That's it. Didn't come to anything of course. He and Jazz were first starting their 'relationship-by-phone' right about then."

 John B. smiled fondly at me then, I think remembering that he and I were taking the same first tentative steps at the same time.

 We retired for the night soon after. If John B. thought I was being a bit distant he didn't remark on it. I was a little upset at the prospect of taking the news of our potential fortune to someone I couldn't help think of as his former girlfriend. Oh, I knew he'd said that they'd been nothing more than friends on Hawaii, and knew that Wilko had said the same thing. But I've heard the phrase often enough: "What happens on tour stays on tour". They'd been close enough that he carried around her hat. And if anything *had* been going on, would Wilko really tell me? I mean, we're good friends, but he's closer to John B. than he is to me. I really do have green eyes, don't I?

Nevertheless, I could see the sense in the suggestion, and after breakfast the next morning John B. rang Drake Professional Services and made an appointment for us to drop in a couple of hours later.

 The drive to Ogunquit was pretty, and didn't take long – about 35 miles southwest along the main turnpike. I'd read up on the town over breakfast (I still wasn't in the mood to chat). It seems to be the LGBTQ 'capital' of northeastern USA, and is reputed to have the nicest beach in Maine. We got to the town a while before our appointment, so decided to stroll around and do some sightseeing.

 I was surprised at how much traffic there was in Ogunquit, especially considering it was well off the main tourist season. We managed to find a parking space near the beach – no mean feat, I gather. From there we walked along something called the Marginal Way (named because it fol-lows the 'margin' of the sea), a nice footpath that mostly hugs the coastline for about a mile, except for a block or two that goes through town.

 Ogunquit seems to attract, well, let's say *characters*. We spotted one girl sitting on a bench overlooking the beach with one of the worst hairdress-ing efforts either of us had ever seen. And bear in mind we'd worked for a man who's hairdresser wife used him for some of her most outrageous experiments. It looked like the haircut of someone with a much smaller skull had been lifted and then relaid intact upon her head. A wide fringe of pink skin glowed around her ears, down and across the back of her neck.

"Do you think she paid someone to make her look like that?" I asked qui-etly.

"I fear so," John B. replied. "Maybe it's a fashion statement."

"In which case, the statement is: avoid being fashionable," I said.

 Later we saw another eye-catching young woman sashaying along the lit-tle section of town that the Marginal Walk took us through. Bear in mind, for all that it was a lovely clear day, the weather was cool. Yet she was dressed in a skirt that was so abbreviated top and bottom it looked more like a low-slung wide belt, and a flimsy top made of less fabric than most handkerchiefs.

I frowned and said, "I think she's a… how can I put it delicately… rhymes with 'flollop'…"

"I'm so glad you're being delicate."

Okay, I was still a bit tetchy. I was probably a little less catty soon after when a well-proportioned young man skateboarded past us wearing even less: a glittery gold derby hat, wraparound sunglasses, and a shiny gold penis sheath. We turned to watch him go by (as I'm sure was his intention), and read "Greetings from San Francisco" tattooed in large decorative letters across his muscular upper back.

"I presume the outfit has something to do with the Golden Gate," remarked John B. mildly.

The walk eventually brought us to a car park that was very full. On the far side of that was a pedestrian bridge over Perkins Cove. What was distinctive about it was that it was a drawbridge, a fact we only realised when we saw it being raised to allow passage of a small yacht under full sail.

Our destination was in a block of shops further along the cove, so we walked along the waterfront rather than the street. It hadn't been long since we'd sailed from the Shetland Islands over to Norway in our own little boat, so we took an interest in the various craft we saw moored and sailing.

At one point John B. pointed out a slim, very sleek motor cruiser with the name *Ondine* painted on her hull as it slipped slowly past.

"I was in a play called 'Ondine' at high school," he said casually. "Variation on the 'Little Mermaid'. She was a beautiful daughter of Neptune who fell in love with a handsome knight, her family didn't approve, lots of magical chaos ensued. I don't remember the details."

"I'm not surprised you remember magical chaos, though. An indication of things to come, maybe."

The office of Drake Professional was in a smart wooden building that had been designed to look 'historic'. A comfortable entrance foyer gave access to four doors - a suite of offices, evidently. We entered and introduced ourselves to the receptionist, an overweight pink-faced young man named Jeremy.

He was a strange mix of obsequious and rude, as if he knew he was supposed to keep customers happy, but deep down he resented how they complicated the smooth running of his day. Well, I've worked in a few 'customer service' jobs myself, so I understand that feeling, although I hope I never disguised it so poorly!

We were shown into one of the offices. No sooner had we walked in than a very pretty young woman threw her arms around John B. and gave a little squeal of delight as she hugged him.

"It's good to see you, too," he said returning the hug, admittedly a bit less enthusiastically, probably aware of the look I was giving them.

"Ariane Cook, I presume?" I said, unable to keep frost from my voice.

"No, that would be me," said the young lady behind a desk. I hadn't noticed her behind the two embracing.

"I'm so sorry!" said the girl who'd jumped on my beau. She gave me a huge smile and thrust out a hand for me to shake. "I'm Glexie. Glexie Hill. You must be Elizabeth."

Resisting that smile would be like kicking a puppy. I shook the proffered hand and introduced myself. The girl behind the desk, Ariane, stood and shook my hand far more formally, and only then reached to shake John B.'s hand in greeting. I did notice that they held the clasp for a moment or two longer than politeness required, though.

Both women were slightly less than my height. Glexie had long wavy hair, a little lighter than my shade of brunette. I suspect it was bleached by the sun, as she had what I admit was an attractive tan. She wore a mid-length blue skirt and a blouse with a floral print that reminded me of a Monet painting. To my eye the blouse was a size too small for her curvy figure, but I'll admit now that my eye was being a bit critical at that moment. Long sleeves hid most of the extravagant tattoo on her arm that I'd heard about. Alright, I could see how Wilko was attracted in Hawaii.

Ariane was more conservatively dressed. A plain black skirt, white top and a black bolero jacket – the sort of thing I'd have worn in my corporate days, although I like to think I'd have chosen a more interesting colour palette. To be fair, the black and white did suit her. A pale complexion, highlighted by just enough make-up, and jet-black hair cut in a curly bob. A pixie-ish sort of face, but very dark eyes that had a striking intensity. You wouldn't mess with the owner of those eyes.

"John B. didn't give much away when he rang, just said you wanted some legal advice about property ownership. It doesn't sound like you need an accountant for that, so I'll get out of your way. I just wanted to say 'Hi' when you arrived. Could we catch up for lunch later on though?"

Glexie's enthusiasm was irresistible. I found myself saying, "Sure, love to," without actually engaging my brain before I opened my mouth.

"Wonderful! Thanks! There's a nice place just along the waterside, outdoor tables – near the bridge," the accountant bubbled.

She gave me a brief, cheerful hug before almost skipping out of the office.

"I'm sorry. Please forgive Glexie. I think since Hawaii she's been finding Maine a bit... stuffy," said Ariane sympathetically.

"The place, or the job, or..." asked John B. cautiously.

"A bit of everything, I'm afraid. Actually getting out into the big wide world seems to have lit a bit of a fire in her."

"And you, my friend?" my wizard asked.

 Ariane gave a little laugh. "Oh, it was always there for me. I'm just much better at restraining it. Thanks for asking – it's good to see you, my friend. Now, Elizabeth, please tell me, what can I do for you?"

 Feeling somewhat more at ease with this young woman's friendly but professional manner, I explained the situation as succinctly as I could. That was no easy task, but I told what I could of the story of Henry St. Clair's journey from the Orkneys nearly six hundred years earlier, the settlement he was thought to have established and left behind, our meeting Wehmisemawa, and the gist of the story she'd told us.

 I held out the locket for her to examine, and said, "I'd like to see if this 'treasure' really exists. But I don't think it will be easy, and I'm reluctant to go to a lot of effort if whatever we find has to go straight into the hands of the government."

 As she turned the gold object over in her hand, Ariane was silently thoughtful for a time.

"A tricky one," she finally said. "If the treasure *does* exist… even if it could be proven to be a 100% St. Clair legacy, given the passage of time, I can't see much chance of you being considered 'sole beneficiary'. Even if we could prove direct lineage. I'm sure there must be others in the family after so many generations. Depending on where it's located, there may be an argument for finder's rights, or salvage rights, if it were you who unearthed it. That might be contingent on the ownership of the property where the treasure is located. Any idea of where that might be?"

 John B. and I exchanged looks. Clearly he trusted Ariane Cook, and I trusted him.

"In an underwater cave, so we're told. Have you heard of an island called Tepatamwa?" I asked.

 Ariane shook her head. "No. But I'm very much a landlubber," she admitted. "I know there are a lot of islands out in the bay. Some are big, with permanent communities living on them. I'd know the name if it was any of those. But many of them are small and uninhabited. Some get visitors, fishing or spotting wildlife. It may be one of them. It could be an old name for something we now know as something else."

"The name means 'Love Island', I think," said John B. "Algonquin word."

"Very good," said the legal officer with a smile. She looked at me. "Do you share an interest in indigenous cultures too?"

"I'm learning," I replied. "I don't have your flair for languages, babe," I told John B., putting a possessive hand on his arm.

 I was still a little wary. Ariane was a good-looking woman and she clearly knew my beau pretty well. If she caught the signal she gave no indication of it.

"A lot will depend on the actual ownership of this island, then, or the part where the cave lies. Although, being underwater some maritime law might come into play. I'll have to do some research, okay?"

 I nodded.

"Two boxes of stuff like this?" she asked, handing back my locket. "The historical value alone could be significant, let alone the intrinsic worth of the gold itself."

"Jewels too, if our little lady is to be believed," I said.

 Ariane looked thoughtful. "I'll have to talk to my boss, Lachlan Drake, after I've done a bit more research. I'm good with property, but he's much better with salvage laws than I am. Don't worry," she said recognising a look of concern on my face, "I'll tell him the bare minimum of what I need to get an answer for you."

"Thank you," I said. "I'd appreciate it being kept as quiet as possible."

 I must have given an inadvertent look over my shoulder towards the reception area.

"And I definitely won't be mentioning anything to Jeremy," she added.

 I laughed, a little embarrassed at being so obvious. "Sorry, there's just something I didn't like about the young man…"

"Understood," Ariane replied. "I wouldn't employ him in a pink fit. He's a moderately good office manager but his people skills are rubbish, although he doesn't seem to realise it. I suspect he's only here because he and Lachlan frequent some of the same bars. Sorry, that's probably unfair, but I do understand your reserve."

"Bars like the *Aye Noah Place*?" suggested John B.

 Ariane rolled her eyes. "Alas, yes."

"Not your sort of venue?" I asked.

"Not quite. Alright in daylight hours, but they seem to prefer a male clientele at night. Women aren't actually excluded, but the regulars there aren't… well, they're not to my taste."

 Suddenly I caught the subtext, and immediately felt safer regarding my beau.

"There are much nicer venues here in Ogunquit, quite frankly," said Ariane. "Say, I probably won't make lunch with you and Glexie – I'll get straight to work on your case – but why don't the four of us get together tonight for dinner and some drinks afterward? There's a wonderful place called *Twinkles*. Awful name, I know, but it's a very nice upstairs eatery with a great piano bar."

 One thing I've learned when travelling is to trust local knowledge. Eat where the locals eat, and drink where they drink. Never mind the tourist information brochures!

"That sounds great, thanks Ariane," I replied. "Okay with you, babe?"

"I'm not sure I'm dressed for a night out with three lovely ladies, but we can always scoot back up the turnpike so I can change," said John B.

Our new legal advisor shook her head and laughed. "You look fine, hon. The t-shirt is clean, isn't it? *Twinkles* is nice, but it's casual. What about you, Elizabeth? I think you look great, but are you comfortable?"

I tried to picture myself in this morning's mirror. I'd wanted to look smart – credible – but not too formal. Green top that showed off my shoulders that JB claims to love, simple A-line patterned skirt in greens and soft browns. It wasn't a competition, I told myself.

But nonetheless I said, "I think we'll pop back to Portland and change first. I'll have been in this outfit all day. It may not bother this bloke, but I'd like to freshen up."

"I get that. Let's say 7:00 then. Time for Glexie and I to get home after work, then come back. We've got a place a little way up along the road to the Yorks."

I checked my watch and said, "That works for me. Now, do you need anything else from me – us?"

"I don't think so. You left your mobile number when you rang this morning, didn't you? I'll call if there's a problem. I'll just buzz Glexie and tell her you're ready for lunch."

The farewell handshakes were probably a bit warmer than when we'd arrived, on my part at least. Glexie met us out in the reception room, and gave Jeremy a cheery wave as we left the building. His answering smile looked fake, but the accountant seemed either unaware or unconcerned.

Lunch was light, but very tasty, and the view over the water was as pleasant as had been promised. We noticed the *Ondine*, now moored nearby. I noticed three crew working on her. Well, two lean men working, and a fatter fellow apparently supervising.

The company was good, and I started to relax as we chatted about golf, beaches and our travels. Glexie explained the origin of her unusual name. Short for Glexandria, named after her great-grandmother who was later realised to be Alexandria but they'd misread her handwriting. Her enthusiasm seemed to dip a bit when we got to discussing life around Ogunquit.

"Oh, it's nice enough," admitted Glexie. "The beach is great, for part of the year anyway. I've known some people here for my whole life, although funnily enough there aren't many I can honestly say I'm close to. Enough to have a bit of fun. I'm looking forward to *Twinkles* tonight, we haven't been there in a while!"

The thought seemed to perk her up a bit from the little slump around discussing her hometown. I thought back to Ariane's comments about the discovery of the big wide world. I sympathized. After all, I reflected, I wasn't long out of my own cocoon that I'd let myself be stuck in for far too long.

The click-clacking of hooves caused us to look around. Along the path was coming an open-top wagon, drawn by two beautiful chestnut horses. The wagon was being driven by an elderly man wearing a top hat, and contained a half dozen Asian tourists, snapping pictures of everything around them. A boy of about twelve whizzed past them on his skateboard. Evidently he realised he was being photographed, because he decided to do some trick riding.

I've no idea what his intention had been, but the result was that he lost his balance and crashed into the side of the left-hand horse. The poor animal must have gotten a terrible shock, because it whinnied loudly and reared. It raised its front half so high it slipped from the wooden sticks that connected it to the wagon, landing with a leg on either side of the timber. By some miracle the boy wasn't hit by flailing hooves, and he managed to roll clear.

But both horses were panicked, and in a terrible tangle veered off the path. There was something I took to be a grassy drainage ditch beside the walkway, and the horses and front of the wagon wound up in it. The old fellow had been pitched off his seat, but the passengers were clinging to their perches and still taking pictures, laughing and chattering in whatever language it was. All part of the show, they seemed to think.

The old chap was trying to calm the horses, but they were having none of it. The mare caught straddling the wood, in particular, was flailing about, teeth bared and eyes wide. The poor wagon master couldn't get near it without risking serious injury.

Suddenly John B. was up out of his seat and striding over to the scene. He pushed aside a few people who'd started to gather and shout ineffectual advice. He waited a moment for the frightened horse to have both front feet on the ground then stepped briskly forward and laid one hand on the beast's chest and the other on its muzzle.

Glexie and I had stood up, and both immediately started to follow him. Instinctively though we both stopped a little way away, not wanting to further startle the horses. The one who hadn't been struck by the skateboarder was less agitated, and after feeding on the other animal's distress, was getting noticeably calmer as John B. soothed the frightened mare.

And he was. He was talking softly, putting gentle pressure on the horse's face to dissuade her from rearing up again. He moved his other hand from her chest and very carefully began to stroke her neck. The mare shook her head momentarily, but he never broke eye contact with her. She was visibly trembling, but at least stood still.

Without turning his head, John B. called to the wagon master. "Can you unhitch her, and back the carriage up? I'm sure someone here can help with pulling the wagon back."

There was no arguing with that voice. Although still shaken, the old man approached the horses gamely, undoing harnesses and bits that connected the animals to the vehicle. Others, Glexie and I included, gripped the sides of the wagon and started to push it back out of the ditch. First though, we had to remove several tourists who evidently still thought this was all being done for their entertainment. John B. was hugging the perspiring mare's head to his chest, one hand still on her muzzle, just below her eyes.

Two burly men who looked like footballers gallantly took over from Glexie and I to help haul the carriage. She and I stepped back to watch, ready to help where and how we could. As the timber and tangled harness pulled back from under her the horse shied a bit, but my wizard just held her a little tighter and rested his forehead against her. She settled.

Glexie said to me quietly, "I saw what he was like with that hawk over in Hawaii. Now look at him. Are there any more like him at home?"

"I don't think there are any quite like him anywhere," I replied.

With a smile she answered, "I believe you. You done good, girl."

"Thanks," I said. I looked at Glexie a bit speculatively, and cautiously began, "I , er, thought you and Ariane…"

"A few people think that. We're just good friends. Mates, you Aussies call it. I'm straight, she's not, we're both looking." I must have looked slightly defensive, because she hurriedly continued, "Well, not *looking*, but unattached and optimistic. And careful."

I nodded. "Careful is good. Better than rushing into a mistake."

"Sounds like a 'been there, done that' observation."

I sighed. "Yeah. Better now." I gave a smile, to reassure both of us after my moment of painful recollection.

Glexie tentatively squeezed my hand. "Like I said, you done good."

I squeezed back and replied, "I think so."

The object of our discussion was gently leading the horse back up onto the pathway. Onlookers were keeping a safe distance, still wary of a spooked look in the mare's eyes. But she seemed docile enough now. In a moment she was resting the front of her head against JB's chest, with her eyes closed, as her breathing finally slowed.

The wagon master had regained his hat, and his composure, and was talking quietly with John B. The mare stood quietly alongside the other horse as the footballer types helped maneuver the carriage back into position so the old fellow could reattach the harnesses. A final word from JB and a pat on the neck, and she click-clacked away apparently happy again. There were to be no more rides that day, though – a fact which caused a stir among the former passengers. It's a good thing the biggest and most belligerent of them barely came up to one footballer's chin.

My wizard came back to our table and sat down heavily. He was drenched in sweat. I don't know how much was his and how much had come from the mare. While I took his hand and let him get his breath back, Glexie dashed inside to fetch a cool drink.

As she handed him the glass she said, "You certainly know how to liven up a lunchtime! Well, that's a story to keep the office entertained this afternoon, thank you!"

John B. gave a wry smile. "Thanks. I'd like to say it was a pleasure, but not quite true. Still, worked out in the end. We're invited to have free carriage rides whenever we want one. More importantly, no real harm done to the horse. Poor thing." He looked down at his perspiration-soaked clothing. "I definitely will have to change before tonight, so that's *that* decision verified."

With hugs all round, even to my sweaty beau, Glexie went back to work. We began to stroll back to where we'd parked the car. As we walked I asked, "You're a regular Doctor Doolittle, aren't you babe? Have you always been so good with animals? Or is it… another side-effect of your, er, bump on the head?"

 John B. looked thoughtful. "I hadn't thought about it. I mean, I've *liked* animals as far back as I can remember. Never had a pet, as such. My Dad was allergic to cats, and Mum didn't like the noise of dogs barking."

 I knew he was referring to his adoptive parents. I presumed there were no pets kept in the orphanage that he'd been in for a while after being found wandering the streets, apparently amnesiac, somewhere around the age of ten.

"We did have a couple of goldfish, but I don't remember much interaction with them," he continued. "I know I was a bit upset when the table holding their tank collapsed. So was Mum, but I think that was more to do with the mess on the carpet."

 I had to laugh at the image. "But the way they seem to respond to you now?" I pressed.

"I really don't know. It's instinctive on my part. I just try to be… gentle. Seems to work."

 He's an intriguing man, to my mind not least because he seems to really know so little about himself. And he seems more sanguine than curious about that. We both walked in silence for a while, each absorbed in our own thoughts.

 As we neared the car park we had an opportunity to look out over the beach, that neither of us were dressed to take real advantage of. Despite the nip in the air, there were plenty of people on the sand.

 I couldn't help notice one girl. I'm sure her breasts were surgically en-hanced. Either that or they could defy gravity. Only just wearing a white bikini, as she promenaded along the sand she had her own entourage of admirers (male and female) beside and behind her.

I suspect the green in my eyes was flashing again. I already had an answer or two in my head as I asked out loud, "What's she got that I haven't got?"

JB answered casually, "She's got nobody holding her hand, who loves her."

There's a reason I love that man. I turned, hugged him, and we shared a kiss to confirm just how mutual the feeling is.

.o0o.

10 MUSING TO THE MUSIC

Twinkles turned out to be more fun than I honestly expected. JB and I were far from the only straight couple there, but the place was genuinely inclusive, in the truest sense of the word. Unlike the *Aye Noah Place*, this felt like it welcomed anyone and everyone.

I even recognised Mister 'Greetings from San Francisco' although that took some time. I knew the face, but he looked different with clothes on. Even though they were short shorts and a very open-necked white shirt.

The food was excellent, just as Ariane had suggested. Both girls had more substantial appetites than John B. or me. It seems to be an American 'thing'. The serving sizes are often daunting.

After we'd eaten, the four of us settled at a small table by the window. We had a panoramic view of the street (not that exciting, I must admit), and were close enough to the grand piano to enjoy the music without having to converse in bellows and sign language.

During the evening Ariane explained what she'd gleaned from Lachlan Drake without, she'd hoped, giving too much away to him. Naturally enough he'd asked questions, in order to give a reliable answer, he explained.

In his considered opinion, if there *was* a treasure that had been abandoned centuries earlier, it would become the property of whoever found it, with due consideration to whoever owned the land on which it was found. If it were state-owned land there were State regulations to apportion the value of the find, but he did observe with a conspiratorial wink that he was "quite certain" many such discoveries were never made known to the government.

"And the family connection?" I asked.

"After so many generations, without a clear line of succession, he pretty much laughed off the idea. If the finder was a descendent it might give them a nice warm glow, but there'd be no other legal benefit," Ariane relayed.

"So, finders keepers," said John B. "I don't know. I'm still a bit sensitive to the idea of some native claim. I can't imagine Wehmisemawa has any authority to speak for her whole tribe, for all that she seemed to take that upon herself. And what about the people who Henry's community inter-married with? The Micmaq, presumably?"

Ariane shrugged. "I don't know anything about this mysterious woman's people. I suppose they could be an offshoot of one of the other tribes in the area. I think there are only a handful of Micmaq in the region now. A lot died off in the great plague of 1617."

At that point the jovial man at the piano launched into a rousing rendition of *Hello Dolly*, encouraging everyone in the place to, "Sing along, y'all, an' sing loud!" It was the perfect mood-lifter after Ariane's sombre remark. It was the start of a bracket of show tunes that got the whole of *Twinkles* bouncing along. The four of us left our table and stood near the front of the happy cluster forming around the piano.

Among the singing crowd I was delighted to spot Lanny and Cowley. The big man especially was enthusiastic about belting out a tune. *Can't Help Lovin' That Man Of Mine* was clearly a favourite. During a brief break between songs I managed a quick "Fancy meeting you here!" or words to that effect.

"We've got a little boat that we bring here for servicing," explained Lanny. "There's a very good chandler in Perkins Cove that we take her to."

Any chance of further chat was lost when the piano player launched into '*Anything You Can Do, I Can Do Better*' (it's from *Annie Get Your Gun* if you didn't grow up on a diet of Hollywood musicals like I did). The 'choir' was split into boys versus girls, as usual. But this being *Twinkles*, there was the added advice, "If y'all don't identify as neither, then jus' sing both parts!”

 Later in the night, when the entertainer was enjoying a well-earned break and the piped music wasn’t too loud, we were able to resume conversation. I introduced the girls to Lanny and Cowley, and was pleased (though not surprised) when they seemed to hit it off straight away.

“I’ve been thinking,” announced John B. “I reckon another visit to Texas Dorothy might be wise.”

 Seeing the blank looks on our two lady friends I briefly explained who and what Dorothy Duncum was – as much as we knew, anyway.

“Ah’m glad she’s been some use to ya,” said Cowley. “Ah know her more by reputation than anythin’ else, but whatever Ah’ve heard has been good.”

“Do you think she’ll know something more about this woman’s people, or the lost settlement, that she hasn’t told you?” asked Glexie.

“I have a hunch she knows about a *lot* that she hasn’t told us,” replied my beau.

 Just on instinct alone, I thought he was right.

.o0o.

11 WHO SAID WHAT TO WHOM

A letter from Peter Baron, a bartender who works the evening shift at the 'Aye Noah Place', to one of his former regular customers:

Dear Cliff

I do hope you're settling in well to sunny Florida. Of course we're all terribly jealous of you, as we head into what will surely be another dreary Maine winter.

But of course we miss you terribly, too, and would really rather you were here to share the bleakness. Or better, that we were there to share the sunshine!

In all seriousness my dear, you truly are missed, and I for one am terribly sorry that your break-up with Bertie was so painful that you felt you had to leave and go quite so far away.

Whatever nonsense Sam McFerris put into Bertie's head about you was, I'm sure, just that. Nonsense. And I really didn't think Bertie was so stupid as to believe a word of it, whatever it was.

Speaking of Saxa, I must tell you this story.

It started with Lachlan Drake. You know that rather shrewish man from Ogunquit who comes into the bar occasionally? Always wears a blue suit with a wide collar. He's a lawyer or accountant or something tiresome like that.

Well, I heard him talking with Sam McFerris about

these two clients he had, or at least that someone on his staff had consulted him about. They'd apparently either inherited or found some very substantial treasure. Chests full of doubloons and gems or something, terribly valuable at any rate. He mentioned that they'd recently arrived here from Australia.

Saxa asked Lachlan to describe them, and of course he then said he knew them. Even suggested he was the one who'd sent them off to Popham Beach, which was where they'd presumably dug up their hoard.

Well, that quietened Lachlan down a bit, I can tell you. The next time I came near them the conversation had turned to fishing, and of course it was a very one-sided conversation, most of which was coming from Saxa.

Not long after, Lachlan left with that nice young fellow from the hardware depot. You know, the blonde one he sometimes goes out with. And around the same time that curly headed fellow that McFerris lives with turned up. Dean something. So the two of them got into some sort of deep and meaningful discussion that I didn't want to hear. Nasty chap, that Dean, I think. I did overhear him say something to the effect of, "I think our large nautical friend will want to know about this."

But it doesn't end there. A little while later Barry Lister arrived with two of his friends. Did you ever meet Barry? Big chap, carrying too much weight for his health I'd say, has a red beard that always looks well trimmed. Usually a terribly jolly chap, although I have heard he has a temper.

Well, Barry and his friends sat alongside Saxa and

Dean at the bar. They're all pals. Actually, I have heard that Dean has something to do with selling things for Barry that may not always be terribly kosher if you know what I mean. But I'm not one to gossip, unlike some.

So, Saxa tells Barry this story of the two Australians who've found a vast treasure under Popham Beach, describing golden goblets studded with rubies and emeralds, and goodness knows what other fancies! He even cited Lachlan Drake 's involvement as some sort of evidence!

Then Dean interrupted, and said something about how Sam's Uncle Cowley had called and given Saxa a telling-off for sending two Australians on a wild goose chase to Popham. Apparently he'd tried to set them straight by sending them to the author woman who lives up past Windsor. Dorothy Duncum. I've never met her, but she's supposed to be terribly charming.

Barry of course laughed the whole thing off, but Sam got quite prickly and said that he'd had it from an 'unimpeachable source' that even now the two tourists were looking to get the hoard valued. I had to move away to serve someone, but I did hear big Barry say something about how that would put his stupid brother in his place. I didn't know he even had a brother.

When I happened to be back near them Saxa was complaining about his own worthless brother. Usually we all hear about his dreadful sister. The only time Bill McFerris is mentioned is when someone else is having a problem with _their_ brother. Isn't that strange?

And that's what I'm trying to tell you, Cliff. I hope I
haven't bored you with all this, but my point is that I
think Saxa's stories are just that. Stories. And Bertie
is terribly foolish for being taken in by them. I know
this probably isn't what you want to hear right now,
but I do think you're better off without him, if that's
the extent of his trust in you.

Please take good care of yourself, and remember
that no matter how warm it is in Florida, there's a
welcome at least as warm waiting here for you back
in Maine.

All my best
Peter

.o0o.

12 OLD STORIES AND NEW

I'm very glad John B. had volunteered to be 'designated driver' on our night out. Far too much of something called 'Georgia tea'. Not as innocent as it sounds – it's a cocktail made of vodka, gin, white rum, peach schnapps and cranberry juice. I blame Glexie for introducing it to me. She and Ariane only had a short cab ride home, so they were both happy to indulge themselves. To be fair to Ariane, she avoided the cocktails and stuck to bourbon and soda. A good quantity of it, but she showed no sign of that beyond enthusiastic singing, and we were all in on that! Even JB, who was drinking two Moxies to every one single malt.

Cowley and Lanny stuck to red wine, and not much of that as I recollect. I think Lanny sets a lot of store in self-discipline, and his partner goes along with it out of loyalty and love, as good partners do.

The next morning was challenging, though. John B. was solicitously worried that "the cranberry juice had given me a headache". Sweet man. I definitely wasn't keen on an early drive to back up beyond Windsor. Breakfast was delivered to our room, and eaten slowly and quietly.

While I was lingering over coffee, JB called Texas Dorothy. After a few minutes of quiet conversation he reported back to me.

Yes, by the description she thought she knew something about the people of the little woman we'd rescued.

Yes, she knew something of the Micmaq who might be the remnants of Henry's lost community.

And yes, we were very welcome to visit her later in the day, and to spend the night there if convenient.

When we packed a change of clothes in a bag and did finally get on our way, our first stop was to top up Yvette's gas tank. The garage surprised

me by stocking a range of good-looking pastries, so I had a selection
boxed up to take with us. I was raised to never arrive empty-handed for a
social visit, and I'd wished I'd thought of it when we first called on Dorothy. I also treated myself to a big bottle of water!

I don't remember much of the drive. There's a fair chance I slept for most
of it. JB woke me in plenty of time for me to knock back a half bottle of
water and clear my head before we rolled up the long driveway.

This time it was Dorothy herself who opened the door. Mac was on her
lap, and the cavoodle came close to bouncing out of it greeting us. The
writer's welcome was as warm as her dog's, albeit a bit less demonstra-
tive. The pastries were well received, and went down well with the coffee
our hostess already had brewing in anticipation of our arrival. Considerably better than the hotel's brew!

We sat in the lounge room and chatted for quite a while. From our description, Texas Dorothy identified Wehmisemawa as being from a people she called the *Muhkeahweesug*, who are, or were, something like the
Native American equivalent of leprechauns.

"Lots of cultures, all over the world, tell similar stories," said Dorothy.

"I remember hearing about the *menehune* when I was in Hawaii. I wonder
what links all the traditions together. Any ideas, Dorothy?" asked John B.

After a curiously long moment's pause she answered with a shrug. "Ah
jus' collect the stories, hon. Ah make sure they ain't lost. Like Ah done
told ya, historian ain't mah job."

"Okay," I pressed on. "So do any of the muhkeahweesug stories that you
know shed any light on anything Wehmisemawa told us?"

Dorothy shook her white head sadly. "Ah'm afraid not. Ah know stories
about 'em, not from 'em. They're a folk what keep, or kept, themsel's to
themsel's. You two are the first people Ah've heard of even meetin' one of
the muhkeahweesug in over a hundred years. Ah reckon as how most

everyone thinks they'd died out. This woman y'all rescued, she an' her kin must dwell wa-a-ay back up in the woods!"

John B. patted my leg. "Doesn't sound like you're going to have to contend an ownership claim from them, at least, pretty lady. Now, what about this 'love island' – Tepatamwa?"

Dorothy grinned. "Now thet *is* something Ah can tell you some stories of. It's a little island up in the north of Casco Bay. Ain't nobody lived on it permanently, probably ever. Partly cos it ain't real big, but more important, especially in the old days, was cos of where it lay. Didn't quite fit in the regular fishin' lanes of any one family or tribe, but close by quite a few. So by a kinda mutual agreement it never belonged to anyone."

"Neutral territory?" asked John B.

"Pretty much. Over years it became the place where folks from different tribes would get together, especially if their kinfolk didn't approve. Or in times when tribes were warrin' with each other. Like when the Tarrantines was fightin' with the Massachusetts. It became the place where the rules didn't apply. Lotsa places didn't have somewhere like thet, so the folks in these parts were lucky."

"Running Bear and Little White Dove could have done with somewhere like that," said JB, who's always been strangely fond of that old song.

"Sure would have," agreed our hostess. "Thet song's based on an old old story, though not many folks know thet. Anyhow, there was a whole lotta much happier stories came off o' thet island. Wars finished, families getting' back together, little miracles like thet. Somewhere along the way, it was the Abnaki name for the place that stuck – Tepatamwa, meanin' love, but truth is they got no more claim on it than any other folks."

"So is it state-owned?" I asked.

Dorothy shrugged. "Cain't say. Reckon you might need to talk to someone of a legal persuasion 'bout that."

As she spoke she pulled a bound volume of maritime charts from her well-stocked bookshelves, almost immediately opened it to the correct page and handed it to me to examine while I answered.

"Well, we sort of have, without actually naming the place, discussed the legal ramifications. We didn't quite get told to ignore the possibility, but there was a definite sense of 'what the official eye doesn't see, the official heart doesn't grieve over', if you know what I mean," I said.

That brought another bright smile from Dorothy as she scratched Mac between his ears. "Sounds like a typical islander attitude, if you ask me."

"A bridge to cross if and when we come to it," observed John B. "What about these Micmaq? Do they have stories about Tepatamwa? It strikes me that they're the other potential players in Henry's story. The ones who interbred with the colonists, anyway."

"We never did get up to see that group that Sings Like Frog directed us to," I said.

"Why don't we all head up there now?" asked Dorothy, catching me completely off guard. "Ah knows some of the folks thet live there, an' Ah'm feelin' a whole lot chipper than a day or so ago."

There seemed no good reason not to, so we finished off our coffee, then JB and I waited while Texas Dorothy took herself off to get changed. Mac sprawled contentedly in my lap while that was happening, with John B. sitting on the floor beside me scratching under the dog's chin. I spent the time fixing the details of the maritime chart in my mind.

"Is the cavoodle coming with us?" I asked as Dorothy wheeled herself back into the room, resplendent in white jeans and a loose white cotton top beautifully embroidered with light blue tribal patterns.

"Better not," she replied. "Ah'll jus' take him outside ta do his business first, then he'll be fine in here with a bowl of water an' a handful of crunchies."

The dog was put on the ground at the side of the house, where he half bounded, half dragged himself into some low-growing foliage that fringed the area. Leaving Mac some privacy, John B. and I gave a cursory examination to the row of ten-gallon drums that stood alongside the house. They held Texas Dorothy's garbage, carefully sorted into food, paper, plastics and metals. A little way out among the undergrowth there was an area roughly fenced with corrugated iron, in which was piled plant cuttings and fruit and vegetable scraps. This was her compost heap, I presumed.

Dorothy explained that someone drove up from Brunswick "every so often" to take away her trash. I worried that such a casual arrangement might lead to a health hazard, but she just smiled her beaming smile and replied, "Oh, Ah get looked after. But thank you for carin', hon."

Mac gave a few barks as if to say he was done. John B. walked into the undergrowth and picked the dog up into his arms, getting some enthusiastic licks to his face as a 'thank you'. We followed Dorothy back into the house, where John B. put Mac down on the kitchen floor, alongside the two white ceramic bowls that held his sustenance for the day.

The little cavoodle looked up at us, his head tilted to one side. There was a reproachful look in his big eyes, as if to say, "You're not going out and *leaving* me, are you?" Each of us in turn gave him an affectionate pat on the head, at which point he then turned and buried his face in his food bowl.

"Right, we're dismissed it seems," said John B. and led the way out to Yvette.

"Nice set of wheels," said Dorothy as she pushed herself up out of her chair to stand, a bit wobbly but confident enough to wave away my offer of help. "Ah'm fine, hon, thanks. Been doin' this for a while now."

She took a few slow cautious steps, and climbed into the front passenger seat while John B. folded up her wheelchair and loaded it into the back of the SUV. I was quite content to be chauffeured in the back seat while Dorothy navigated.

We made a bit of small talk for the first part of the journey. Eventually though I felt bold enough to ask what had happened to put Dorothy in her wheelchair.

"Oh, mostly jus' getting' old, hon. Ah had a fall a few years back, down some stairs in a lighthouse. Landed on my back an' broke somethin' whereas Ah'd prob'ly have just gotten a big bruise a mite earlier. Ah s'pose Ah could change, but Ah reckon Ah ain't done with this ol' one jus' yet."

I didn't really know what she meant, but I had the sudden sense that this was not a conversation she would casually share with anyone else. Why was she so comfortable with us? It was as though she assumed we'd understand. But we didn't, and I said so.

She looked over at John B. in the driver's seat and said thoughtfully, "Of course. There's a whole lot you don' remember, ain't there?"

"I remember most of my life since I was about ten years old. But before that, nothing," he replied carefully.

"Ah was meanin' earlier than thet. Ah was meanin'… well…"

"Past life memories?" I suggested.

I could see Texas Dorothy studying me intently in the rear view mirror. "Of course it's a mite different for you, hon. Y'all have a *family* history."

"Well, sure. I've told you a chunk of it, how I traced back through the Orkneys to Henry St. Clair – that's what brought me here."

"An' this was on your father's side," she confirmed. "Ah see it in your eyes."

"Wehmisemawa said something similar," observed John B. quietly. "The green eyes are a family trait?"

"Ah reckon so. You ever seen anyone else with eyes thet are quite thet colour?"

 I had to admit, it hadn't occurred to me. But on reflection, no. I've met other people with green eyes, but never quite the same shade. In a lyrical moment John B. had told me it was like gazing into emeralds that went on forever. At the time I just thought he was being romantic, but there was something in Texas Dorothy's voice that hinted at more.

 Curiosity about more than my own past was niggling at me, though. "You said it was different for John B.?" I prompted. "What makes him special? Other than being incredibly special to me!" I hastily added, reaching forward to squeeze my beau's shoulder.

 Texas Dorothy again took a moment to reply. "You know we was talkin' about how so many cultures have stories about a race of little folk thet came before 'em, like the muhkeahweesug?"

"Leprechauns," I replied.

"Menehune," John B. offered.

"Yep. Same in different parts of Africa, an' all over the world. Well, did you ever notice thet all over the world they's also got stories of people who can do magic? Not whole races, but individuals."

 John B. was nodding. "Like Coyote, the trickster. Chang Kuo in China. Argula in Western Australia. I'm sure I remember other characters in African stories, and Scandinavian."

"You're well read, suh. An' there's some a lot more recent than thet."

"Are you saying John B. is one of these people?" I asked.

 The storyteller shrugged. "Little Wehmisemawa called him Wetassawam-etewa. Reckon she thinks so. Seems like thet there time you hit your head, you done woke something up thet was inside you."

"That fits with what I've been thinking since it happened. The night I became a wizard."

"The night John B. Stewart became a wizard. Mm." With that, Dorothy seemed to go quiet.

My memory had been prodded though. "Wehmisemawa also mentioned a John Dimond. Who's he?"

"Feller who lived round these parts back in the 1700s. Settled down in Marblehead, but s'pposed to have gone where he was needed. Lots o' stories about John. It weren't long after all the troubles in Salem, so nobody wanted to 'ccuse him of witchcraft. He got called the Marblehead Magician. Funnily enough, the local high school sports teams are still called the Marblehead Magicians."

"Gone but not forgotten, eh?" I said.

"Thet's my job, hon," Dorothy replied with a smile.

"Tell us a John Dimond story please?" I asked.

Dorothy wriggled back into her seat. I suspect there was little she liked more than hearing the words, "Tell us a story, please…"

"Folks would often call on John Dimond to find things thet were lost or had been stolen. He didn't have a perfect record, it's said, but then maybe some folks weren't tellin' the truth, either. There was one time when poor ol' Widow Brown had her firewood stolen. Now she'd spent a long time cuttin' an' stackin' it herself, ready for winter. Winter can get right cold round here, so thet was hard on a poor ol' woman. She came to John an' told him what had happened. While she was sittin' there, John Dimond closed his eyes and went into a kinda trance, accordin' to Widow Brown.

Then he opened his eyes and said a name. A feller named Fergus, thet lived over on the other side of town. Now this feller had a reputation for trouble, so the Widow weren't keen on confrontin' him. But John Dimond said she were to leave thet to him.

Now, nobody were ever quite sure what John Dimond said to him, but the story at the time was thet all through thet night Fergus was seen walkin' the streets of Marblehead with a heavy log on his back. Like enough it wasn't one log, but a whole stack o' them, because next mornin' Widow Brown's firewood were all back, stacked up neat an' proper behind her cottage."

"That's nice!" I exclaimed. "Worthy of you, babe!"

"Thank you, pretty lady," said JB, wrestling the car left around a sharp corner onto a little track Texas Dorothy had indicated.

As she'd recounted John Dimond's story I realised we'd passed the spot where we'd encountered Wehmisemawa. Before long the narrow track opened out onto an open space about half the size of a football field. On two sides of the clearing was a collection of rough conical buildings. Tee-pees I suppose, although these were made from bark, not the animal hides we see in movies and TV shows. I could see a couple of SUVs parked dis-creetly behind them. Much rougher than shiny new Yvette, but eminently practical for the track we'd just travelled.

There were perhaps two dozen people visible in the clearing. Men and women, and a few children, all dressed in a mix of traditional and contem-porary clothes. As we drove into the clearing, Dorothy motioned for John B. to park over to one side. As Yvette rolled to a halt, several of the group strode over towards us, looking stern, if not exactly hostile.

But the moment that Texas Dorothy was recognised, the expression on every face changed to a welcoming smile. I got the wheelchair from the back of the car and set it up while John B. helped the white-haired woman from her seat. The tribesfolk gathered around her, chattering excitedly, far too fast for me to understand even if I had learned more than a word or two of local language.

It was funny, though. I'd swear that I heard some words that I recognised from our time in both Scotland and Norway. What languages had they absorbed earlier in the history of their tribe?

 I was privately pleased to find that John B. wasn't much better off, for all that he already had a better knowledge of Algonquin to draw on.

"It's the speed, and the accent," he told me later. He was good enough to explain some words to me though, and I've reproduced them here as best I can.

 Dorothy introduced us to her friends, and there was much embracing and clasping of forearms – the equivalent of a handshake, I quickly realised. We were ushered over to sit in front of one of the teepees. Close up, I realised just how substantial the structures were. The bark looked rough, but it was strong, flexible, and I was assured, very rainproof.

 The storyteller explained the purpose of our visit, which elicited looks of considerable surprise. Several of the older people of the tribe, men and women, took themselves off for a private conversation. Meanwhile Dorothy entertained those who remained, especially the children, with a story about an owlet that fell from her nest and was protected by different creatures until a kind person climbed the tree and returned her home. She quickly got John B. and I involved by having us provide sound effects, including appropriate animal noises. JB's worried mother owl was especially poignant, I thought.

 When the elders returned, one stately man (whose air of dignity was surprisingly undiminished by a Marvin the Martian t-shirt) sat on the ground alongside me.

"This is Miskwamikletonakani, the *sakimawa*, or chief of these people," explained Dorothy.

"Miskwa – something to do with bears?" I ventured, taking the chief's proffered hand.

"Beard colour like bear," he explained in awkward English.

"The word *miskwa* can mean both 'bear' and the shade of red of their fur," said Dorothy.

It was appropriate enough. And it was a shade of red that also carried overtones of some Celtic blood, I realised. The chief took my hand, and looked into my eyes for what felt like a long time. Finally he solemnly said, "*Ehe. Yes. Kimoci menehstepatamwa, atamepyeki wapanwi, nana-hilizbeth.*"

I'm afraid I must have blinked like an idiot. Both the chief and Dorothy smiled, then the storyteller translated: "Thet which is secret, hidden, under the water at the east of the island of lovin', properly belongs to Elizabeth – to you, hon."

"Thank you," I said quietly and sincerely, my gratitude immediately echoed by my beau.

"You are welcome to stay, watch… uh… *nimyiweni*…?" The chief looked helplessly at Dorothy, but it was JB who responded first.

"Dance?"

Texas Dorothy gave one of her dazzling smiles. "Thet's a right honour. What happens here is somethin' more than a dance. It's a… well, it's an education, an' folks outside the tribe very rarely get to see it."

"We're honoured," acknowledged John B., clasping the arm of Miskwa-mikletonakani.

Members of the little Micmaq tribe gathered themselves into a circle. Only a few wore anything like a costume over the clothes they'd already had on. An older man and a young woman with striking red hair – more vibrant even than the chief's beard, started to beat out a rhythm on drums that were hollow logs.

At first the dancers moved in a clockwise circle, arms legs and bodies all in a seemingly random but coordinated set of gestures and gyrations.

After the whole circle had gone around four times three of the dancers broke from the ring and moved into the centre. One man wore a head-dress of black and red feathers; the other two (one male, one female) wore extravagantly beaded necklaces and bangles.

I noticed that all three had their eyes closed, and their movements were gradually shifting from rhythmic, in time with the drumbeats, to something jerkier and more spasmodic.

Beside me, John B. and Texas Dorothy were conversing quietly.

"I'm reminded of a corroboree I saw in Central Australia, and of a 'real' hula demonstration I saw in Hawaii," said my beau.

The authoress nodded. "Y'all might consider Morris dancin' in the same way. Long before them dances were about entertainin' the tourists, sorry, giving them an appreciation of local 'culture', the movements had much more importance."

"To both the audience and the dancers," suggested JB, to another nod.

I was intrigued. "Teaching, you mean?"

"Thet's a part of it, yep. In a kind of a way," replied Dorothy.

As I watched the three central dancers with their eyes closed, seeming to become lost in a kind of trance, I asked, "What then? Hypnosis? Subliminal imagery?"

"Imagery, yes," replied Dorothy. "A memory aid, like them wampum bands Ah showed ya – the movements reflect places and objects, and each of those represents somethin' important to be passed along the generations. It's another way of passin' on stories, besides just tellin' them, or writin' them down. But there's more. The dance awakens, or p'rhaps Ah should say activates, power in the dancers, and their unconscious reaches out. *That* is what influences the watchers."

We went quiet then, transfixed by the movements at the heart of the circle. The fellow in the beads darted around the circle, tapping one dancer then another, seemingly at random, before whirling back to the centre. Then the two men danced close to each other, clashing the backs of their forearms together in a rhythm twice the speed of the continuing drumbeats.

"Fighting?" I breathed.

Miskwamikletonakani leaned closer to me and whispered, "*Pakamewa esaweskwi.*"

"Sword fighting," translated Dorothy.

That struck me as odd in this culture. "Why…?" I began.

Pointing to the man in the beads, Miskwamikletonakani softly said, "*Myalaci, kemotwiweni. Myalimechkwi. Nimata sonkiteheweni.*"

"The first man is evil, a thief. He's got bad blood. The other man, the chief's brother, is a man of courage."

By now the woman was circling the two men, dancing counterclockwise with sinuous movements of her spine, but with her arms spread wide. As she ducked low at one point, the man in the feathered headdress suddenly lurched backwards from his 'swordfight'. It looked for a moment as though he'd fall over her, but as he left his feet he stayed balanced, his back on her back. She carried him for a lap of the circle, before he rolled off and stood crouched. The woman resumed her sinuous movements and closed in on the other man, her arms still spread well apart.

"*Kehte mankhboh kentapyeskawi,*" explained the chief, indicating the woman. He spread his own hands. "*Axpihtesiweni!*"

"She's an ol' big lizard what's goin' under the water. An' she's *real* big!"

As the woman circled him again, the man in the beads began a complicated series of movements that included running his hands up and down the length of his body, and turning in small circles with his arms making sweeping motions up over his face.

With a puzzled expression on his face, Miskwamikletonakani said, "*Maci-napehkwani, kimoci askikwamani...*"

Reflecting his puzzlement, Dorothy translated, "It's a bad ship, secretly made of metal. Ah don't have the faintest idea what thet's about..."

Then the man in the headdress was at the side of the woman at the centre of the dance. Suddenly she snapped her arms together around the beaded man, who dropped to his knees and bowed his head. The dancers in the circle all took a pace in, and extended their arms to the middle as they reduced their pace to a slow even step. The woman-who-was-lizard and the man-of-courage faced each other over the kneeling thief, and each placed their left hand on the other's left shoulder. They both stamped their left foot in time to the drumbeat. Twelve times, and with each stomp the kneeling figure slumped lower until he fell sideways to the ground. The circling dancers gave a loud cheer, and the drumbeats stopped.

The circle began to break up. As it did, the three who I thought of as the 'principal performers' all seemed to shake themselves, stretching and flex-ing as if waking up.

"*Mankboh tahkwantanwa macinapehkwani, neksiwanatesiweni. Myali tahpenewa. Nimata sawalentakwesiweni,*" explained Miskwamikleton-akani to a blank look from me.

"Phew!" exclaimed Dorothy. "Near as Ah can say it, the big lizard bit the ship an' destroyed it. The evil one was drowned. The lizard an' the chief's brother shared a blessing."

"Who was blessing who?" I asked.

Dorothy smiled as she answered, "Goes each way, Ah reckon."

"Have you seen this dance before?" was my next question.

As the authoress watched the dancers drift back to their teepees in little chattering groups she answered slowly, "Ah'm not sure thet anyone's seen thet dance before."

With his hands clasped in his lap, Miskwamikletonakani turned to face JB and I, smiled and said solemnly, "*Metewacyemwani.*"

Before Dorothy could interpret John B. nodded and said, "A mystical story."

The chief stood, and leaned to embrace Dorothy. As I got to my feet he embraced me too – it was like being hugged by a gentle bear. Finally he again clasped my wizard's arm. It seemed that our audience was over.

"*Sonkiteheweni, maskawesiweni, nimati,* said the chief.

"*Maskawesiweni, lepwahkaweni, nimati,*" my beau replied.

Most of the little tribe gathered to help, then to wave goodbye as we got Texas Dorothy and her chair back into the SUV and drove away.

"What did you and the chief say to each other?" I asked JB as we wound our way back down the narrow track.

"Just courtesy," he replied. "He wished me courage and strength, I wished him strength and wisdom in return."

"Not quite 'wished', hon," corrected Dorothy. "More like a recognition of the characteristics in each other. Especially when addressin' each other as brothers."

John B. gave a wry little smile. "Fair enough. It just seemed the right words to say."

"They was indeed, hon, they was indeed. Thet there was a right interestin' afternoon! Thank you both."

"Our pleasure," I replied, answering for JB as he grappled Yvette around a particularly nasty bend.

 It wasn't until we were back on a relatively main road that I asked the question that had been bothering me for a little while. "You called that dance a 'mystical story', and the suggestion was that no one had ever seen it before, even amongst the tribe. What does that actually mean?"

 Texas Dorothy was silent for a time before finally answering. "Ah think maybe sometimes stories kinda hang in the air, just outside of our time an' space, till it's their time. Then they finds a way to be told, by somebody what's got their mind in just the right place. A writer, a poet…"

"A dancer," I said.

"Thet's it. An' certain stories, they got a bit of magic in 'em. Maybe it's them thet demand to be told, at a certain time an' place."

 The drive continued in silence for a while. I think each of us were mulling over that strange story and what it could mean. If I could have seen into the future I'd have known, but then I'd almost certainly have made some different decisions.

 Pre-destination? Fate? I don't know that I've ever believed in any of that. But the more I hang around magic the more I wonder about a lot of things I never used to think about. That's a good thing. Mostly.

.o0o.

13 A SHOT IN THE DARK

Extract from statement to Det. R. J. Fisher, Portland Police, by Mr. Juan Roca:

I am visiting Maine from San Diego. I have been fishing here for two weeks.

Last night I went to nightclub for some drinks. I have been unhappy since boat I hired was attacked and my family jewellery stolen *(Note: see earlier report by Sgt. B. J. Haynes).* I did not know at time that club was for men only – I just want drinks.

A little after ten I had gone out into alleyway to relieve myself. Men's room was very full, and I had had several tequilas so my need was quite urgent.

From further along alley I heard sound of men arguing. One said something about not wanting to know about what was going on. Another man said, "You are lookout, so go and look out."

I hid in shadows behind dumpster. Something in second man's voice frightened me. I only saw back of man who was called 'lookout' – he was about my size, white shirt, curly hair, red I think. Light not so good for telling colour.

Then argument started again. I heard different voice, quite high and angry, say something like, "I only agreed to meet you because you said you would make it worth my while. But you have got nothing to offer me. I am one who knows their secret. I don't need your 'resources'! I am quite resourceful myself, you know. Matter of fact, I am sure…"

Then scary voice interrupt, and said, "Resource this."

There was sound of shot, but muffled like it was fired close against target. I have heard such sound in my own country. Also what came next – sound of body falling on ground.

Scary voice said, "Thank you Bill. Well executed." I think he was making bad joke.

Then another voice, I think maybe this Bill, said, "Are we going inside?"

"No, no one will ever know we were here," was answer.

I realised men were coming along alleyway toward me, so I moved further behind big trash dumpster. I realised I could see them as they approached. One skinny man, dark hair. One much bigger man, short beard. Something familiar about him, I am sure I would recognise him if I saw him again. I will watch for him and tell you if I see him.

I waited for men to go past, leave alleyway and join lookout I as-sume. Then I went along alley to where I had heard them arguing and talking. In shadows I tripped and fell over body lying there. Man in suit, lying on back. It was hard to tell in dark, but I think he was shot in head. I hurried back into nightclub.

I still have no cell phone so I asked barman to call police. He told me he want no trouble, called me drunken Mexican and told me to leave. Got security man to throw me out of club. I saw no sign of big man or skinny man outside, for which I was very glad. I walked straight to police station to make report.

POSTSCRIPT by Det. R. J. Fisher: The body of Juan Roca was found by the waterfront two days later, killed by single bullet to the brain, identical to the murder of Lachlan Drake. It seems plausible that Mr. Roca encountered Drake's killer and was foolish enough to reveal that he recognised him. Other than ballistics, there was no evidence at the scene of this crime, either. Mr. Roca's vague descriptions have proved of no use. Both cases remain open.

.o0o.

14 MEN OF LEGEND

 As interesting as the Micmaq dance was, the big takeaway from the visit for me had been Miskwamikletonakani's assertion that whatever had been hidden away under Tepatamwa Island was rightfully mine, as far as they were concerned. But I didn't talk about it in front of Texas Dorothy. Not because I didn't trust her, but I wanted the planning of our next move to be a conversation just between JB and I. This was our business – well, technically mine I suppose but I chose to make it ours – and I wanted any decisions to be ours alone.

 We'd stopped to buy some lobster on our way home to Dorothy's place, together with a few other "fixin's" as she called them. John B. volunteered to cook dinner, and put together a lovely dish of fettuccine with a lobster cream sauce: ever so slightly thicker than a lobster bisque but just as rich.

 As we relaxed in the lounge room afterwards, I asked Dorothy to tell us another John Dimond story. I was intrigued by this man who seemed to have some mysterious connection to my wizard, not just by my reckoning but also according to some more mystically inclined locals.

"One of the things often told about John Dimond was that he had a special feelin' for the weather. Thet ain't no easy thing, cos New England's weather ain't never been easy to predict.

Folks would talk about John climbin' up to the top of Old Buryin' Hill. He'd bought up a big chunk of the woodland around the base of the hill, leavin' room for folks to come an' go to the old cemetery thet gave the hill its name. But if'n folks saw John climbin' thet hill, they knew it were likely there was a big storm comin'. And more'n likely it would come in over the Bay.

He'd wander about among the old headstones, talkin' quiet. Some said he talked to himself, other folks said he was talkin' to them what lay under the stones. As the wind got stronger so his voice would get louder.

Sometimes a few brave souls would follow John when he climbed the Buryin' Hill, and keep a watch from what Ah guess they hoped were a safe distance. They told as how, as the winds got bad John Dimond would stand among the graves an' shout out toward the water, out at the fishin' fleet miles out to sea.

"Captain Smith of the *Elizabeth Anne* – do you hear me?" were the kinda thing they said he shouted. "Keep to starboard four degrees, run true to Halfway Rock!"

For hours they say, he'd shout commands from one skipper to another, callin' 'em by name. It was said thet the ships thet sailed safely into Marblehead Harbor after a storm were always those thet Dimond had directed, an' whose skippers had listened to him. A few skippers of the time said they'd 'heard' John's voice over the howlin' winds an' followed his commands almost like they was in a trance.

Mind you, if'n there was any skipper John Dimond had taken a set against for some reason, then God help thet man in a storm. John would stand among them graves and curse the feller. Most times it's reckoned, any skipper thet was condemned like thet was lost at sea, an' never seen again."

Texas Dorothy leaned back in her chair, smiling as we applauded her story. Just as I opened my mouth to speak, Mac sat up suddenly in his basket and gave a couple of sharp barks, just as there was a crash from outside the house. One of the garbage drums falling, or being tipped over? There was a growl, and then there were a few more crunching, crashing sounds, as if something were rummaging, or stomping, through the rubbish.

My nose wrinkled. I thought maybe I caught the scent a few seconds after Mac. Dorothy reckoned it was more likely he'd caught it earlier and not been bothered until something else disturbed him. The smell was rank. It was something like a mucky barnyard, with heavy overtones of stale sweat. JB and I went to jump out of our chairs to check outside, but Dorothy waved for us to relax.

"That sounded way too big for a fisher cat," said John B. "Do you suffer from *miskwa*?" he asked.

 Dorothy smiled in amusement. "Oh, Ah don't get bears in my trash - that would have been Dooley."

"Who?" I asked.

"Let's call him a prominent local identity. Ah rarely sees him, but he turns up from time to time. Actually, he's the reason Ah don't get troubled by bears. His scent lasts a long time, and it frightens them off."

"I understand about the scent," I answered. "It'd put me off hanging around wherever it lingered!"

"Worse still if'n you got a really keen sense of smell like most critters that ain't human," agreed Dorothy. "Still, he cain't help it, Ah reckon."

"No, I don't imagine that regular bathing or hair washing matter greatly to a *wintikowa*," mused John B. "That's what, or who it is, isn't it? Bigfoot, wendigo, sasquatch – any one of a few names. Although 'Dooley' is a new one on me. Why 'Dooley'?" he asked.

 Just for a moment I thought that Texas Dorothy looked… wistful perhaps, before replying, "Ah noticed early on, he often walks with his head hangin' down. Prob'ly sniffin' out a trail, but it made me think of the old song about Tom Dooley."

 Looking at my beau I said, "I'd have thought a better question would be 'why does he keep turning up here?' Or do all your neighbours get the pleasure of his visits, Dorothy?"

 Our host casually replied, "Oh no, he pretty much just comes here, from what folks tell me. As to why, well, for one thing Ah'd like to think I have tastier trash than my neighbours. Specially after a friend fixes up a fine dinner like'n we had tonight! Two, Ah've got prob'ly the most isolated place in these parts. An' three, Ah openly admit to believin' he exists, but

Ah'm neither scared of him nor interested in hurtin' him. Ah've collected plenty of stories about him and his kin from all over the world. Includin' plenty from down your way."

"Ah, the dear old Yowie. Know of him, certainly, but never had the pleasure," said John B.

'Give it time, if I know you,' I thought to myself. Out loud I said to Dorothy, "And you reckon Tom Dooley knows that he has your sympathy, or that you've written about him?"

"It's kind of hard to tell just what he knows. Ah do think he senses Ah'm on his side, though. Ah reckon most critters know who's with 'em and who's agin 'em, deep down."

I thought of John B. and that frightened horse, and the fisher cat, and the hawk I'd heard so much about. "I reckon you're right," I said.

It wasn't until considerably later that I learned there'd been other visitors to Texas Dorothy's place that night. One of them actually told me about it.

Out in the darkness, while we were relaxing in the lounge I think, a few men were creeping up Dorothy's driveway. Somewhere down the drive they'd parked a Jeep that they'd stolen.

It wasn't Dorothy they were there for. It was us. Well, me. They knew about my treasure. A bit, anyway – they knew it existed, and they knew that Texas Dorothy knew something about it. Finding her was easier than finding me.

Seeing our Yvette in the driveway made them cautious. The plan had been to just boldly march up to the door and confront Dorothy, but now they were wary of whoever was visiting, not knowing it was JB and I. That got them skulking up to the house, with the idea of listening or looking surreptitiously in.

They were creeping up on the side of the building nearer to the woods, keeping to cover, when Dooley came out from the trees and started into the bin full of food scraps. Apparently, and not surprisingly, they couldn't believe their eyes.

"Shiver me timbers, it's bigger'n you are, Nook!" is what their leader said.

 As described later, and admittedly he was only seen in the dark, Dooley was well over seven feet tall, even walking in a slouch. He was covered in shaggy dark hair and "smelled like a very old bilge pump".

 They didn't know whether the big creature saw them or heard them, but suddenly it growled and loped a few long steps in their direction, arms raised threateningly.

 The young man who told me this story admitted that if some of the more bloodthirsty members of their crew had been present, they might have made a stand and fought. He didn't think that would have been a good idea, though, and fully endorsed his captain's decision to let discretion be the better part of valour.

"If that be the watchdog she be keepin', I reckon we'd better think of another strategy, maties."

 And so they were gone, without us ever knowing they'd been there. Thanks, Dooley.

.o0o.

15 TO SEA, TO SEE

We left Dorothy's house fairly early the next morning. I slept deeply,
rather to my surprise given the beast prowling outside. Dreams of treasure
and tribal dances may have had something to do with it.

There were wheat cakes to go with coffee for breakfast, and then JB and I
said fond farewells to our hostess and her ever-affectionate cavoodle.

We spent the drive back to Portland making plans. Miskwamikletonakani
had given us a good explanation of how to navigate to Tepatamwa Island,
which we'd confirmed on the relevant map that Dorothy had amongst
her burgeoning bookshelves. We realised we'd have to hire a boat. No
big problem, but mildly annoying when we already own a good one, the
Fior Ghaol (Gaelic for *True Love*). At the time of writing she's securely
berthed in Norway and thus of absolutely no use to us in Maine. Still, as
JB pointed out, we were in a good place to find a boat.

"I wonder if a little local knowledge would help?" I mused. "At least
mark us as less likely to be taken advantage of. Not that I expect we
would be, but a familiar face or voice might be a bit handy."

"Sure, that makes sense," agreed my driver. "Are you thinking of Lanny?"

"Funnily enough, no, although he'd be a possibility, too. I was thinking
we should fill Ariane in on what we've learned, and that if she knew anyone in the boat-hire business it would kill two birds with one stone. I can't
imagine anyone taking advantage of her!"

I really did mean that more diplomatically than I suddenly realised it must
have sounded, but if John B. noticed he didn't react.

"Good thinking," was all he said. "The office may not be open yet. Give
her a call when we're back at the motel."

So that's what I did. Ariane was suitably impressed at everything we'd discovered. A bit bemused by some elements of the story, but shrewd enough to say, "I think life around John B. Stewart must be very interesting at times."

She wasn't able to advise on the matter of boat hire ("I am *very* much a landlubber, I'm sorry.") but did suggest that Glexie should be more able to hclp. When the accountant was put on the line she confirmed that, yes, she knew just who to see.

"Name a time, hon, and we'll come up to Portland and see you," she said enthusiastically.

I appreciated the offer, but what about work?

"Aw shucks, it's a quiet day. Lachlan hasn't even showed up. Ariane and I can take the time to come look after a couple of good clients. Jeremy is always talking about how he can run this place all by himself. Today he can, eh?"

And so it was not a great deal later when we all met at a waterfront café. I'm sure JB felt like an old-fashioned sheik sitting at the table surrounded by three gorgeous women (his words, not mine) but by now I was comfortable with the friendship of the girls from Lachlan Drake's office.

Ariane was particularly pleased by the endorsement of the Micmaq people. She's very conscious of what we in Australia call 'native rights' and was fascinated by the story of our meeting with Miskwamikletonakani and his people. As she'd already indicated, though, she couldn't help much with the matter of a boat.

Her housemate, on the other hand, was as good as her word. After coffee and snacks (John B. is developing a definite taste for whoopee pies that I fear won't do his waistline any good) Glexie led us to a little timber yard. There she introduced us to the business owner, Arnold Janesmann.

He was a big, fair man with thinning blonde hair – I suddenly imagined a Viking going bald. Unlike many of the men we'd encountered in this area of Maine, Arnold was Very Heterosexual. Not aggressively or unpleasantly so, but his office was absolutely festooned with photos of his wife and two kids. I hadn't seen one like it since the workshop of a mechanic I knew back in Canberra.

It turned out that Glexie had handled his accounts for several years, and had saved him a lot of money. That money had helped finance his other passion (beside his family) – the restoration of an old wooden lifeboat and its steam-powered engine.

He couldn't get away from the business to take us out on the Bay himself. I was privately rather glad of that. No offence to Arnold, but the less people who knew details about our endeavour, the happier I'd be. But Glexie had been very interested in his restoration project, to the extent of getting actively involved and learning to drive the boat.

I did wonder about how Arnold's wife felt about that, but the more I watched the accountant deal with people the more I was struck by just how genuinely likeable she was. Certainly, I could recognise what both Wilko and Ariane saw in her, but I also saw that she seemed to have absolutely nothing predatory in her nature.

Arnold took us to the shed where his boat *Emma* was kept under lock and key. She'd been named for his daughter, which came as no surprise given the photos of the pretty blonde girl all over his office. A private little slipway led from the back of the shed straight onto the water, which was ample proof that Arnold's business was doing well. Real estate like that doesn't come cheaply anywhere!

Happy with the promise that we'd bring the *Emma* back as soon as possible, Janesmann took himself back to work, leaving the four of us to our mission.

Well, three of us, really. Ariane was emphatic that she wasn't at all comfortable with being on a boat. ("I'm okay *in* the water, just not *on* it," she said.) So it was agreed that she'd wait ashore for us, checking back into the office and meeting us at the boatshed in three hours, unless we called earlier to indicate otherwise.

The steam-driven *Emma* was completely unlike our own *True Love*, but Glexie knew her well; I like to think I'm quite adaptable and capable on any boat; and John B. is useful for more than just 'ballast' as he described himself. We wouldn't have successfully made it from the Shetlands to Norway otherwise! I'd committed the directions on Texas Dorothy's chart to memory, together with Wehmisemawa's description. The weather was clear, if brisk, and the forecast was for it to remain that way, so I was confident that a three hour round trip was a generous estimate.

With hugs all round, Ariane waved us on our way, promising to be at the slipway waiting for us mid-afternoon.

"I'll ring you if anything happens to delay us, or better yet we're all done sooner than expected!" I called over the noise of the engine that Glexie and John B. had got going.

He was already streaked with black from firing up the small boiler that powered us.

"I wish you luck on your adventure!" she shouted back.

My sooty wizard grinned, waved at the shore, and then blew me a kiss. "I wish you – us – fortune, pretty lady," he said quietly.

John B. and I had swimwear and towels in a canvas bag, ready to go looking for the cave below the waterline. We reasoned that the treasure had been put there in a time before scuba equipment had been invented, so it should still be accessible without such gear, as long as you knew where to look. (I hadn't considered the possible water temperature at that point – silly me!)

I kept us heading east-northeast until I spotted a small island dominated by a distinctive hill that I'd been watching for, at which point the *Emma* was swung onto a more northerly course. Soon after I set us more wester-ly, starting a zigzag course between several little islets and lumps of rock.

 John B. looked out from under the tin-roofed shelter that covered the rear third of the boat.

"Looks like we're headed into some fog, sweetheart," he warned.

 He was right. There was a big bank of the stuff rolling toward us. It was as though we were approaching a wall of grey cotton wool. Anything could be behind that wall.

 It earned a shrug from Glexie. "Happens round these parts, hon. They can come up real quick, and real thick. And this looks like one of them. We'd better slow down and keep a look out. *Emma*'s got a pretty shallow draft, but some of these channels can be a bit treacherous. Incredibly deep in parts, but then you'll find a sudden spike of rock poking up just below the surface."

 I nodded. "Division of labour, then. Babe, you look after the boiler, Glexie the steering, and I'll park myself up here in the prow and watch where we're going."

 It meant cutting our speed right down for safety's sake, but nobody bregrudged the caution. That was working well, and while we weren't making quick progress it was safe and steady. It also meant that, being up front, I was the first to see the apparition that suddenly loomed out of the fog.

 I saw it. I didn't quite believe it. Did you ever see the old Errol Flynn movie "*The Sea Hawk*"? It was a Saturday afternoon TV favourite of my mother. What was coming towards us looked like Errol's ship the *Alba-tross*, cut down in size. It even had a skull and crossbones flag flying from the middle mast, the tallest of three.

 I think I managed, "Umm…"

Glexie whistled, and John B. just said, "Now there's something you don't see every day," as he let the *Emma*'s speed slacken.

 It took some sharp steering on both vessels to avoid a collision. Suddenly the three-master was alongside us, and a voice boomed.

"Ahoy! Stand fast ter be boarded!"

.o0o.

16 PIRATES. REALLY.

To avoid a collision John B. slowed our converted lifeboat almost to a halt, letting the engine idle gently. A single line was thrown from the strange boat, obviously by someone with skill, because it lassoed our little smokestack on the first attempt. The *Emma* was bumped against the pirates' hull with a strangely echoing thud. A rope ladder was thrown from above and down it clambered two men who, again, could have stepped straight off the set of *Sea Hawk* or *Captain Blood* or any other swashbuckler you might think of.

The first to land in our boat was the man who'd bellowed at us. He was about JB's height, but a bit heavier. Not fat, but solid. His hair was tucked up under a black tricorn hat, and he had an outrageous blue paisley cloth tied around his face as a mask, although it didn't hide all of the bushy red beard. He wore long leather boots, black breeches, a white shirt and a knee-length red coat, beautifully embroidered. Firmly gripped in his left hand was a long curved sword. To complete the ensemble there was a parrot clinging to his right shoulder. It was a weird looking specimen – an almost fluorescent pale apple green with a pink 'collar', long tail, and a large powerful beak. It had the maddest white eyes I've ever seen on a bird.

Arriving only a step behind was a much slighter man, more plainly dressed in a blue and white striped t-shirt to go with the breeches and boots. He wore a plain blue bandana on his head, and another covering most of his face. No cutlass for him, though. He held a large, professional looking automatic pistol.

You know, before I met my beau, I think I'd seen one real gun in my entire life, carried by a payroll guard in one of my early office jobs. Since we got together though, I've seen quite a few, most of them pointed at me, and this was one of the most intimidating.

John B. got up and took a couple of steps forward. The gun was swung to point directly at his heart.

"Aar, I'll ask ye ta stand still, me hearty. We'll relieve ye of yer valuables and be quietly on our way, thank ye," said the bearded man with absurd politeness.

 The green bird fluttered off the pirate's shoulder and landed on the *Emma*'s deck just in front of John B. It hopped onto his leg, walked up his thigh, casually climbed up his shirt and perched on my beau's shoulder. He turned his head and he and the bird looked into each other's eyes. The parrot tilted its head to one side. John B. mirrored the movement.

 Suddenly the bird dived towards the wizard's neck and with a quick snap of its large red beak sheared through the leather cord that held the Viking styled pendant I'd given him in Norway. The parrot went to fly back to the pirate with the cord in its bill. JB's hand shot up and caught the silver object so the bird was left with only the cord as it fluttered onto its master's shoulder.

"Neat trick," observed John B. evenly.

"Aar, he's got a good eye, has Teef," replied the bearded man with a broad grin. If he was disappointed to have not acquired the talisman he didn't show it.

"A beak that sharp, 'Teef' is more than a pun, isn't it? More like a warning."

"Let's just say it seemed appropriate."

"I hope the parrot Teef doesn't end up getting swallowed," said John B., his voice even throughout the whole exchange.

 Although his face was masked, there was a grin evident in the pirate's voice as he replied, "Well said, me hearty. For that, and yer quick reflexes, ye can keep yon trinket."

"Rather more meaningful than a 'trinket', mate," said my beau coldly.

"Thanks, babe," I said, thinking to myself that I was glad I'd resisted the urge to wear Henry St. Clair's locket.

"Ah, all the more reason fer ye ta retain it then. But me lad Billy-boy here hates to leave a job empty-handed, so I will ask ye to give me whatever other such valuables as ye be carryin' with ye."

The man in the stripes, 'Billy-boy', held out a hand towards me, obviously expecting meek compliance.

"I wish you'd change your mind about that," said John B., much more calmly than I felt.

At that point Glexie stepped out from under the little shelter at the rear of our boat, saying, "Come on – do we look like we're the sort to be carrying valuables?"

"Aar, I happen ta know that looks can be deceivin'… lass…"

The pirate's voice trailed off as he actually looked at Glexie properly instead of glancing in her direction. He just stood and stared, probably with his mouth open behind the mask if I'm any judge.

Billy-boy was also staring, but at John B. and I through narrowed eyes.

"Are they Australian accents?" he asked suspiciously.

I saw no reason to lie. "Yeah. I've got to say, as a welcoming committee you guys are different, but y'know, not that welcoming."

"Boss, remember the story Blood told you?" Billy asked the man who was evidently his captain – a man who was presently quite distracted.

"Eh? What? Aar – yeah. Yeah, I do, matey." He paused for only a moment of thought before an impulsive decision. "Ladies, and you bucko, up the ladder thank'ee. Ye'll be joinin' us fer a bit, I'm thinkin'."

 That wasn't the response his crewman was expecting, I think. He looked like he was about to question the order but the captain shook his head.

"Me mind's made up, matey. If they're who ye be thinkin' of, then we can deal with 'em better on our own deck."

"What about this one then?" Bill asked, gesturing a thumb towards Glexie. "We can't leave a witness."

"Indeed we can't, matey, indeed we can't. Ye'll be joinin' us as well, me fine lass."

"Hey! Do I get any say in this?" our accountant protested.

"No," said Bill simply, and motioned her towards the ladder. "Any more than I do," I heard him mutter under his breath.

"Ahoy, lads – stand by for three boarders! Restraints at the ready!" the captain shouted up.

 Two more masked faces appeared, looking over the side of their ship.

"What…?" began one crewman, wearing a shirt and bandanas that were a red version of Billy-boy's outfit.

 He was interrupted by his much larger companion, who elbowed him warningly and called, "Aye aye, boss!", getting an irritated glare in response.

"Not quite what I'd had in mind, sorry sweetheart," my wizard said to me softly as he turned off *Emma*'s motor at the captain's direction.

"It's okay babe. We're still alive. We've been in worse spots. I think," I tried for a reassuring grin before leading the way, scaling the rope ladder.

It was clear to me that, eccentric as these 'pirates' may be, they weren't bluffing. The eyes behind that gun were cold and menacing. John B. followed me up the ladder, then Glexie. Billy-boy came after her, one well-practiced hand keeping the gun trained on her as he climbed with the other. After standing there, obviously admiring the view as Glexie ascended, the man in the tricorn hat slapped his belly and shook his head as if to regain his concentration. Then he sheathed his blade and climbed up onto his own deck.

As each of us came up over the edge of the hull we were grabbed and quickly secured, wrists and ankles, in well-tied lines. These guys didn't just look like old-fashioned sailors – they knew their stuff.

The man who took John B. was massive. At least a foot taller than my beau, broad across the shoulders, and a substantial girth, although I don't think a lot of it was fat.

Glexie was being tied up by another large man (although nowhere near the size of the giant beside him) when the captain came aboard. The red-bearded man gave him a sharp poke in the ribs.

"Belay the roughness, Blood!" The captain looked at Glexie, a smile in his eyes. "Do we need ta tie ye up, lass? I'd rather not… but aye, p'raps it's best fer now," he admitted with a glance around his crew.

The man in the red stripes pointed down at the *Emma* and said, "With these on board now, do we just sink that?"

His captain appeared thoughtful, and looked over the side at the remodeled lifeboat.

"No, I think not, Bish. That's a fine piece o' workmanship, that, and it'd be a damned shame to scupper her for no good reason. Let her drift. She looks seaworthy enough. She'll fetch ashore somewhere, or someone'll take her in tow. Unhitch her and let her away."

The man addressed as Bish shrugged. He was evidently the man who'd tied and thrown the lasso, because with just the right flick of the wrist he disengaged the line from the smokestack.

 The captain called to a lookout stationed up the main mast, "All clear, laddie?"

"Aye aye, skipper," came the reply.

 He must have excellent eyesight, I thought, as the fog was quite heavy.

"Slow and steady, south south-east," ordered the captain.

 The giant saluted, and took over the wheel that had been lashed in place up on the raised poop deck. It looked like a car steering wheel in his huge hands.

 It was clear that we three weren't expected to be going anywhere, as the captain signaled that the bandana masks could be removed. Some of the small crew looked unhappy at this, for all that breathing foggy air through the cloth must have been awkward. The big man who'd tied Glexie made a placatory gesture to his companions that I realised indicated, 'Be patient, they won't live long enough for it to be a problem'.

 The crew members weren't actually introduced to us as we sat with our backs together amidships, but we got to know them soon enough so I'll describe them for you now.

 Our captain called himself Redbeard, for reasons that became obvious when his mask came off. Imagine Ned Kelly with long red hair in a pony-tail. He was much younger than I'd expected – surely not much more than thirty at most. His given name, I discovered, was Edward St. John Lister, but I never heard him use it.

 When the other large (not giant) individual removed his mask he was re-vealed to look like a fleshier version of Redbeard. That made sense when I learned he was the captain's brother, as well as his adjutant, first mate and most importantly book-keeper! Christened Barry, the signature

B. Lister had prompted the nickname 'Blood' from his older brother who could no more resist a pun than could my beau. He had a much more florid complexion than his captain, and a far more neatly trimmed beard that skirted around multiple chins. It reminded me of an orange ribbon tied tightly around a pink balloon.

 Similarly punnily, the giant, Paul Lear by birth, was called 'Nook' (rhymes with 'kook'), and introduced by Redbeard as "our not-so-secret weapon". Clearly the big man didn't object, the nickname tattooed prominently on his forearm. In case he ever forgot himself, I wondered? He was well over two metres tall (a bit above seven feet if you prefer) and tipped the scales at around 500 pounds in US parlance. About 230 kilos, if you speak in metric. I think his size was a result of a condition called acromegaly, which would quite possibly kill him eventually. I soon learned he was less simple than he seemed.

 The two similarly dressed men weren't related. They didn't even look alike. The thin one in blue was Bill – William Wadsworth. The other, stockier bloke, the lasso thrower addressed as Bish, was Bysshe Brentford. Named for Percy Shelley, who his mother apparently admired greatly. Their names inspired the collective nickname Redbeard had given the pair: the P.O.E.T.s – Pirates Of Extreme Treachery. They were the 'enforcers' of the crew. Bish had some sort of military background. He'd been a Marine, or SEAL or something. He was good with explosives and guns as well as a rope, I learned. Bill was from a good old local family, grew up 'hunting, shooting and fishing' (as we'd call it at home) but with a particular passion for firearms.

 Rounding out the small crew was the man up above looking down from the crows' nest. As you'd expect from someone in that job, he was a slim, lightweight fellow. He had flaming orange hair, quite a different and brighter shade to the Listers. Redbeard hadn't needed to bestow a nickname on him. He could hardly have outdone the man's parents who'd christened him Inigo Montoya McCallum. He'd been conceived in the back seat at a drive-in movie theatre during the film *The Princess Bride*. It's a great pic if you haven't seen it. The character for whom McCallum was named is a master swordsman who repeatedly goes into combat with the refrain: "Hello, my name is Inigo Montoya – you killed my father, prepare to die". Our Inigo's father was in fact not dead, but apparently could sell you a good funeral insurance policy if you'd like one.

I suppose technically there was another member of the crew. The parrot Teef, of a type called Alexandrines I'm told. They're intelligent birds, readily trained. I don't think most have the evil eyes that Teef had, though. It was like an insanely ravenous seagull and I'm frankly glad the bloody thing didn't talk. I doubt I'd have liked anything it said.

So there we were, three of us sitting tied like Thanksgiving turkeys, to use a pertinent local expression, with the *Emma* drifting away to a future that was as uncertain as our own. Even if Ariane raised an alarm when we didn't get back on time, how would anyone know where to find us?

I twisted about to look hopefully at John B., thinking that this was a good time for a bit of magic. He nodded in response.

"I wish these ropes would be removed," he said. He paused a moment then whispered, "I've got an idea." Loudly he called to the captain, "Hey, Redbeard! I wish you were the sort of bloke to accept a challenge!"

The pirate strode over to look down at us (not that he'd been far away, keeping a very watchful eye on Glexie).

"Arr, I might well be, matey. What do ye have in mind?"

.o0o.

17 CROSSING SWORDS

John B. and the pirate captain stared at each other for several seconds, perhaps gauging each other. It was my beau who spoke first.

"You seem pretty keen on that cutlass of yours. Well, I reckon I know one end of a sword from the other. How about a duel? I win, we go free. You win, we'll go along with… with… whatever it is you've taken us along for."

The first mate sputtered, "You must be joking! Red, they've seen our faces! You can't possibly agree…"

"Avast there, Blood! Have ye no faith in me, brother? Aye lad, ye have a deal."

I was struck by the oddity of Redbeard calling John B. "lad" – I'd have sworn the pirate was the younger of the two by a few years at least. I must confess I was also unconvinced by the wisdom of my wizard's 'plan'.

With a flourish of his cutlass Redbeard severed the lines binding John B.'s wrists. My beau untied his ankles, stood and stretched. As he flexed his wrists and rolled his shoulders, the captain called up to his outsized helmsman.

"Ahoy there, Nook! Toss us down yer sword, me hearty!"

"Aye aye, boss," replied the big man without demur, and he lobbed his cutlass down onto the deck at Redbeard's feet.

With the point of his toe the captain flicked the weapon up at John B., who caught it cleanly by the handle.

After a couple of experimental movements, John B. shrugged. "Not a type or weight that I've used before, but I reckon I can adapt," he said more calmly than I felt.

 At a gesture from Redbeard, Teef flew from his shoulder and perched on a coil of cable, white eyes apparently watching intently. The two men took a pace towards each other, and the fight was on. Their styles were very different. Redbeard looked like he'd learned his sword-fighting from a lot of Hollywood movies. It was energetic, with lots of shouting and dramatic jumping, diving, and lunging. John B., I realised, was using the fencing technique he'd learned from his old friend Edmund in Norway.

 Edmund had a pair of badly damaged knees, and had developed his own fencing style predicated on maintaining a solid base, most of the movement coming from the waist and shoulders – concentrating on effective defence and looking for the opponent's weaknesses and mistakes.

 I realised as I watched that John B. had learned a lot more in his practice sessions on Edmund's farm than I'd given him credit for. The cutlass was a very different weapon to the rapier he'd learned with, but the strategy remained effective, and his focus was impressive. He seemed oblivious to Redbeard's histrionics, saying nothing but maintaining a resolute parrying of the pirate's wild slashes and thrusts.

'Wild' is a good description of Redbeard's way with a sword. He was a powerful man, and I could see that each parry jarred John B.'s shoulder and arm. He'd jump back and change position between blows, each of his striking moves preceded by a big backswing.

 Every so often John B. would make a thrust, or at least a feint of his own, usually while Redbeard was in the act of moving back. It kept the pirate just slightly off balance.

 This went on for some minutes, with the crew as fascinated as Glexie and I were as spectators. Most of them, anyway. From the corner of my eye I noticed Blood turning away from the action and slipping an incongruous mobile phone from his pocket. He was in furtive conversation with someone, but I didn't pay him much attention – I was too concerned with my beau.

His strategy of patient engagement, or perhaps I should say non-engagement, was clearly frustrating Redbeard. Just as clearly, the pirate was starting to tire – a key element of Edmund's teaching.

The captain swung a mighty backhand slash at his opponent's head, which John B. evaded by swaying backwards from the waist, but simultaneously turning his body to follow the direction of Redbeard's blade. JB brought his own cutlass down hard on the hilt of the pirate's sword.

The blow didn't quite dislodge Redbeard's weapon, but it was enough to throw the pirate off balance and send him sprawling on the deck, and that was sufficient to jar the cutlass free. The blade skidded across the deck, the pirate trying to reach for it in an awkward, frantic dive.

Sword raised, John B. took a pace towards his prone opponent. I suspect he had it in mind to keep Redbeard from regaining his cutlass – I really do not believe he'd have struck him in the back – but that question was suddenly moot.

In a moment that would have done his movie namesake proud, Inigo slid down a line from his crow's nest and landed lightly on the deck between JB and his captain, parrying John B.'s sword with his own cutlass.

"You're good, sir," he acknowledged, "I can't take a chance on you coming at my captain from behind, however."

"Hadn't been my plan," grunted JB as he stepped back to reset his defensive posture.

"Perhaps it's the company I keep," admitted the lithe redhead with a smile as he went on the attack.

This was an entirely different fight. Whereas his captain had relied on power and furious energy, Inigo's movements were precise and economical. He preserved his energy just as John B. did, but moved lightly and quickly, forcing my beau to keep shifting position and balance in a way that Redbeard hadn't managed.

Although his defence was still holding firm, I could see that JB was tiring himself. Well, it was his second fight in minutes, I thought, and it wasn't a discipline he had much experience in! And Inigo was good. Very good.

Redbeard had rolled over and sat up, watching with keen interest, barely noticing as his parrot fluttered back to its usual position on his shoulder. If he had any qualms about his lookout taking over from him in the fight he didn't show them. Even Blood had finished his secretive phone call and was paying attention.

That was John B.'s undoing. As Inigo circled him, blade a flashing blur, the wizard took a careful step back as he parried. That pace brought him within range of the first mate, who calmly bludgeoned him with a convenient belaying pin. Entirely by luck JB didn't fall onto the edge of Inigo's cutlass, or his own.

"Aar, that weren't necessary, Blood!" admonished Redbeard loudly.

"No! I had him beaten!" agreed an outraged Inigo.

The captain's brother shrugged and replied, "Better safe than sorry. I think these two may be too valuable to risk losing." The portly bookkeeper tossed Nook's sword back up to the helmsman and was looking at me as he continued, "The accents got me wondering, and I've just had their descriptions confirmed. Redbeard, I think this pair are the ones who've got a handle on that treasure we heard about."

*

I later learned that back in Portland, Ariane was getting worried. She'd tried calling all three of us in turn when we were tied up, which only succeeded in prompting Bish to remove our phones and stash them away somewhere. I heard them ringing a few times subsequently, from somewhere below us.

125

Our legal advisor had been anxiously watching her watch, and the sea, for a while. It was past our guessed-at return time, but more to the point, she said, she had "a bad feeling".

By late afternoon that bad feeling was a whole lot worse. The lack of a response from any of our phones only exacerbated that. It was past 4:30 when Ariane made her way to the police station.

Now, I admit I wasn't there, but I really *cannot* imagine her as the hysterical type. So when Ariane tells me she was entirely calm and reasonable, I don't doubt her at all.

Calmly and reasonably, she advised that she wanted to report Glexie, John B. and I as Missing Persons. The bald little man behind the counter (her description) was apparently prepared to look her anywhere but in the eye. Ariane's eyes can be quite intimidating, I admit, but I don't know that that was the issue in this instance.

The desk officer took a few initial notes before asking how long we'd been missing. He looked up disbelievingly when she told him.

"How long for?"

"About three hours," she repeated.

"Lady, are you kidding? Come back in about three weeks."

"They're out on the Bay somewhere!"

"Alright, maybe not three weeks. But at least wait overnight."

"They may drown overnight if there's been an accident!"

"If there's been an accident they may have drowned already," observed Sergeant Sensitive. "If they haven't turned up by tomorrow morning I'll get our boat to look out for them. Can you describe their boat?"

"The *Emma* – it's a converted lifeboat, steam powered, painted white. It's got a little metal roof structure over the back bit."

"The stern. Okay. If there's no sign of your housemate and her friends by ten o'clock tomorrow, call in and let us know."

 The interview clearly over, Ariane could only grind her teeth and leave the station, trying hard not to slam the door as she left.

 Out of courtesy, her next move was to call around to see Arnold Janesmann, who surprised her by seeming quite unconcerned. He'd spent plenty of time out on the waters of Casco Bay, he explained. It was very easy to lose track of time, especially if the objective was to look around some of the smaller, uninhabited islands. Glexie had explained that she'd wanted to show the visitors some of the local birds and wildlife, so it seemed entirely reasonable that they might get distracted.

 Even if they inadvertently were caught out in the dark, the *Emma* had a stock of lights, blankets and even a small amount of food that would see them through until morning. He trusted Glexie – if he didn't, he wouldn't have loaned them the boat, would he?

 As much as that should have reassured Ariane, it didn't. Armed with a packet of sandwiches and what she later described as "one of the worst cups of coffee in history" she settled on a bench at the waterfront to wait. With the going down of the sun she retrieved a blanket from her car, wrapped it around her shoulders, and resumed her position under a bright street lamp.

 Maybe she was radiating a 'Danger – Do Not Approach' aura, or maybe it's a credit to Portland that nobody interrupted her vigil.

.o0o.

18 ALL AT SEA

John B. was still out cold. Nonetheless Blood took the precaution of getting Bish to tie my beau's wrists together.

"Not that I don't trust him, ladies, but I prefer to be cautious," he said, his smooth words belied by the surreptitious kick I don't think he saw me notice him plant into JB's ribs.

Redbeard noticed though, and admonished his brother. "There be no need for that, Blood. Ye've made yer point." He bowed to Glexie and I, but I wasn't the one his eyes were fixed on as he continued, "Apologies for me brother. He's inclined to act a bit hasty. I think his temper overcomes his manners sometimes."

Blood smiled a smile so thin it could have sliced bread. "Apologies. Yes. As I was saying, brother, I believe we've stumbled upon the couple that our… associate ashore informed us about."

The captain turned his attention to me, perhaps a little reluctantly. As he watched me thoughtfully my beau, unceremoniously dumped on the deck at my side by Bill, began to stir. He's had a few head knocks I think, but seems to recover quite quickly, claiming a harder-than-average skull.

Redbeard scratched his chin under the luxuriant mass of hair, a gesture oddly like John B.'s habit of scratching at the stubble where his own beard routinely fails to make much progress.

"So, ladies, what be bringing ye out on this fair bay? Be ye… *lookin'* fer something?" he asked.

To my surprise, Inigo was kneeling beside John B., solicitously examining the fast-growing lump on my beau's head. The lookout had a gentle hand on his erstwhile opponent's arm, a mark of respect for a capable foe, I assumed. When neither Glexie nor I answered immediately, he spoke.

"I know it was dark, captain, and I only got a fleeting look inside, but I'm pretty sure these are the ones we spotted in that place up past Brunswick."

"I've no idea what you're talking about," I said, which at that point was true.

The captain continued to scratch his chin. "I be inclined to trust yer eyesight, Inigo. And speakin' of which, I'll be havin' yer back at yer post, thank'ee."

The young swordsman saluted, let go of John B.'s arm, and clambered back up the mast like a monkey. Redbeard rocked back and forth on his boot heels.

"Arr, funny that. We'd gone up there to look for the old writer-lady, not expectin' to find yer. Truth is, I doubt we'd have recognised yer anyways, although ye were the reason fer us to come a-callin'. Well, not so much ye as yer treasure. Here was I turnin' my mind to how ter look for ye or yer hoard, settin' out fer a quiet day at work, when shiver me timbers – we just about sails slap-bang right inter ye. It's a funny old world of coincidences, eh me hearties?"

John B. had recovered enough to mutter darkly, "Mine aren't always for the best, it seems."

The pirate either didn't hear, or ignored the comment, instead asking me, "What *was* that thing we encountered up there?"

"No idea," I replied. "I keep telling you, we've got no clue about anything you're talking about."

"We're all at sea, you might say," added John B., earning a chuckle from our captor.

"Arr – I allus said we should keep our activities on the water. We be much

better'n we are on land! And here ye've delivered yerselves to us anyway.
Fate's allus kinder to me when afloat. Now, as to this treasure of yer's…"

"What bit of 'no idea' isn't getting through to you?" I asked as angrily as I
could sound. "I don't know who you think we are…"

Blood answered. "We think – indeed, I feel rather more strongly than
that, that you are the two Australians who've come to the area to collect a
very substantial old family treasure. We understand you've had some concerns about the attitude of the local authorities to your doing so. I propose
to relieve you of the burden of those concerns."

"It be in our nature, y'see," explained Redbeard. "Pirates and treasure go
hand in hand. Or they should, by rights."

"Um, speaking of which, pirating seems to me to be an… odd choice of
occupation," said Glexie.

The captain's face fair lit up when she spoke to him. He was oblivious to
his brother's glowering reaction as he answered.

"That ink on yer arm would be worthy of any of my crew, meself included. It enhances yer beauty, right enough," sighed Redbeard. "Alright
then, me lovely. I'll tell ye my story, and then ye can favour me with yer
own. That seems fair, do it not?"

Before any of the three of us could answer he launched into his tale, clearly hoping to win over the tattooed girl.

"About three hundred years ago, 'Black Sam' Bellamy were the scourge
o' this coast, up an' down from Canada to nigh on Long Island. Then one
dreadful night in April 1717 his good ship, the *Whydah*, went down off
of Cape Cod. Tis said Black Sam an' over a hundred of his faithful crew
died that night. Only an old Welshman an' a local Indian survived. Black
Sam an' his hearties were known to have a mighty hoard of gold, silver an'
jewels."

John B. interrupted. "I've read of Black Sam, and of his treasure. Didn't someone find his ship, and its contents, off Cape Cod back in the eighties?"

"Aar, that be true, bucko, but Black Sam weren't fool enough to be leavin' all his booty on the *Whydah*. I reckon when the old girl started to take on water he set off in one of his small boats to find a safe harbour for to put most of his hard-earned spoils in. Reckon he made it a fair ways north too, comin' out o' that storm."

"Stellwagen Bank, Tillies Bank, somewhere like that," said Nook quietly, listening from the helm.

"Aye, me hearty, old Black Sam went to the bank with his treasure, that's for sure. And it were a few years ago, when I was workin' hand to mouth as a salvage diver that I happened on a good chunk o' Sam's keepin's. And I knew right off, a pirate's fortune were meant to be spent on piratin', so I got meself this proud beauty and set out to add to me new found wealth."

"What was found in '85 was reckoned to be less than a sixth of what Black Sam Bellamy actually had, and that haul alone was thirty million dollars' worth," observed my wizard.

"That may be so, that may be so," agreed the captain.

"Be nice if he ever told anyone else where he found the damned thing," I heard Bish mutter, which earned a soft grunt of agreement from Blood.

Glexie almost smiled at Redbeard as she said, "It sounds like you don't really need to go around stealing from people."

"Aar, it be Black Sam's legacy, lass, and I'm not the man to argue with the fate that's been delivered to me. And now then, ye've heard my tale, as promised, so I'll be hearing yer own," he said, turning his gaze to me.

I tilted my chin as I looked back at him. "Actually, I never said anything about any sort of a deal to 'swap stories', as you put it."

"Ye disappoint me, lass, truly ye do," the captain said as he shook his head. "Bish, Billy-boy, set up the plank."

 Both of the POETs looked at each other. Bill tapped at the gun in his waistband.

"This'd be quicker. Or not. I can shoot off one bit at a time…" he offered.

 Redbeard's face flushed dramatically. "That's *not* how we work on the *Ondine*!" he roared.

 The thought, 'Another coincidence,' flitted across my mind momentarily. A small flash of memory of Ogunquit, a boat we'd seen, and the name of a play that JB remembered.

"There be traditions to piratin', and that sort of carry on ain't amongst them," he continued angrily. "Now, be about the job I've told ye to do!" He turned back to me, face still dark, and said, "Of course, that's not to say I'm not about to use the old ways. They're effective enough at getting' ye to tell me what I wants to know, I'll warrant."

 He called up to his giant helmsman, "Nook, give the wheel to Blood. I can use yer strength on deck. Yer know what to do – remember the drill."

"Aye aye, cap'n," responded the giant, stepping back to make room for the captain's still-scowling sibling.

The POETs set to work pulling a long plank from somewhere out of my line of sight. I did notice they surreptitiously sought, and received, a silent nod of approval from the first mate. The captain's authority wasn't as absolute as he thought, I realised. Maybe I could use that.

The plank was set up to rest, seesaw-like, on the starboard railing. The deck end was lifted and nailed to a barrel that Nook had carried into place.

Clearly it was heavy, as even the huge man had made an effort to lift it.

"And now…" Redbeard began ominously.

"Not the girl?" asked Nook, half questioning, half protesting.

 The captain put a calming hand on the outsized arm and said, "No, matey. Tis the lass I be wantin' answers from."

"Sensible," agreed Blood from the wheel, in a voice that carried a trace of surprise at the admission. "From what we've been told, it's her treasure. She'll be the one to know where it is."

 Suddenly it dawned on me that Redbeard had never divulged the location of his own cache of treasure, even to his brother. If he did actually re-member where he found Bellamy's hoard (and that was questionable, I re-alised – Redbeard wasn't the most stable of individuals) he wasn't letting on. Perhaps he considered it his 'reserve' in case the pirate business dried up or got too awkward. Equally obviously, if their roles were reversed Blood wouldn't be sharing the information either. It didn't occur to either brother that JB and I wouldn't keep something like that secret from each other.

"That's right," agreed the captain. "Nook, the laddie, please," he said and gestured with his cutlass at John B.

 The giant lifted my wizard with less effort than he'd required for the bar-rel, and deposited him, standing, on the deck end of the plank. The point of Redbeard's cutlass poked into the back of the purple t-shirt.

"No more delays, lass. Tis a simple question. Where be yer treasure? Tell me and yer feller lives. Stay quiet and it's the briny for him."

 I saw JB rock unsteadily on his feet as the boat pitched. Even through the fog that was still about, I could tell the sky was darkening, presumably with clouds as it was still well before sunset. There was a storm looming.

"Don't do this!" exclaimed Glexie.

"I won't. If yer friend here tells me what I wants to know. Or if ye do, should ye know."

Glexie and I shared worried looks. Was this madman serious?

Suddenly John B. laughed. "Name, rank and serial number only, ladies!" he shouted. "Be seeing you!"

He ran – well, took a few rapid strides – and launched himself off the end of the plank and into the water.

Redbeard and Nook stood with mouths open. Glexie screamed. Quite possibly so did I.

.o0o.

19 NOT SUCH MONSTERS OF THE DEEP

We all heard the splash as John B. hit the water, but it took a moment for anyone to react. Redbeard was the first to move, running to the side of the deck and peering over the rail.

"Can't see a blamed thing!" he exclaimed. "Mister McCallum?"

The lookout was gazing aft. John B. would already have been well behind us.

"Not through this fog, cap'n!" There was genuine emotion in the young man's voice.

"What in hell possessed him to do that?" asked Bish.

Clearly the notion of self-sacrifice was beyond his understanding. Although I didn't cotton on to that immediately either, really. I was much more concerned with my beloved beau's survival. He'd launched himself into the water with wrists tied, and as far as I knew he wasn't an especially strong swimmer anyway. He'd be okay. I hoped it. Trusted it. Believed it.

Redbeard turned away from the railing, and knelt in front of Glexie and I.

"Ladies – please believe, that wasn't what I'd had in mind…"

"We've still got the one who knows where to find the treasure, hey?" observed Bill.

His 'poetic' partner Bish slapped him on the shoulder. "And just lost leverage on her, dimwit."

Bill's lip curled in a snarl, but a short whistle from Blood at the wheel seemed to defuse the tension.

I realised though, that Bish had expressed just what I thought had prompted JB's unexpected move. I tried to imagine what else he could have been thinking. A miraculous escape, to be followed by a remarkable rescue? Well, his magic had worked miracles before – I was living proof.

Glexie hadn't had quite the same experience of John B. as I did. There were tears streaming from her eyes. Redbeard reached out to put a consoling hand on her arm, but she pulled away from him with a sob and buried her face in my shoulder. Our bonds prevented the embrace we both wanted, damn them. The pirate looked crestfallen.

From above came Inigo's voice: "Storm brewing, cap'n. A big one by the looks of it."

"Alright lad. We'll get ourselves home, and batten down the hatches there," replied Redbeard.

"Won't you at least look for John B.?" pleaded Glexie.

The pirate stared at her. He knew how hopeless that would be, but nodded.

"Aye, lass. Alright." He called up to the helm, "Blood, turn her about and head for home. Lads, no more than half speed till Inigo thinks the storm's too close. Keep yer eyes out fer the man overboard."

"Put us where we can see over the side too," I said.

Both Redbeard and Teef looked at me with head tilted to one side, before the captain replied, "No, I don't think so, lass. I'm not going to risk either of ye being mad enough to try followin' him into the depths. Yer both far too valuable fer that. Each in yer own way." That last sentence was muttered softly and thoughtfully, perhaps as much to himself as to me.

*

My instinct, or faith in JB's magic, turned out not to be misplaced, although I didn't know it for quite some time.

Later he confirmed for me that yes, his plan had been to "take some pressure off me" by ensuring that the pirates couldn't use threats to him as a means of getting me to reveal what I – we – knew about Prince Henry's legacy. As he'd run along the plank he'd muttered, "I wish I could have a mysterious getaway, then help Q and Glexie."

His intention was to land as far away from the *Ondine* as he could, then swim underwater as far as possible to avoid being seen, and then trust that he'd soon find land before exhaustion set in. It sounded to me like the plan of a man who'd just been whacked on the head.

What actually happened was bizarre, even for my wizard.

As he described it, he'd only gone a little way underwater before he "bumped into something". He assumed the rough surface belonged to a submerged rock, or even a hill on an underwater island, hidden by the incredibly murky water. But then to his shock it moved under him.

Caught unawares, he sprawled face first on a big broad curve. He knew he was rising through the water at a steady if not rapid rate. Then suddenly he'd broken the surface, and was able to suck in some big mouthfuls of air. Pungent air, like the air above a bucket of prawns left out in the sun, he realised, gagging.

He would never have been able to discern the grey-green surface he was lying on from any distance through the fog, but up close as he was he realised what it resembled. Sharkskin.

Startled by that thought he twisted himself to see more of what he'd landed on. The curved surface, he suddenly realised, was the broad back of some living thing. But it wasn't a dorsal fin that was rearing up a few feet in front of his head. That should have been a relief, but hardly so – coming up out of the water was a nubbin of a head, on a neck that was long and getting longer.

'How the hell did I get to be in Loch Ness?' he wondered.

Hampered by his wrists being tied, John B. could only cling to his awkward perch by pressing his knees into the creature's flesh as best he could. Quickly he realised that the coarse skin was chafing through the denim of his jeans, and would soon be treating his own skin just as roughly. Inspired and motivated by that thought, he maneuvered his body to bring the binding ropes against the abrasive surface, and rubbed hard.

The strategy worked. Even the hardy maritime cords were no match for the tiny sharp-edged scales that made up the animal's skin. As the fibres parted, John B. grabbed at them and coiled them around his hands, protecting his palms from the savage surface as he held onto his improbable 'steed' and took some of the pressure off his knees.

There was nothing rough about his passage through the water. The waterhorse, as he immediately christened the creature based on an old Scottish name for Loch Ness' fabled inhabitant, swam smoothly. Was it – she, he impulsively decided – even aware of his presence? Feeling positive, with a grin he patted the broad back. For a moment the long neck twisted and the wizard looked up into a glittering eye, a black gash gaping in a yellow orb. A wide mouth opened in a head the size of a beer keg, and John B. could see a row of sharp teeth. Not long fangs, they were more like the teeth of a cross-cut saw. He tensed himself for a desperate jump if that great head was to suddenly lunge at him, but the waterhorse showed no sign of aggression. Did she... *wink* before turning her head away again?

Bemused, John B. settled as best he could on his unexpected ride.

'At least I'm up out of that bloody chilly water,' he mused. He wasn't much bothered by the cold, but the immersion wasn't pleasant even for him. He relaxed a bit, and contemplated the memory of "a big old lizard" in a Micmaq dance. The journey continued for a little while, silently cutting through the fog. Then a scraping sound came up from below, and there was the jolt of a sudden stop. The wizard could make out a stretch of sand not far to his left.

"I guess this is my stop," he said. "Thanks for the lift, old girl."

After an affectionate pat on the great beast's shoulder, John B. slipped off into the bay. It was only a short swim to reach a point where he could stand in chest deep water, but in the time it took to do that and turn to look back, his gigantic reptilian benefactor had already gone.

'She's the shy type,' he mused. "I'm glad she made an exception for me!" he chuckled aloud as he made his way ashore.

He'd been deposited at a small sandy island, quite possibly submerged at a high tide, he thought. Even at a slow and cautious walk it didn't take long to walk around it.

The fog was thinnest at the slightly elevated centre of the islet, so that's where he sat down. Perhaps he'd have a moment of inspiration, or perhaps there'd be another surprise.

"I wish something else useful would present itself," he said calmly as he settled into his preferred comfortable cross-legged position.

He'd closed his eyes and relaxed into some meditative deep breathing. It was a shamanic practice he'd learned from a Hawaiian friend, and he swears by its value.

Centred and calm, John B. had no idea of how much time had elapsed when he heard a scrape and a soft thump. The return of the waterhorse? It didn't sound big enough. He opened his eyes and realised that the fog had thinned. He could see to the perimeter of his little sanctuary, albeit not clearly yet. Away to his left was a white shape.

Still calm after his meditation, he ambled down the gentle slope. He found a dinghy. It looked new, but battered. Both the prow and one side were dented and charred, as if they'd been too near to some sort of blast. No motor, alas, but a serviceable oar lay on the floor, along with several chunks of burnt and broken material: metal, fiberglass and wood, all further evidence of an explosion. On the stern of the little craft he found a carefully hand-painted name. *Harriet*.

"I don't know who you are or where you've come from, Harriet, but I'm very pleased to see you," he said and gave a gallant bow to the welcome little boat.

He looked out over the water, and thought of Alice In Wonderland, as the little girl had conversed with the Cheshire Cat. He recalled the cat asking, "Where do you want to go?" to which Alice replied, "I don't know."

"It really doesn't matter which way to take, then, does it?" answered the cat.

'The difference is, I know where I want to go,' mused the wizard. 'I want to get to Q and make sure she's safe. But I can't just go off randomly.'

He noticed his feet were getting wet. 'Tide's coming in. Right, there's a direction – get to the mainland and then set out for a proper search.'

Without further hesitation he pushed the *Harriet*'s dinghy off from the islet. She was obviously seaworthy enough to have made it to that little shore, she would carry him back to the coast. He clambered aboard, hefted the oar, and set off.

Instinct and magic would see him where he needed to be, he had no doubt of that.

.o0o.

20 RIDERS ON THE STORM

Of course John B. was right. He dismissed it publicly as more luck than good judgement. I wonder if our friend Wilko's frequent rejection of any notion of 'magic' has gotten to my beau more than he admits. Whatever agency you thank, the *Harriet*'s dinghy caught a helpful current. With only moderate use of the oar, as a makeshift rudder as much as anything, the little boat and its passenger made good time across Casco Bay. She ran aground on a stretch of beach a few miles north of Portland.

The coast road ran along not too far away. With no clue of where he was, he initially turned the wrong way and headed north. He'd wasted the better part of a half hour before finding a sign that told him he should have gone in the other direction. With a sigh and a shrug he turned around. The light was fading as he plodded south.

John B.'s optimistic thumb was mostly ignored by passing drivers. He didn't really blame them, realising how bedraggled and unpromising a figure he must have looked, even in the rapidly fading light. He did manage to hitch one ride for a mile or two, sharing the back of a pickup truck with a collection of well-used gardening equipment.

The driver dropped him off on the outskirts of Portland as night fell. The wizard estimated that the lift had pretty much made up the time he'd lost walking in the wrong direction. That seemed a fair trade-off for the clippings and grass stains that now added to his disheveled appearance.

Notwithstanding the time spent meditating, my beau admits that he was too tired to be walking rapidly, despite how worried he was about me and Glexie. 'Trudging' would be a better description. But he also admits that his pace quickened a lot when he got near to the slipway and saw Ariane sitting on a bench under a streetlight.

She was looking out to sea, and he was approaching from the street behind her, so she wasn't aware of his presence until he called her name. They didn't describe their reunion to me, but I'm willing to bet it was something like running into each other's arms and holding a long embrace. And you know, I don't mind at all.

Looking over JB's shoulder, Ariane's first question was, "Where's Glexie? And Elizabeth?"

I think he slumped a bit in her arms then. A few spits of rain were starting to fall.

"It's a long story," he managed.

There was a small covered area nearby. Cinder block with a metal roof, over a table and bench seats. The light barely spilled under the roof, but at least it was shelter from the elements. The pair sat side by side, her blanket wrapped around them both, holding hands while John B. told his long, strange story. In return, when he stopped for breath she explained what she'd been doing as she waited and worried. Of course, she also asked questions as he went along, but if Ariane had any incredulity at all about his description of pirates and the waterhorse she didn't show it. She strikes me as a very sensible, grounded woman, but I know she was very aware of my wizard's strange experiences in Hawaii.

As they sat the weather continued to deteriorate. The wind rose, thunder crashed and the rain got heavy. John B. went from glancing out at it occasionally to staring. Just as he was describing the voyage of the *Harriet*, Ariane reckoned his voice just trailed off and his eyes glazed over.

He let go of her hand, stood up, and walked out into the storm. On a little grassed hillock he sank into that cross-legged lotus position he's fond of, pressed his hands palms down on the ground at his sides and tilted his head back. In flashes of lightning she could see that his eyes were closed and his lips were moving.

Worried about delayed concussion, or perhaps something stranger, Ariane walked out into the storm and knelt beside John B. He didn't respond to her at all, even when she put a hand on his shoulder. He seemed as oblivious to her as to the rain that soaked them both. But at least now she could hear him, even if the words meant nothing to her.

"Bear left. Bear left. Seven degrees to port. Run with it now… run with it… Hard aport, now! Hard! Good, now you can tack back…"

 If Ariane's local knowledge included tales of John Dimond she didn't make the connection right then. She just hoped that any rogue lightning bolt would hit the metal roof of the shelter, or the lamp post, but not them.

*

 Our search efforts out as sea were, of course, fruitless, although I do have to give Redbeard credit for trying. He seemed genuine, even if some of his crew were obviously less committed. The captain stood right at the prow, watching the water. I couldn't see his first mate anywhere – I gathered that he was 'below'. Nook was at the wheel, the POETs stationed at either side amidships, and the sharp-eyed Inigo up in his lofty perch. He had probably the least chance of any of spotting anything, given how dense the fog had become, but that was changing rapidly.

 The thick bank of mist was breaking up quickly as the wind behind us intensified. It was shredding, like fairy floss being torn at by a greedy child. The sea beneath us was getting rougher by the minute, too.

"I don't like this at all, lads," exclaimed Redbeard. "Inigo! Reckon we can outrun it?"

"No!" was the simple reply from the lookout.

"Maybe if we'd made speed earlier," growled Bill.

"Belay that, Mister. Ifs and maybes are for games of quoits. If this storm be as rough as she feels I reckon she'd have caught up anyway." The captain cupped his hands around his mouth and bellowed to his crew, "Make her tight!"

143

At a run, Redbeard took over Nook's place at the wheel while the giant rushed to help Bill and Bish with hauling in rigging and taking in sails. Soon we were running under just a jib and a closely reefed topsail, and Nook had rushed back to lend his weight to his captain's as they wrestled with the wheel as the heavy sea caught the rudder with great pounding thuds.

The rain was a torrent. Between that and the waves that leapt onto the deck as the *Ondine* rolled in the wild waters, everything and everyone was soaked. I don't think I've ever felt more frustratingly helpless. I'm not suggesting that Glexie or I could have added much physical assistance, but bound and forgotten as we were, there wasn't even the distraction of trying. We could only lie there cold and huddled, hoping that the lines binding us were truly securely lashed to whatever stays we'd been tied to. Otherwise we'd be swept off in one of the foamy masses that raced across the deck, or pitched overboard by one of the dizzying rolls the ship suffered when hit broadside by a wave.

The storm's fury was getting worse. The pirate crew was under terrible strain as the *Ondine* trembled under them. Suddenly there was what I can only describe as a voice in the air, audible even over the raging weather. And it was a familiar voice. I could hear John B. Stewart.

And so too could Redbeard.

"Bear left. Bear left. Seven degrees to port. Run with it now… run with it… Hard aport, now! Hard! Good, now you can tack back…"

Redbeard heard, and he listened. Whether Nook could hear too, or whether he just followed his captain's lead, the pair of them threw their considerable combined strength into hauling the *Ondine* onto the lines that were being directed.

At one point, a sheet of lightning illuminated small islands on either side of us, both scarcely more than a boat-width away. It would have been a narrow channel to navigate under smooth sailing. In the grip of the storm we flew along it like a ladybug caught by the jet of a garden hose. I'm a pretty good sailor, I reckon, but this was seamanship of astonishing skill.

We shot back out into something more like open water, still being tossed like a cork in the wind and the waves. And still my wizard's voice came over the sound of the rain.

"Five degrees to starboard. Five, no more. Hold that line now. Hold. Hold. Reef ahead. Hard aport! Hard as she'll go! That's it – you dodged it! Now bring her back starboard."

Sometimes the lightning came as bolts that may have struck either water or land – maybe even trees on some of the islands – there was no way we could tell through the waves, the rain and the pitching of our vessel. Other times it was a great sheet in one part of the sky that lit up our surrounding watery hell like a moment of daylight.

It was at one such moment that Redbeard looked around wildly. Teef had somehow crawled down to shelter inside his coat. I could see an occasional glimpse of the top of the green head pressed against his chest. The pirate's hat had long ago been blown away into the distance. His long hair had come untied and was plastered across his face so that I was amazed he could see at all, but see he evidently could.

"Run with the wind. Veer to port. Five degrees, make it eight," were the instructions of John B.'s disembodied voice.

But after his look around in the eldritch light of the storm, the captain threw his head back and roared defiantly, "Aar, I know where I be – I know this passage! To blazes with ye, sir! I'll rely on no-one but me own good self!"

With a mighty effort, he and his massive crewman powered the wheel around and forced the rudder to turn the *Ondine* sharply to starboard instead. We must have been making for some landmark he'd spotted, but the change of direction proved disastrous. A massive wave slammed into the side of the boat opposite Glexie and me, and as we watched horrified, splintered the timber and tore a great section of bulwark away like ripping off a piece of wallpaper.

The ship rolled sideways again – surely the deck stood at ninety degrees for some seconds. The sea poured across us like a waterfall, then suddenly somehow the ship righted herself. The strain was too much for the main mast though. It had creaked and groaned through the storm so far, but now there was a tremendous crack and it started to bend like an elbow about one third of the way up.

Incredibly, Inigo had stayed at his post the entire time, but now he had no choice. He sprang up like a jack-in-the-box from the wicker basket that had been his station. For a split second he was in open sky, his light form caught like a leaf in the howling gale. A desperate outflung arm caught some of the rigging that still had an end attached to the boat and was snapping about in the air.

Redbeard vaulted down from the wheel and grabbed the lines that his topman clung too, heaving them in as best he could. The lookout fought the wind to drag himself hand over hand until his captain was able to reach out and clutch a desperate arm. They threw themselves to the deck and tried to roll to the faint shelter of a surviving piece of bulwark.

With a terrible sound the deck heaved under us, and a great crack appeared in the planking, running in a jagged line between Redbeard and where I lay wedged with Glexie. There was another loud splintering sound as the forward mast started to give way near its base. The top few feet of the aft mast had already snapped of and gone spinning into the darkness.

"Below! Get everyone below!" shouted Redbeard.

If you can run in a crawling posture, that's pretty much what Inigo managed, moving as quickly as he could. Bish had dived out from behind the capstan where he'd been sheltering, and was prying open a hatch cover in the forward deck. Between the splintering of the timbers and the icy water that continued to crash down around him, it was a struggle, but with

Inigo's help the cover was raised just enough.

Bill scuttled crablike from wherever he'd been securing lines and sails as best he could, and dived into the darkness below the hatch. With a nod from Inigo, Bish swung himself after his fellow POET. The lookout used his knee as a wedge to keep the trapdoor from closing and turned frantically to see where his captain was.

The bearded pirate had dived and slid across the wet deck to reach me and Glexie. A long knife made short work of the lines binding us, but he kept a firm hold of us both while he braced his feet against the bulwark beside us.

He looked up over my head to where Nook still stood, legs wide, braced like a tree as he strove to hold the ship steady. It was an incredible effort, but a doomed one. As we rode and pitched down sideways out of another wave there was a sound like a cannon being fired. Suddenly the wheel spun freely in the helmsman's grasp – so freely that the giant lost his balance and would have been swept overboard had he not managed to hang on to a spoke of the wheel. The rudder, or perhaps the mechanism controlling it, had been sheared off. The *Ondine* seemed destined for destruction, and us with her.

The captain motioned with his head for Nook to get forward. To my amazement the giant snapped off a sharp salute in reply. He stopped in his staggering progress, though, to take an enormous handful of the back of Redbeard's coat. It must have almost crushed the parrot against the captain's ribs, but it secured his skipper who was in turn supporting his erstwhile prisoners.

Tied as we had been, then buffeted by the storm, I doubt that either Glexie or I would have been able to move ourselves effectively. The combined efforts of the two big men saw us carried like wet kittens to what I thought was unlikely sanctuary.

With one massive hand, Nook gripped the edge of the hatch cover, holding it sufficiently open for Inigo to slip below. Realising that Glexie was barely conscious, I pushed her towards the opening ahead of me. Reluctant, but understanding the situation, Redbeard went down the hatch first, allowing Nook to lower the object of his affections into his arms.

 The giant gave me an incongruously pleasant smile and indicated that I should go next, and he'd come after to secure the hatch behind us. I was still looking at his face as my questing foot found the rungs of a ladder. I expected to be clambering down into a dark and damp hold. It wasn't a nice prospect. What I found when I looked down was something quite different.

.oOo.

21 WHAT LIES BENEATH

It wasn't damp, and it wasn't dark.

It was a cabin. White walls under curved windows, carpeted floor, edged with comfortable-looking couches, illuminated by several lights. Their slight flicker and a barely audible hum indicated that they were powered by a generator. What had probably, in the original design, been an open area had been modified to create this enclosed room. Oblong windows framed a metal door aft of the cabin, and a light forward bulkhead opened into the cockpit. A curtain into that space had been pulled back, and I could see that two steps led up to a couple of chairs which sat before a panel full of controls, dials and gauges. A viewscreen or monitor was mostly hidden by a broad figure in front of it.

Blood was in one of the chairs, his back to us. After ensuring that Glexie and I were settled on one of the couches, as comfortable as we could be in the still wildly pitching cabin, and doffing his sodden coat to allow Teef to clamber back onto his shoulder, Redbeard stepped past the curtain to stand behind his brother.

"Control?" asked the captain.

"Barely. Stabilizers are working flat out. We do have some steering, even without the main rudder. Bow thruster isn't working. The cruiser's damaged but serviceable. More than can be said for… the other."

With a weary sigh Redbeard dropped heavily into the other chair. Through the wall panels we could hear the sounds of timber cracking with each roll and toss of the ship.

"No choice but to jettison, eh matey? Another bad wave and some of this wreckage could drag us under at any moment," the captain said sadly. He called back over his shoulder, "Everyone secure yerselves. Lads, say yer goodbyes to a fine lass what's served us well."

Bill and Bish, Nook and Inigo, all took seats on the couches on either side of the cabin, bracing their feet hard against the floor. Seeing that, I did the same, though Glexie was too out of it to notice. The giant had sat beside the two of us, and his arm reached around both our shoulders to hold us securely.

On the bridge I could see that Redbeard had grasped a T-bar handle and was removing a locking pin. He squared his shoulders and with a sharp jerk pulled the handle down. It was difficult to hear or feel anything over the storm, but I think I caught some popping sounds and a grinding noise, different to what I'd heard of the damage before.

Where there'd been nothing but darkness in front of the bridge moments earlier, suddenly a view opened up. The same sort of sight as suddenly appeared at the sides and aft. Wild waves. Foam and water lit by lightning. Almost immediately the view was obscured by the torrential rain that hammered the windows.

The penny dropped. We were in a boat that had been within a boat. This modern craft had lain inside the shell of the pirate ship *Ondine*. That's how she could move so quietly. I guessed it also allowed for fast getaways in any direction, whatever the prevailing wind. It was outrageous, audacious and brilliant all at once.

But now the shell was ruined, and of necessity had been somehow jettisoned. I supposed there must have been a mechanism to allow what Blood had called 'the cruiser' to slip in and out of its camouflaged skin, and that's what Redbeard had reluctantly released. A little piece of the Micmaq dance reverberated in my memory. What else had they got right?

I realised that Nook was sniffing hard. Not quite crying, but his distress was obvious as he looked at his captain's back.

"He loved her. That was a real hard thing for him to do," the big man said quietly.

None of the crew looked happy. Bish's mouth was set in a grim line,

Bill's frown more downturned than usual. The normally ruddy face of Inigo was pale as he stared forward at the window. Even the parrot seemed to have its head bowed.

"I'll take the helm, Blood. We're not too far from home, by my reckoning."

The mate nodded, and the captain flicked a switch. Evidently there were two wheels, like the arrangement on an airliner. The younger brother made no move to get out of his chair, though.

"I suppose you'll want to rebuild her," he said. "That's going to be expensive…"

"We've managed it before, matey. But not right now, please."

It was the softest I'd heard Redbeard speak. Nook had clearly been right.

The sleek motor cruiser was better able to handle the storm than its anachronistic shell had been, but we still battled under the conditions. Several loud cracks and crashes told their own story.

And then it was over. Almost but not quite as suddenly as it had struck, the storm passed on. The gale fell, and with it the waves. No more thunder and lightning. There was only rain, still heavy but not pounding as it had been.

"Damn that for timing," growled Redbeard.

He punched a button and the bright beam of a searchlight burst from the front of the cruiser. I realised we were approaching an island. The captain cut our speed, but I still thought we were in danger of running headlong into one of the low cliffs that loomed ahead. He pressed another button. I guess it was a radio control device, because a small part of the 'cliff' in front of us pulled back like a stage curtain.

Motor cut, we slid in to berth. The crew had abruptly come to life and were scurrying up the ladder to get to the foredeck, or out the door at the rear of the cabin to make the boat secure. The stage curtain was already rolling back into place.

 Redbeard took Glexie, still dazed but improving, by the hand and led us out the rear of the cabin onto a transom and boarding platform still slick with rainwater. I followed, Blood coming last and securing the door behind us.

 We alighted onto a small dock where Bill had already securely tied what I'll call the inner *Ondine*. Several floodlights provided illumination. I realised that what we were in had been a narrow inlet leading into a short cave. The walls of the inlet had been roofed over to extend the cave, and the entrance disguised to make it undetectable to any passing vessels. Like the disguise of the *Ondine*, it was an ingenious effort, and must have been an expensive one. Black Sam Bellamy's legacy must have been really big.

 I confess I'd been feeling overwhelmed, by the storm and by our circumstances, and by the apparent loss of John B. When I heard his voice in the tempest, I think I'd had the thought, 'Everything will be alright – JB's magic will fix things'. Then I thought of what Redbeard had shouted, about relying on no-one.

The leader of the pirates led us down a short corridor to a door fixed into the natural rock of the original cave. Behind us, Blood was turning off lights. As I prepared to face yet another unknown I gave myself a good mental kick in the backside. Trusting my wizard's magic was fine, but it was unpredictable. I didn't know where he was, or how long it would be until we found each other, although I was utterly certain he was still alive. I knew it was time I started using my own initiative, too.

.o0o.

22 HELP WANTED

"Run with the wind. Veer to port. Five degrees, make it eight!" Ariane heard John B. shouting over the storm.

He repeated himself, louder and with more force. And again, the agitation in his voice obvious as he rocked back and turned his face up to the sky. Oblivious to the torrential rain hitting his face, he held that pose for several seconds, then slumped forward, pounding his fists once into the ground in front of him.

It was as though a connection had been broken. Like the person on the other end of a phone conversation had suddenly hung up. To Ariane's eyes the wizard seemed to shrink, curling in on himself. After several moments of silence and stillness from him, the legal officer realised she had to go out to him.

Ignoring the storm, she ran over and knelt beside him. His breath was coming in ragged gasps, and he made no protest as she put a hand under his arm and guided him to stand upright. He swayed alarmingly. With an arm around his shoulders she led him, stumbling, back under the shelter. Her steady hands guided him as he almost fell onto a bench.

'I'm no medical authority, but this looks like shock kicking in after he's staved it off for God knows how long,' was Ariane's perceptive thought. She quietly sat beside him and simply held him in silence for a while. Ariane had seen John B. at a low ebb before. I know she was present when he came back from being thrown over a cliff in Hawaii. He wasn't as battered and bruised this time, but she saw enough now to be worried anyway. A big part of that worry was also for Glexie, and for me.

Gradually John B.'s breathing returned to something like normal. The storm was passing, and with it, the wizard's apparent affliction.

Cautiously Ariane asked, "Are you okay, hon? Do you need a doctor?"

It took a little time for John B. to answer. Time in which he managed to get the inside of his head straight.

"What we need is a boat, and a clue. Not necessarily in that order," he finally replied.

"I don't know that I can help with either."

"You're helping just by being here."

When the two of them told me about all of this I was very glad I hadn't bought my beau a new beanie to replace the one she'd given him. I knew she'd never threaten the love we shared, but I knew now what he saw in Ariane, and that she was worth remembering.

"A clue," he repeated. "Where to find Elizabeth and Glexie. Where that mad bloody pirate would have taken them. I lost him – them – in the storm, but I have to believe they got to some sort of shelter."

"I've got no idea what you're getting at, hon. But you think they're safe?"

"I think… I think I'd *know* if anything fatal happened to Q. I remember how I felt in Norway, and I'd recognise it now."

"Norway?"

"Elizabeth was shot in the back. Survived by a miracle."

He didn't mention that he was a great part of that miracle, but continued thinking aloud. "I'm sure she's still alive, and if she made it through the storm I reckon Glexie would have, too."

Her normally pleasantly husky voice was deeper than usual as she replied, "I hope you're right, hon."

"The question remains though, where on earth, or on water, are they? On the Bay somewhere, maybe, I guess. But it's a big area, and I don't even know where to start looking. Should we go back to that police station you went to?"

Ariane shook her head. "I had enough trouble getting that coot to take me seriously before. I don't think he's going to be receptive to a story about pirates and a sea monster. Probably lock you up and test you for drugs. What about that island you were aiming for? I know you didn't actually get there, but would it be worth trying?"

John B. scratched at the stubble on his chin. "Ariane, you're brilliant," he replied. "If there's any possible way of her doing it, that's where Q will head for. Even if she has to take that scurvy crew with her, I reckon she'll figure on outwitting them somehow."

"Okay," said the dark-haired girl uncertainly. "Can you find your way to it?"

"Not a hope," he admitted. "It was Elizabeth who committed the directions to memory. I'd need to copy a map."

"I've got maps in the office, but the name Tepatamwa wasn't recorded on any of them."

"Mm – not surprising. But I do know someone who has a map, and would know where to look on it." He patted his pockets forlornly. "Those bloody buccaneers cleaned me out. The keys for Yvette are gone."

"Don't fret honey, I've got a car, remember? As long as you can navigate us to where this somebody is, we'll be fine."

"Sure. Sure. It's late and I'd love to call her – it'll be later still by the time we get up beyond Windsor along the Sheepscot River. But my phone is with those pirates too, and no, I don't have her number committed to memory."

"Past Windsor? It *is* going to take a while to get there. Have you got a name for this woman? I've got resources in my office that might include a number for her. If she can talk us through directions while I've got a map open in front of us, that'd be a lot quicker."

"I've already said that you're brilliant, haven't I? Good plan, my friend. Let's go find our girls."

Ariane led the way to her parked car, and they headed for Ogunquit as quickly as possible, determination and hope on both their faces.

*

Meanwhile… (I've always wanted to write that in a book.) Meanwhile, up in the woods by the Sheepscot River, Texas Dorothy had had her own unusual evening.

She'd seen the storm clouds in the distance, and knowing that her electricity supply wasn't always reliable, had fed Mac early and lit a number of candles at strategic points around the house.

Those in the lounge room were scented, and she'd been sitting there enjoying the fragrance of sandalwood when there was an unexpected knock at her front door.

She was surprised to be visited by Sam McFerris. She had a certain admiration for him as a raconteur, and he'd been to her house once or twice before. It was quite dark outside and the first raindrops were splashing down as she invited him to sit in one of the armchairs.

She winced inwardly at her own generosity when she realised her guest hadn't exactly dressed up for the visit. His shirt was faded and torn, but was still less obviously old than his baggy canvas pants which were grimy and stained with an assortment of oil and grease.

He spun some convoluted explanation for his presence. Something about how, inspired by meeting us, he was investigating his own family connection to the early native inhabitants of the region. I suspect he was hoping to find the place unattended.

"I thought you mentioned being descended from the Popham colony?" she'd asked.

That was a different branch of the family, he explained. A maternal grandmother was of Indian blood. Not talked about much, as that particular ancestor had come 'from the wrong side of the blanket'. But he was wondering now if there might be any connection with the tribe that Prince Henry had befriended. Perhaps Dorothy knew something that might be of interest to him?

He may even have used the words 'of value', which Dorothy admitted would have been ironic. At one point when she'd been in the kitchen making coffee she'd heard Mac barking meaningfully. When she'd wheeled herself back into the room she'd noticed that the wampum shelf looked slightly rearranged. She'd examine it more closely later, but she suspected one of the smaller beaded bands was missing from the apparently random tangled pile.

Dorothy was discreet enough not to tell Saxa anything significant about what we'd learned. The island was never mentioned. She talked in vague terms about how it was thought that there were some remnants of the 'old tribes' way back up in the woods. McFerris had replied that this made sense, and doubtless explained his natural affinity with that part of the country.

"I've always known that I'm a born woodsman," he'd said, and recounted a few tales of his experiences that, to Dorothy's practiced ear, sounded familiar. Teddy 'Miskwa' Burns familiar, perhaps.

It seems they only caught the fringe of the storm up on Dorothy's property. Some wind, and quite a bit of rain, and that was easing off when her uninvited guest not-so-subtly suggested he'd like more coffee before going out to "brave the elements".

Graciously the writer agreed. When she entered the little kitchen, she got a whiff of a familiar pungent odour. 'More than one visitor tonight, Ah reckon,' she thought to herself as she rinsed the cups.

She was patiently waiting for the kettle to boil when she heard Mac start to yap again. Before she could act on the thought to quietly wheel herself back into the lounge there was a loud growl, far deeper than Mac could muster, and a mighty crash against the outside wall. It sounded like the slap of a very large hand.

Then there came a loud shriek from the lounge, and Mac's barking became more frantic. She got out of the kitchen as fast as her wheels would carry her, in time to see Sam rushing out the front door, frenziedly beating at flames that were leaping at the top of his legs and burning his buttocks.

His hands and the lingering rain appeared to have extinguished the worst of the blaze by the time he'd reached the end of the driveway and jumped into his little beat-up sedan. It must surely have been a painful drive she mused as the small car sped away in a spray of wet gravel.

Mac had settled down as Dorothy rolled back into the lounge, and there was no further sound from outside. Dooley had probably departed, as quietly as he usually came and went. Looking about the room, the story told itself.

Papers that had been on her desk were strewn on the floor, as if dropped while being read. The desk was against the outside wall, at just about the exact spot, she realised, as the wendigo had so forcefully made his presence known. McFerris must have jumped back in alarm, and almost sat on one of the scented candles. The sturdy object had landed on the floor and lay in a puddle of rapidly congealing wax.

Fortunately, it must have been extinguished as it fell, but not before igniting some of the oil or whatever was ingrained in Sam's old trousers. She looked out in the direction of the driveway.

"Pants on fire," she said with a chuckle, before rolling back to the kitchen. She'd much prefer a coffee on her own now, and a biscuit each for her and the faithful cavoodle.

Texas Dorothy was privately a bit annoyed at her own naivety in trusting McFerris, even to the limited extent that she had. She'd let her fondness for a good story cloud what was, in hindsight, his obvious dishonesty. Still, she doubted that anyone would believe Sam if he ever tried to tell the story of what happened. She figured that that would only add to his discomfort, even after the burns themselves healed. Probably the worst fate he could imagine for himself.

She was apparently still chuckling to herself when the phone rang.

It turned out that Ariane had been as good as her word. Equipped only with the name 'Dorothy Duncum' and the vague address 'Sheepscot River', she'd spent twenty minutes examining files – electronic, paper, and microfiche, and finally produced a contact telephone number for the rather reclusive writer. John B. was impressed, and said so.

"We all have our own talents, hon," the legal officer replied with a smile as my beau dialed the number.

As soon as Dorothy answered he apologised for the lateness of the call, but said that it was important. He had a very strange experience to relate, and needed her help.

"Funny thing. Ah've had a right strange experience here tonight ma self," she replied, and began to tell the story of Saxa's visit.

He interrupted her as politely as he could. Much as he'd like to hear the story of Sam's misfortune (and of course later did), his question really was urgent.

After a momentary pause, Dorothy asked, "Somethin' bout thet lovely lady o' yours?"

John B. proceeded to tell as abbreviated a version of recent events as necessary, culminating in a request for her to open up the maritime chart that showed Tepatamwa Island, and describe its position so that he and Ariane could identify it on a chart they had in front of them.

"Sure 'nough. Ah can do that. Let me just put this here device on 'speaker' so's Ah can talk to ya while Ah rustle up the chart."

The authoress did so, and chatted while she rummaged in a bookcase, then leafed through pages of charts. Ariane tapped a button on her office phone to activate a similar function so she could also follow the directions. John B. 'introduced' his dear friend and legal advisor.

"Nice ta hear your voice, young lady. Thanks for helpin' ma old pal there - sounds like he been needin' ya. So, John B., pirates, ya say? Not many of them around, this day'n'age. Not round these parts, least ways."

John B. missed or ignored the 'old pal' description and lamented, "It must be a side effect of this magic thing. I've said it before – I'm flypaper for freaks. Wannabe gods, psychic vampires, nutjobs who want to rewrite history, now throwback pirates – they seem to keep finding me."

"Or the other way 'round," suggested Dorothy casually.

"Pardon me?"

"Y'all are drawn to them. Like a antibody to a infection."

"Trust me – I do *not* go looking for these people," he answered with feeling.

"Not consciously, Ah'm sure. Now, Ah got the collection o' charts here. While Ah look for the right one, y'all can tell me more about meetin' Cassie."

The wizard immediately recognised that as the local equivalent of the name 'Nessie', and recounted his experience.

"Nice to know the ol' girl's still around. Ain't been a reliable report of her for a good while. She got seen quite a few times back in the 1800s, when the big fishin' fleets used to be out on the Bay."

"But ma'am, those sightings were nearly two hundred years ago!" exclaimed Ariane over the speaker phone, her surprise momentarily overcoming her polite silence.

"Y'all can live a very long time when ya learn to keep your profile low, ain't that right John B.?"

The wizard looked quizzically at the phone. "Um… yes. Yeah… that makes sense."

Whatever train of thought he was about to embark on was immediately derailed when Dorothy said, "Right. Got it."

The sound of her finger tapping the chart was audible over the speaker in the Drake Professional Services office. Disregarding any concerns her boss might have (and knowing nothing of his demise), Ariane was carefully marking the route on their copy of the chart as the authoress described it. This document would be leaving the office with them, and could always be replaced with a 'clean' copy later.

Once she was sure that Ariane and John B. had the directions clearly marked and understood, Texas Dorothy seemed to overcome her natural tendency to chat and bid her callers farewell.

"Now, y'all better take care. Ah knows ya got power, John B., but Ah reckon there's still troubled waters ahead of ya afore this'll be all over. Ya be sure'n get this rescue right. Thet there girl o' yours is important."

"All three of these girls are important to me, Dorothy," replied the wizard, earning a silent but grateful smile from his current companion.

"Ah know, Ah know. Yer a good man. Ah know ya've had yer moments in the past, but yer good at heart, an' thet's what matters. And Ah knows thet Elizabeth's a big part o' thet. Now, ya better git to work. Y'all have got a tough task ahead of ya.”

 Before anything more could be asked or said, the authoress hung up her phone. Ariane was looking at John B. strangely. Not unreasonably, I’d say.

“I thought you said you’d only recently met Dorothy Duncum. Sounds like you’ve known each other for a long time,” she observed quietly.

 My beau looked just as puzzled as he said, “Yeah, it does, doesn’t it? A question for later, though, I reckon. Like she said, we’ve got a task in front of us.”

“Mm, true. Well, it’s like you said back in the park, honey – now we’ve got a clue, we need a boat. I don’t have Glexie’s sea-going contacts, but we could hire something.”

 John B. shook his shaggy head. “I doubt it. I don’t know about here, but other places I’ve been will only rent boats out to someone with a licence. Elizabeth is the sailor of the two of us – I’m officially just ballast, or crew on a good day. Based on earlier comments, I don’t imagine you’re a qualified skipper?”

“No chance,” she replied with a wry grin.

 The wizard was looking out the office window towards Perkins Cove. Texas Dorothy’s words were still rattling around his head looking for some past to connect to, but suddenly they were elbowed aside by a more recent memory. Memory of a conversation in *Twinkles*. In his mind he heard Lanny French’s voice.

“We’ve got a little boat that we bring here for servicing. There’s a very good chandler in Perkins Cove that we take her to.”

“Do you remember the two older blokes we introduced you to at the piano bar that night?” he asked the dark-haired girl.

"Slim, rather dapper man? And a big fellow with a great singing voice.
Yes, I remember them. Oh yes – they mentioned having a boat! Can you
get in touch with them?"

"Another job for your detective skills, I'm afraid, my dear. And I've
got even less to go on as far as where they live. Maybe around Popham
Beach. Maybe Portland? Not around here though, I don't think."

The legal officer shrugged and went to work. Fortunately, 'Cowley
Honeywell' was not a common name, even in these parts. Finding it on a
document with 'L. French' listed as 'partner' was exactly the confirmation
they required. It took a little over half an hour.

John B. was about to reach for the phone and dial the number she'd managed to extract. Ariane stopped his hand.

"It's late. They're not young men. Even if they are still awake, it's not
like we could do anything at this hour. Let's call and talk to them first
thing in the morning."

The wizard sighed. "I guess you're right. We can only do what we can,
and we're doing that as it is."

"We've done pretty well so far. A few hours sleep is probably a good
idea, for both of us. Do you want to come back to our place? It's close.
There's a couch you're welcome to," she added.

My beau gave a grateful smile. "You're right. And that's an offer too
good to refuse."

And when they tell me that's where he spent the night, you know, I absolutely believe them.

.o0o.

23 LIVING ON AN ISLAND

When I came out of the boathouse cave I stepped onto a wide paved walkway that led between a jumble of rocks, some of them quite large. The pavers were wet, but not slippery. Nonetheless, Redbeard kept a supportive hand under Glexie's arm. No such chivalry for me, I noticed.

I tried to walk slowly, ignoring the rain, and take as much stock as I could of my new surroundings. It was mostly only footlights illuminating the path, so I couldn't see much on either side anyway. What's more, Blood was on the path behind me and I didn't want to be any closer to him than I could help. Occasionally I noticed a dim flash of light above me, reflecting off what I realised was camouflage netting.

Within only a few minutes, the path opened onto a small unpaved courtyard, ringed by single-storey buildings. Simple bungalows, mostly. A couple of sheds, and directly opposite the path, something that reminded me of the old longhouses we'd seen in drawings or reconstructions in Scotland, Shetland and Norway. That was where we were headed for. I couldn't be sure, but I suspected all of the roofs were camouflaged, too.

The 'longhouse' proved to be a meeting room/dining hall, with a kitchen at one end and toilets at the other. The other four members of the crew were already assembled and waiting. Well, 'assembled' is too generous a word really. They were standing around dripping when we walked in. Blood was close at my heels, shutting the door as soon as he'd entered.

Redbeard indicated that Glexie and I should sit while he addressed his men.

"Not a good day, me hearties. But we're alive. We've got resources, we can rebuild."

"If what we've heard is true, then those resources can be substantially increased," said Blood, looking meaningfully at me.

"Aye, matey. That could be useful, at that. First things first though. Get dried, get some warm food into us all."

Nook spoke up. "The stew's bubbling in the galley, ready to eat."

A rich smell wafted from the kitchen, confirming his observation. It turned out that culinary duties were done on a roster system, and it had been the big man's turn. Before they'd set sail, he'd prepared a basic but hearty beef stew that had been simmering in a slow cooker for hours.

"Good lad," said his captain, and patted the massive shoulder affectionately. "We'll need to get the cruiser shipshape before we can do much about reconstructing the real ship."

Blood nodded. "I'll take her in to Ogunquit in the morning. I think the damage isn't too serious. With Misters Brentford and Wadsworth to help the job ought to be done in a day."

"More hands to make lighter work, brother?"

The mate shook his head. "You and Mister Lear are too conspicuous to be seen in town, you know that. Mister McCallum could be handy, but I thought it better if he stayed here to help keep an eye on our – guests."

"We'll think about it over dinner. Get ye all to yer cabins and be back here pronto."

As the crew went to leave Redbeard grabbed Inigo's sleeve.

"Some warm dry clothes for the lasses, eh – if ye please? Ye'd be about the closest size, I think."

The topman saluted. "Aye aye, cap'n," he said with a genuine smile. His expression clouded a little as he looked at Glexie. "Er… I'm not so sure about the size though," he said cautiously as he eyed her generously endowed figure.

Certainly, unless his shirts were extremely loose on him they'd be uncomfortably snug on the accountant. Both of them blushed as Redbeard made the same assessment, an eyebrow raised in amused contemplation.

"Aye, laddie, ye might be right. Stop by my cabin, pick up something warm." He smiled. "And per'aps a bit fancy, eh?"

"As you wish." Another smart salute, and Inigo was gone.

While Redbeard only had eyes for my friend, I glared at him. "What happens to us now? Are we to be clapped in irons? Sent to the brig?"

Teef squawked and flapped his iridescent wings, apparently enthused at that idea. His ambulatory perch grinned.

"Aar, ye know, we don't actually have a brig. Never needed one. Not got anythin' ye might call guest quarters, either. Still, ye'll need to sleep somewhere…"

Big Nook had just come back into the longhouse and had been making a beeline for the galley. His hearing was obviously pretty sharp, because he stopped and ambled over to us.

"You can use my cabin for them, captain. It's got a big bed in it."

I could believe that, given the size of the man. It was a kind offer. There seemed nothing blood-thirsty about this particular pirate, at least. His skipper tugged thoughtfully at the facial hair that had given him his chosen name.

"Yer a good lad, Nook. I might hope that…"

He looked at Glexie, more longing than lascivious though his thoughts were clear on his face. The accountant met his gaze eye to eye and shook her head, not extravagantly but emphatically.

"No," he said, mostly to himself. "I'm reluctant ta move any of me crew out of their quarters. We've got a lot o' work ta be doin' in the comin' days, and sleepin' here won't give 'em the rest they're going ta need. You especially, me hearty, need yer own bed for a decent night's rest.

"Come tomorrow we'll fit out one o' the storage rooms ta tide ye over till somethin' more permanent is arranged. Fer tonight ye'll be in here. We've got camp beds packed away that ye can use."

"Permanent?" Glexie and I asked, almost in unison.

"Ye've seen the faces of me and all me crew, lasses. I can hardly have ye runnin' ta the authorities, can I?"

I realised then what solution to that problem was favoured by Blood, and I suspected, the POETs. Encouraging Redbeard to come up with an alternative suddenly seemed a good idea. A pity I hadn't yet thought of one.

"Ye'll be with us until ye've led us ta yer treasure, at least, me fine ladies. After that, we'll just have ta see."

I threw my head back. "Even if I knew what you were talking about, why would you think I'd do you any favours after you've fed my boyfriend to the fishes?"

I made no attempt to keep bitterness from my voice. Privately I believed John B. was somehow still alive, but I wasn't going to let that show. Mention of my beau's fate stirred Glexie, too. Tears welled in her eyes, but her mouth was set in a defiant line.

"Aar… well… truth be told, that, ah, didn't quite go as planned…"

"Really?" Glexie's voice was cold, and that seemed to really disturb the captain.

He turned to his outsized crewman and patted him on the arm. "Be about yer business in the galley, Mister Lear."

There was a look of some concern on the big man's face, but he saluted and moved off as instructed. The captain tugged at a handful of his own beard.

"Aye, lass. I'd thought…" His voice was uncertain, as if he wasn't quite sure what he'd thought. Perhaps that was the case.

"I'd thought that ye'd give up yer treasure ta save him, right enough. Worst came ta worst, I'd have stalled till I knew we weren't far from one o' the little uninhabited islands, and put him over the side then. Give him a chance. Without makin' it too obvious. Never imagined he'd dive off like he did. I be… truly sorry."

Either he was genuine, or he was one of the finest actors I've ever seen. He reached to wipe a tear from Glexie's face, but she pulled away from his hand.

"Tis a raw wound, aye," he said sadly. "But there's nothin' ta be done fer it. I understand yer grievin'. But now, more than ever, we be wantin' that treasure."

"Then you're doomed to disappointment," I replied flatly.

Inigo reappeared, dressed all in black and carrying an armload of clothes which he placed on the table beside us, together with a couple of big thick towels. I glared at the two pirates.

"Well?" I said. "You don't expect us to put on a show for you while we get changed? For you and whoever else wanders in."

Inigo blushed fiercely, and even his captain reddened.

"Man the door, please, Mister McCallum. I'll turn me back fer a bit – don't take too long, mind ye," he said, giving a little bow.

Satisfied that Nook was too engrossed in his cooking to be an audience, Glexie and I shrugged at each other and got on with it. The towels were impressive, and very welcome. Under other circumstances I admit I would have been delighted with the clothes, too. Our pants were some sort of wool blend, warm but not too heavy. Inigo's taste in shirts evidently ran to silk – I'd noticed a black silk collar protruding above the neck of his sweater, and while the one he'd loaned me was plain it did feel fabulous. A dark skivvy hid the lovely white shirt, but I did get to enjoy the feel of the fabric.

Redbeard's own wardrobe had furnished a white linen shirt for my friend, with warmth provided by a another richly embroidered red coat, some inches shorter than the wet bedraggled one our host was still wearing. It was made of boiled wool, lined and decorated with silk. A final courtesy was a pair of thick wool socks each.

I can't fault Redbeard's chivalry. He never turned around to sneak a peek at us, nor was there a reflecting surface for him to be surreptitiously watching. He talked thoughtfully.

"Perhaps a partnership of sorts. We let ye keep a share of the treasure when ye lead us to it. Get ye back ta Australia with it, ye get on with yer life there, and we get on with business here."

"And I just forget it all happened. Forget the sound of John B. hitting the water. Take a cut of the treasure and be content, is that it? Even if there *was* a treasure, do you really think I'd accept that?"

The captain sighed. "Best offer ye be gettin', I think."

"And what about me?" asked Glexie. "I've got no desire to live in Australia, no offence, Elizabeth."

Redbeard sighed again, but said nothing. I think we both knew what he hoped for, but surely his grasp on reality couldn't be so poor as to think she'd really willingly join his 'merry band'?

Bysshe Brentford was rapping at the door of the longhouse just as we finished dressing. At a nod from the captain, Inigo let him in. Bill arrived shortly after. Their colour choices seemed to be consistent, Bish in a snug maroon sweater while his partner in crime wore a faded blue pullover that hung loosely on his lean frame. I strongly suspected that there was a gun tucked somewhere under the folds of the jumper.

"I'll be back," said the captain, in a vague approximation of Arnold Schwarzenegger as he left to at last change out of his own sodden clothes.

Eyeing Glexie and I warily, the POETs sat at a table on the opposite side of the longhouse to us, and began a quiet conversation.

They exchanged agreeable nods with Inigo as he strolled past on his way to sitting with us. I suspect he was on a gentle form of guard duty. I gestured around the room, with a wave that I intended to include the outside area as well.

"This is quite an extraordinary set up," I said.

"Redbeard is quite an extraordinary man," replied Inigo with a smile. "Oh, I know he comes across as a bit strange, but he's really very clever, in his own way. The tactical psychology behind the pirate ship and outfits. Using the fog to 'hit and run' on our raids. The design of this base – it's quite invisible both from the air and the sea, you know."

I nodded. "All of which must have cost a small fortune. I can't see that he'd *need* any treasure from me. Even if I had some," I added hastily.

"He's determined now, you see. That's what he's like. Once he sets his mind to do something, or to get it, he will not quit until he's achieved it. I think that's how he defines 'need' in his head."

Glexie tapped her fingertips on the table.

"Well if he's set his mind on getting me, he's in for a long wait," she said bluntly.

"I know the circumstances are difficult," said Inigo apologetically. "But strangely enough I really think you could do worse. The captain's a bit rough around the edges, but he's got a good heart, deep down."

"Your loyalty is commendable, at least," Glexie admitted.

"It's been earned. He's loyal to us, we're loyal to him. He's protected us all in different ways over time. His brother and Nook since they were kids – Red was the one who stood up to the bullies."

"Nook was bullied?" asked Glexie in surprise, but softly so as not to catch the big man's ear.

"Look at him. He's *different*. Different gets picked on, especially in numbers," replied the lookout. I suspected he too had been considered different.

The accountant stared at tonight's chef as he tended a simmering pot of potatoes. I sensed she was just starting to see the pirate chief in a new light. The flicker of one, at least. She looked uncomfortable.

To deflect her musings, I asked Inigo, "So how did you come by this nameless lump of real estate? Old family property, or seized like any other form of booty?"

"I suppose you'd call it 'seized'. As far as I know it was just lying out here vacant. Maybe the government owns it, but if so they've never shown any interest. That's Blood's department really. He does all of the administrative work. His brother *has* money, but Blood is better at handling it, I think. Certainly, he's more interested in it."

The flame-haired young man watched the door, and saluted as the two brothers entered, conversing quietly. Like the rest of the crew, Blood had changed to something more like conventional attire, in this case a bright red roll-neck pullover and jeans that were too tight around his ample waist. Only his older brother maintained the piratical motif. Another pair of long boots and black trousers, a loose linen shirt, and now a long frock coat in black and gold brocade.

 Redbeard had two camp beds and pillows under one arm, and sleeping bags slung over a shoulder with Teef perched awkwardly among their folds.

 The lookout turned back to me and said, "Oh by the way, this island isn't nameless. Welcome to Tepatamwa."

.o0o.

24 TURKS BUILDING A BRIDGE

Their intentions had been good, but John B. and Ariane were victims of their own exhaustion. Whatever alarm she'd set, they both slept through it, each in their own rooms.

My wizard woke first, completely disoriented, struggled to get up from the couch he'd sunk deeply into, yawned, and fell back to sleep.

It was mid-morning before Ariane emerged from her room. It was Saturday morning, so whatever 'body clock' got her to work on time, five days per week, had automatically switched itself off. The shock of seeing the hour on her bedside clock snapped her into wakefulness. She'd rushed out into the lounge to check on her guest, apparently only just remembering to throw on the short black Chinese robe that hung on her door. (We found in later conversation that she has the same preference in nightwear as I do: none.)

Rousing John B. didn't take long, once she got his eyes open. The urgency of their problem crashed in on their minds quickly, shredding whatever cloak of sleepiness that still shrouded their brains.

But the lateness of their rising turned out to be costly.

While Ariane was making coffee and quickly heating a couple of croissants, my beau was using her phone to call the number they'd tracked down the night before. Lanny answered soon enough, but explained that Cowley had left for the day. He'd gone out for a day's birdwatching, and never took his cellphone with him for fear of disturbing something he'd spent patient hours waiting for. There was a particularly elusive finch that had been reported in some woodland several miles away, and it would be a coup to 'tick it off' in his book, apparently.

Lanny listened while John B. told his unlikely story. The older man was incredulous in parts – well, you could hardly blame him – but he wasn't dismissive. He asked reasonable and intelligent questions, his measured tone doing much to keep my wizard calm and focused despite his agitation.

Our history-minded friend certainly picked up on that agitation though, and I suspect that may have gone some way towards convincing him of the truth of John B.'s wild tale. Ariane's contributions to the conversation doubtless helped too. There's an air of sincerity about that woman that is carried in her husky voice. You can't *not* take her seriously.

The problem was that, as much as Lanny was willing to believe them – more than willing, and more than willing to help – it was Cowley who owned and operated the boat. His own role was remarkably like how John B. described himself on our *True Love*, sometimes crew but mostly ballast. He was sure his own beloved partner would be sympathetic to how they felt (Ariane not bothering to correct the usual assumption about her relationship with Glexie – after all, she did love the girl even if they weren't lovers). Sure that they'd do whatever they could to help, including setting out onto Casco Bay. But without actually consulting the "big fella" it was impossible to make any arrangements.

He promised that as soon as Cowley came home, whatever unpredictable time that turned out to be (some of these birds were notoriously unreliable), he'd relate their situation. Could he call them back, at whatever hour of the afternoon or evening?

Of course. Ariane recited her cellphone number., Lanny meticulously repeating it digit by digit to confirm.

The call ended, the two finished their now-cold breakfast in silent contemplation. It was Ariane who spoke first.

"It was positive, at least. We can't move as quick as we'd both like, but it gives us time to plan."

"Fair enough. I'm reminded of the story of the Turks building a bridge."

She looked puzzled. "You've lost me."

"A story I heard, out of the Second World War. Given two weeks to build a bridge, the Turks would spend ten or twelve days apparently doing nothing but scribbling notes and making piles of stuff, while the Brits would be trying to sink piles, float pontoons or whatever. Then suddenly the Turks would erupt into a frenzy of activity and everything would come together. Their bridge was done, while downriver the Brits were still falling in the water. I don't know if it's actually true, but it's always impressed me as emphasizing the importance of planning and strategy – not always my long suits, I'm afraid."

"No time like the present to learn, hon. We have to get this right."

 They were clasping each other's hands again, without even noticing.

"Right you are. First things first, I suppose. We should both get dressed. I could do with a change of clothes if you wouldn't mind a drive back to Portland?"

"What? Oh!"

 Suddenly the legal officer realised that she was in only a flimsy robe, while her guest was in his underwear, with damp jeans and t-shirt on the floor, piled on the towel she'd given him the night before. Her alabaster white skin doesn't blush readily, but she reckons she felt a definite flush of pinkness right then.

The long-sleeved black t-shirt she soon wore with jeans of the same colour was probably a more conservative choice of outfit than usual. Conscious or unconscious self-discipline. The multi-pocketed white fur-lined vest that completed the ensemble was entirely practical.

 Still, she'd recovered her equilibrium enough to smilingly observe while driving to Portland, "I suppose I should be glad we weren't on a video call to your friend!"

Her passenger laughed. "True enough, fair lady! I think we gave poor Lanny quite enough to take in as it was!"

"Speaking of whom, how much confidence do you have in him? Them?"

"I don't know either of them well, obviously, but my limited experience has been positive. If Lanny says they'll help, I'm inclined to believe him. Cowley's no fool, but I think he's inclined to go along with pretty much whatever his partner wants."

"Like someone else I know."

"Mm?" John B. raised an eyebrow.

"Honey, you've trailed halfway across the world, maybe more, chasing Elizabeth's family history."

"She has a book to write. I reckon it's a worthwhile project."

"You love her. If she wanted to write a book about the moon you'd probably be trying to find a way into NASA or something. I'm not criticizing, hon. Anything but. A bit jealous, maybe. I'd like to be loved like that."

 The wistful note in her voice wasn't lost on my beau. He put a hand on one of hers, not squeezing so tight as to interfere with her steering, but enough to be expressive.

"I wi-"

"Don't!" she interrupted sharply. "I appreciate the thought. Really. But I don't know quite what it is that I want, other than in a vague sense. However your magic works, it seems a bit... unpredictable."

"That's certainly true," he admitted. "In another place and time, you and I... well... a 'what if', maybe. Can I wish you happiness, at least?"

 She pulled the car to the side of the road and wiped a tear from her eye.

"Another place and time, yes." She caught her breath. "I'm sorry John B. I think the stress, the worry about Glexie, all catching up with me… Happiness would be – a good wish. Thank you."

My darling man put his arms around another woman and held her as she cried into his shoulder. I know first-hand how comforting that can be, and I don't begrudge her a moment of it.

When Ariane had regained her composure they resumed the journey. At our motel room John B. was all for a quick change of clothes, but she insisted he take the time for a shower.

"Not for my sake, hon. For yours. I know it helped wash some tension off me this morning."

If John B. thought that a bit inconsistent with her moment of distress at the side of the road, he was too diplomatic to say so. He left the legal officer reading one of his books of mythology while he took her advice and headed for the bathroom.

Soon after, he emerged, clad in clean jeans and a purple t-shirt emblazoned with a black Celtic knotwork motif. We'd bought it as we travelled through Scotland. He was toweling dry his hair, which would have done nothing at all to improve its shagginess. Poor boy – he does try sometimes, but I'm afraid he seems fated to look untidy.

"That does feel a lot better," he admitted. "You were quite right."

"Of course," she replied. "I usually am, you know."

The two friends smiled affectionately at each other.

"Whatever you say, ma'am. Now let's get started on building this bridge."

They did some shopping in Portland. Ariane had given a lot of thought to John B.'s description of the pirate crew, and to the sort of reception they'd get if – when – they encountered them again. She took them to a discreet little gun shop and bought herself a good German-made automatic pistol.

 It was a little surprising to her when John B. refused her offer of a similar weapon.

"I don't like guns," he said simply.

"I'm not a fan either, trust me. I've never believed in 'peace through superior firepower'. But if there's a realistic prospect of finding myself on the wrong end of one, and that certainly seems to be the case, then I want to be able to defend myself."

"Personally, I'd rather find another option."

"Yes, but you have your magic to rely on."

"It's there for you too, you know."

"And I appreciate that, my friend." She patted her new parcel. "But I like to have a Plan B."

 Eventually they made their way back to the cozy home outside Ogunquit, where they spent the rest of the day waiting to hear from Cowley. They occupied some time studying the maritime chart, trying to commit the directions to memory.

"It's not quite all Greek to me, but I'm sure it'll be a lot more meaningful to Cowley if he's spent much time out on the Bay. I've only seen it once, and I wasn't paying that much attention. There's a big difference between two and three dimensions," admitted John B. with some concern.

"You sounded like you knew your way around during the storm. You were calling out some pretty definite directions."

 The wizard blinked. "Really? Wow. It's a shame I don't remember anything of it."

"Nothing?"

"Nope. Sorry mate. Sometimes my memory is like a bloody big Swiss cheese – full of holes."

 The look Ariane gave him was more thoughtful than doubtful. "I've seen and heard you pull all sorts of facts and information up out of that memory."

 He shrugged. "Data I'm okay with," he conceded. "Language, history, facts. I'm pretty good for a game of Trivial Pursuit. It's myself that my brain goes missing on."

 He proceeded to tell Ariane of how he'd been placed in an orphanage as a child, after being found wandering the streets with no idea of his own identity.

"Nothing?" she asked, shocked.

"Not that I've ever recalled. The only clue was the name 'John B.' that was scribbled inside the collar of the purple t-shirt I was wearing. The woman running the place guessed I was about ten, but I didn't know. Not then, not now. Sitting in the office of the orphanage is the first memory I have."

"That's… weird. And sad."

"I've never missed what I've never known. I was adopted a little while later, which I appreciated. Lovely Scottish couple I've called my parents ever since. Had a pretty average suburban childhood. Grew up into a pretty average sort of bloke. Well, until I hit my head and woke up this magic thing."

 The dark-haired girl smiled. "I don't think you are at all 'average', my friend. With or without your magic, I reckon you'd be something special."

"Thanks." He looked back down at the chart. "Now, where were we…?"

It's a measure of how much John B. had come to trust our new 'legal advisor' that he'd revealed so much of himself. It's not a story he's told many people. Wilko knows a bit, and I think John B.'s housemate Darren. I believe I'm the only one he's explained detail to – such detail as he knows, that is. The only one in a long time, anyway. I know there's an ex-fiancée in his past. I guess he would have spoken to her about it. Or maybe not, and that's got something to do with her being an ex.

Eventually Cowley did call. Lanny had told him a remarkable story. He didn't need to hear it all again, but he did have a few questions. John B. answered them honestly and succinctly, which I'm sure helped his cause.

"We-e-ell, outlandish as it sounds, I don't reckon that's a story ya could make up. I'm happy to help ya," Cowley said. "More than happy. I'm honoured ya saw fit to ask us."

If he was aware that John B. could think of no other options he was good enough not to say so.

"Ya have a chart for finding this island, ya say? I've never heard of Tepatamwa, but there's hundreds, maybe thousands of little pieces of land out there so that don't mean anything. Ain't no point in trying to do much of anything now, sorry. I know ya must be keen to get going, but it'll be dark too soon for us to be out there searching for your girls."

Reluctantly, John B. and Ariane had to agree. They'd maintained their faith that they would 'know' if anything happened to Glexie and me, and realised they'd just have to hold onto that faith for another night.

"Ma little boat's tied up down at Ogunquit. I had to get some seals repaired, and I ain't gotten around to bringing her back north yet. Can we meet ya at the marina in Perkins Cove tomorrow morning?"

John B. didn't mention just how coincidentally convenient that was, simply agreeing to the arrangement. They organized a rendezvous that would allow the two older men plenty of time to drive down, but would still get them out onto the Bay as early as possible. Lanny made it very clear he'd be coming out with them.

"Um, there's every chance this could turn into a risky business you know," John B. warned. "These characters I met, they're dangerous. I don't know if we'll run into them or not, but if we do…"

"We-e-ell, if we do, it'll be their problem. Don't ya worry, young fella. Lanny and me, we've seen some action in our time. We know how to take care of ourselves."

The wizard could hear a throaty laugh of agreement in the background. He appreciated the support, but could only wish that the two men would be as safe as they predicted.

"I'll see you tomorrow morning," he said. "I wish us success."

.o0o.

25 TABLE TALK

I reckon both Glexie and I could have a career in playing poker. Neither
of us showed a flicker of reaction to Inigo's casual bombshell. Not that he
even knew he'd dropped it.

We didn't get the chance to converse privately until considerably later,
so I wasn't sure what was going on in her mind. But I know the news of
where we were sent my brain spinning. Our old friend Wilko has called
my beau a "walking improbability field" on more than one occasion. It
seemed his extraordinary talent for coincidences was rubbing off on me.
Here I was, on Tepatamwa, where I'd wanted to be. But now what?

Not much was said over dinner. The POETs and Blood sat at a table on
the other side of the longhouse from us. Redbeard's attempt to sit beside
Glexie was thwarted when she quickly moved herself to the end of the
bench seat and I stayed resolutely at her other hip. He settled for sitting
opposite us, but his attempts at conversation were mostly met with silence.

Inigo diplomatically concentrated on his meal. I did make a point of
thanking the cook when he joined us at our table. The stew was pretty
basic, but it was rich and warming, and after all that had happened during
the day, really satisfying.

The big man grinned. "Don't expect the same tomorrow, miss. It's Bill's
turn to cook. He only knows how to fry stuff."

"Aar, sad but true," agreed his captain. "It'll be his usual sausages, I be
thinkin'. Still an' all, he takes his turn, like we all do."

I'd realised that, despite his eccentric demeanour, Redbeard actually ran a
well-disciplined operation. A tight ship, he'd have called it. Duties were
rostered, and not just the kitchen chores. The place was kept tidy. Clothes
were clean. The bathroom and toilet at the opposite end of the longhouse
from the galley weren't exactly immaculate, but they were a lot cleaner

than I expected from a half-dozen blokes. There were some strange contradictions and surprises in this crew.

 Meal over, the captain called his men together to make plans for the next day.

"What I'd like, o' course, is ta set about collectin' this treasure."

 The crew en masse looked at Glexie and me. We said nothing, both keeping our faces as expressionless as we could.

"Ah well, all in good time, lasses. Be sure of that." There was a definite note of warning in his voice, and I don't believe it was just for the benefit of his more fractious crew members. "We've got some rebuildin' to do, me hearties. Blood, I think yer notion of takin' the cruiser into Ogunquit with the two lads is a good one. Nook and Inigo, you and me will make a start on our new ship. I've still got the plans. We can start pullin' together supplies tomorrow. See what we've got here, an' assess what we're goin' ta be needin', put together a list. We've done it before, we can do it again."

"And what about us?" I asked.

"Aye, I know – I did say we'd set up a cabin for ye…"

"Ah, just lock 'em in one of the tool rooms," snarled Bill.

 Bish smacked him on the arm. "No, you dope! Don't give them access to sharp stuff!"

"Alright, empty it first! Or lock 'em in one of the other little storage huts, with the toilet paper and tinned stuff."

"Oh, that'd be handy if we went on a baked bean-eating frenzy," said Glexie, smiling sweetly. She was definitely recovering her nerve.

 Redbeard was chuckling at her response. "No, I don't reckon so," he said. "This is an island, Mister Wadsworth. Where could they go? Ye'll have the boat, and as healthy as these lasses look, I doubt they could swim to anywhere useful."

 In my mind I saw the chart we'd been navigating by, now drifting around out on Casco Bay somewhere. I knew he was right. He'd chosen the location for his secret base well.

 Glexie was looking at me as she said, "It seems like we're going to be here a while until we can get it through their thick heads that we don't know what they're talking about. I don't know about you, but I'm not keen to spend all my time tied up like Christmas parcel." She turned her gaze to Redbeard but didn't give him the smile he was hoping for. "If you're right about us not being able to get away from this island, and I admit that seems likely, we might as well be useful here in some way. No, Mister Billy-boy, I'm not suggesting we be allowed to play with sharp objects."

 Some of the crew smiled or smirked quietly while Wadsworth scowled. I added my smile.

"I've never tried my hand at boat-building, but hey, I'll have a go."

"Ha! Shiver me timbers but ye've got spirit! Both of ye! Nay lasses, I'll not have ye settin' about with hammers and weldin' tools, not just yet anyway. But aye, there are some jobs I'm sure we can find ye. A decision for the mornin', I'm thinkin'. Been a long day, with more ahead. Mister Lear, I'll give ye a hand cleanin' up in the galley. Good hearty meal, that, by the way, thank'ee. We'll make sure everythin' is looked away nice an' secure."

 He said this with a nod of acknowledgement to Bysshe Brentford, who might have worried about our unsupervised access to kitchen knives.

"Now, to yer duties if ye've got 'em, otherwise to yer cabins," the captain ordered.

To a man, the crew saluted. Very nearly, so did I. He might have been
mad, but he was charismatic. The POETs and Inigo upped and departed almost immediately. Redbeard and Nook gathered up the plates and
headed for the galley. It struck me that part of the captain's secret was that
he made it obvious that he wouldn't expect any of his crew to do anything
he wouldn't tackle himself. (Although if he'd ever spent much time in a
crow's nest I thought it must have been when he was much smaller.)

Allowed the freedom to set up our beds wherever we wanted in the
longhouse, Glexie and I chose to be as far from the door as possible. We
dragged tables to create a little bit of privacy. I was sure the building
would be locked from the outside, but we weren't keen on having anyone
wander in on us overnight, wanting a casual cup of coffee or something.

While we laid out our sleeping bags, the portly first mate came over to
watch and speak to us – low and menacing.

"Tell me where to find your treasure."

"What treasure?" I asked, without meeting his eyes.

"I see. And you?"

Glexie shrugged as she smoothed out her sleeping bag. "Don't look at
me. I just drove the boat."

"You're both still resolute then." He bent closer. "My patience is not
boundless, ladies, be warned. Far from it. I will have that fortune. My
brother's lovesick foolishness will not shield you much longer. His patience has limits too, but regardless of him, I will extract the information I
seek."

"Oh yes?" I said casually.

"Oh yes. I might wait until my brother's doe eyes are elsewhere, or frankly I may not even bother to wait that long. His notions of chivalry are

inconvenient, impractical, and annoying. You women are vexing me, and I do not take kindly to being vexed."

"Oh, I am sorry." I'm sure I sounded as insincere as I felt.

"You shall be. Expect pain. Disfigurement. Expect to beg to tell me what I want to know, just to make it stop." Blood stood up straight and gave a small mocking bow. "I will speak to you again tomorrow evening., ladies. I look forward to a pleasant conversation."

 He turned and strode out, leaving the two of us to look at each other.

"Do you think he's serious?" I asked my companion, letting my concern show now that he'd gone.

"Serious enough that there's a river of ice down my spine, hon. What do we do?"

"Try to sleep on it, I guess. I've got no doubt John B., wherever he is, will be trying to do whatever he can…"

"Ariane, too, I'll bet."

"Of course. Between them, anything is possible, but let's face it, they've no idea where we are. I think we have to rely on ourselves, and I'll be better able to do that after I've slept."

 Unable to stifle a yawn as she lay down, Glexie agreed. "You're right, of course. But after everything that's happened today, God only knows how I'll be able to sleep."

 I think it was less than a minute before I heard her softly snoring. I know Redbeard and Nook were still putting pots and dishes away, because that was the last sound I heard before I must have followed her a few seconds later.

.o0o.

26 WORK

I'd like to report that after a good night's sleep we woke up full of great ideas for how to liberate ourselves. Alas, that wasn't the case.

At least we hadn't been disturbed. I'd heard Blood and his two unpleasant off-siders come in, breakfast and leave for Ogunquit without letting on I was awake. It also meant I caught their quiet conversation about hearing from someone – the person who'd identified John B. and I over the phone when we'd first been picked up off the *Emma*. They'd contacted Blood, and were apparently demanding a share of the treasure they were sure had been found by now.

The word 'demand' hadn't gone down well. Blood was determined that whoever it was would be dealt with.

"I've agreed a meeting this evening before we come back here. The repairs will be done in plenty of time." This was a statement, not a request. "I'll put ashore at that little cove near Popham Beach where we've made drops before. You wait on the cruiser – I won't need your help for dealing with this one. It shall be over quickly."

"Sure?" asked Bill, a note of disappointment in his voice.

"Over?" asked Bish, a little uncertainly.

"Yes, and yes. There are other fences when we require them. Men who will know their place. Now come, gentlemen. We have things to do."

I lay awake tossing that conversation around in my head. It didn't bode well for someone, but I didn't know who. Well, whoever it was had helped drop me in this mess, so I wouldn't be too sorry. I must have dozed off again.

We were both woken not long after, I think, by the other three pirates coming into the longhouse. They were soon busy reheating the sausages that had been left in a pan for them. We were offered a share, but neither of us fancied the pool of grease that the snags appeared to be swimming in. Toast to accompany coffee would be fine, thank you very much, gentlemen.

The prospect of more of the same that evening wasn't appealing either. When I offered to grill the dinner sausages, and make up some mashed potato, even some gravy if they had the makings, the enthusiastic agreement from the three sailors made it clear that Bill's day on cooking duties wasn't looked forward to by anyone. Probably including Bill.

"You're willing to trust me with kitchen implements?" I asked wryly.

"Aar, if'n I never trust ye, then how can I expect ye to ever trust me?" Redbeard replied.

I didn't say anything in response, but I let the thought settle in my mind for later consideration.

We had a busy day. The pirate chief was as good as his word in identifying a cabin for Glexie and I. It wasn't huge, but it was well insulated and dry, and at least had a toilet if not a proper bathroom. We were promised privacy in the use of Redbeard's own shower when required. His promises thus far had certainly been kept, so we cautiously accepted.

While Inigo joined his captain in the longhouse poring over the plans that had been brought out, Nook made short work of emptying out the building we'd been allocated. He could carry barrels and boxes single-handedly that would have been a struggle for Glexie and I together. He pried open the shutters on the one window. They didn't seem to have been opened since the building was first constructed. He was quite willing to sweep the place out for us before we moved our bedding in, but I realised there really were other priorities for him.

We were prisoners, yes, but well-regarded (by this half of the crew, at least) and it seemed wise to nurture that, not take undue advantage of it. Besides, time to ourselves while we tidied, dusted and generally made ourselves a nest meant Glexie and I could talk privately about what we might do next.

By mid-morning we were well on the way to being as comfortable as possible. Our camp beds were supplemented by a low table set between them. A chest of drawers had been provided too. Our own clothes would go in them after drying in the sun. Neither of us missed the implication, though, that this was being considered as more than a very short-term arrangement.

When our giant benefactor had gone to start hauling together the equipment and materials that Redbeard and Inigo were listing, we tried to come up with ideas.

"I certainly don't intend to spend the rest of my life stuck on this island!" Glexie said emphatically.

"Are you sure? I think our host is keen to make it a desirable option for you. In his own odd way, he'd be quite a catch. Not unattractive, wealthy, a career, if an unusual one," I teased.

She surprised me by taking a while to answer.

"There's some truth in that. But being whisked off at sword-point is not my idea of being wooed. And I can't forget the sight of John B. on that plank. Bluff or not, that's not something I can forgive."

"Of course, and believe me, I get that. Sorry if I sounded like I was making fun of you."

"No, no, not at all. I know you were joking, and I know we have to keep our heads up. And like I said, there's some truth in what you said. How can we use it to our advantage?" she asked, bluntly practical.

"To keep us alive, for a start. I don't think Little Brother has any interest in you except maybe as a means of pressuring me. Nook and Inigo aren't likely to hurt us, but I'm remembering what Blood threatened last night. I don't reckon he'd say that and not mean to act on it. Captain Redbeard is our best insulation against his first mate and those other two low-lifes."

 Perched on her cot, Glexie nodded. "So, you think I should play up to him a bit more?"

"No! God, no – I'm not trying to pimp you! That's not what I meant at all…"

"But I'm thinking about it now. You're absolutely right about Blood. He's like a fat shark, waiting to strike, and Redbeard is our best protection."

"Maybe, but he can't be our only defence, either. We've got to find ways of looking after ourselves, until we can get away."

 We pondered getting away. Surely the sleek cruiser couldn't be the only boat on the island. What would they do in emergencies? How did they bring in the large supplies they'd have needed during construction, both of this base and the phony pirate ship – things like lumber and pipes?

"Let's make ourselves as useful as we can, especially today," I said. "See what we can learn about the layout, resources, anything we could possibly use. If there are any other vessels, at least we both know how to operate them. If we can figure a way of quietly disabling the *Ondine* when they bring her back it'll buy us more time to escape."

 Glexie nodded. "What about weapons? I think you're right about defending ourselves."

"Tricky," I admitted. "Firstly, I don't think Redbeard is silly enough to leave us unsupervised around anything very useful. Although, if you can somehow provide a distraction while I'm in the kitchen later, maybe I can quickly snatch a couple of decent knives. But these guys are all fighters, remember. You and I would be relying on luck and surprise. We wouldn't get more than one opportunity.”

 My room-mate looked at me thoughtfully. “Y’know, you’re reminding me of Ariane right now. She’s a planner and organizer too. Not me, I’m afraid. I’m more impulsive than that.”

“Restrain it. Impulsive could get us killed. For now, let’s learn what we can.”

“Okay. I wish I knew what Ariane is up to, or how we could get a message to her.”

“It’s an optimistic thought, but keep an eye out for an unattended mobile – sorry, cellphone. Yours, mine, or anyone’s that we can use quickly and quietly.”

“Good thinking. Even a quick text, or a call to 911 that might be traceable,” she suggested.

“That’s the idea. I wish I knew what had happened to John B., too. In my heart I know he’s alive, but my head would like to know where he is and what he’s doing. Still…” I grasped Glexie’s shoulder and squeezed. “Come on girl, you and I can start looking out for ourselves.”

 Glexie and I threw ourselves into being Useful. It was only during the course of activity that it happened our names were mentioned. No-one had asked us before – we’d been ‘ladies’, ‘lasses’, or ‘you’. First names only, we were careful of that. Although how many ‘Glexies’ could there be? Of course, the origin of that oddity had to be explained, but the crew were politely amused by it. Redbeard naturally was enthused as well as amused. She could have introduced herself as Rumpelstiltskin and he’d have still called it the most wonderful name he’d ever heard. If he had any notions of applying a nickname to ‘Elizabeth’ I trod on them immediately. There is only one nickname I’ll answer to, and that only from one very special person.

 We kept busy. We fetched, carried, tidied and helped keep a check on the list that had been prepared. I'd hoped for access to the galley over lunch, but no such luck.

It was an odd meal, barely deserving of the word in my view, but I suspect it had some origins in the seafaring lore that lay behind so much of Redbeard's chosen life. We each sat down to a plate of biscuits, a mug of tea and a shot of rum. The biscuits were heavy on cereal and whole grains – the type of thing I've seen marketed as 'breakfast biscuits' – but with a strangely meaty flavour, as if beef stock had been used in their manufacture instead of water. Stranger still, they were quite palatable. Certainly, nobody left any, even Nook whose plate had been piled high.

I'm not normally keen on rum, either, but this had been nicely spiced and slid down well after a hectic few hours' work. The whole meal was designed to sustain as much as satisfy, I think, and it worked.

There was more of the same labour throughout the afternoon. I'd soon established that we were based on the western side of Tepatamwa, which was some slight relief as far as keeping the treasure's location secret was concerned, but I was watchful as we moved about. Having sought out and assembled all such relevant tools, timbers, fittings and equipment as the various compound buildings could provide, the five of us conveyed it all south to another part of the island.

We set it all down under trees that fringed a small shallow inlet. Its peculiar 'L' shape meant it was all but invisible from the sea.

"Another bit of your creativity?" I asked Redbeard as I helped him to safely put down a long length of brass that I thought might be destined to edge a part of some new bulwark. The parrot fluttered down to stride back and forth along it, as if asserting ownership.

"Kind of ye to suggest so, but nay. A happy circumstance, built by nature to be a good little dry dock. One more way I just know I be followin' the destiny Black Sam intended."

"Your destiny is what you make it," I replied. "I think that you're using circumstance to justify choices you'd have made anyway."

"An interestin' philosophy, lass. I think ye've got it wrong way round, but. Circumstances bend ter accommodate me."

Just for a moment I thought of John B.'s magic, and how it seemed to work in that same way. "That's a shamanic thing, I'm told – shaping reality by force of will. Consciously or otherwise."

Redbeard stopped and looked appraisingly at me. "Ye be more than a pretty face, Elizabeth."

The malevolent bird squawked and flew back to his shoulder, snapping its beak at me as it passed.

"Most women are, I think you'll find," I said, and pointedly led the way back along the track we were using. The captain followed thoughtfully behind.

By day's end we'd built a tidy pile of materials and equipment at the tree-line of the natural dry dock, and tucked it all securely under tarpaulins. The ferocity of the storm we'd fallen victim to was rare, but rain and storms of less violence were not.

There was still no sign of Blood and the POETs after we'd all showered and regathered in the longhouse. I guessed that Redbeard knew nothing of his brother's planned assignation with the 'fence', but I saw no advantage in revealing it. Maybe it would go wrong, and I'd be rid of the fat shark's threat.

I made good on my promise to improve on dinner. The sausages weren't the best raw material to work with, but simmering them in an onion gravy was a better option than Bill's default pan of grease. Inigo sat on a stool nearby, offering assistance if required. Peeling potatoes was handy but otherwise help wasn't needed. More importantly, he never took his alert eyes off me. Unfailingly polite, of course, but there was no chance of my secreting any of the impressively sharp cutlery.

The five of us ate well, still leaving plenty for the others when they finally graced us with their presence. Redbeard didn't stint on provisions. Glexie insisted on doing the galley clean-up since I'd done the cooking, so of course Redbeard insisted on helping her. Her eyes requested chaperoning, and Inigo stepped up. His captain almost dismissed him, but when the object of his affection insisted that, "It'd be so much quicker with three of us, then we can all relax," he relented.

Nook had lumbered off to the bathroom when suddenly Blood and his minions joined me at my table. The POETs opposite me, the mate sat uncomfortably close to my side. I really wished I'd been able to purloin a long knife – his well-padded ribs were right at my elbow.

"Ready to talk?" he asked quietly.

"Happy to chat," I replied cheerily. "We've had a busy day here. How was yours?"

His smile was so thin it would cut flesh. "Fine, thank you. Let me share with you how it concluded. I spent some time with a man of your acquaintance. Dean Parsons."

"Never heard of him," I said with a shrug.

"I will concede he's not someone many people would be proud of knowing. That is no longer a concern for anyone. Parsons was very emphatic about knowing you, and gave a detailed description of you, your boyfriend, and a historic treasure that you've claimed."

"Sounds like a fantasy. Or a lie."

"I think not. His insistence that he was 'entitled' to a share very strongly suggests otherwise. When I refused, he was foolish enough to attack me. Parsons was not the first to presume that my size makes me slow. Do you know that an elbow, applied with sufficient force to the right point, can fracture vertebrae and sever the spinal cord? Mister Parsons learned that. And learned that it is not wise to cross me."

"Really?" I tried to still sound casual in the face of the POETs' grins. They'd evidently watched what had transpired.

"Really. Your erstwhile friend – I'm sorry, acquaintance – it was the last thing he learned. I hope the lesson was clear in his mind as he lay on the beach unable to move. He didn't take long to die."

"Heh heh – no wonder!" chortled Bill.

"Indeed. I was standing on the back of his head, ensuring he could inhale nothing but sand. You see, young lady, I am entirely serious when I tell you not to cross me. I frankly do not care about my brother's infatuation. For the sake of loosening your stubborn tongue, I will piece by piece destroy your pretty friend as you watch. He will find someone new to fixate on. Or not. With your treasure at my disposal Edward's value to me may well be at an end."

Any further intimidation was stalled when Nook returned to the table, squeezing Bish and Bill along as he sat down.

Blithely unaware he asked, "Has Elizabeth told you about how much we got done today? And how about you guys? Is the boat fixed? You were away long enough."

The mate waved a fleshy hand airily. "Oh, it took a bit longer than I'd expected. More things needed fixing than first realised. Everything is fine. And will only get better from here, won't it?" he said, smiling at me.

The others were emerging from the galley. Although the table I was at wouldn't accommodate them, I waved them over to sit nearby. I hastily jumped up and moved to sit beside Redbeard, much to Glexie's relief, and surprise.

Her surprise went up several notches when I next spoke.
"Y'know, Captain Redbeard, I've been thinking about our conversation earlier. About destiny, and circumstances. Alright, I'll concede there is something of my family history on one of these islands. I don't know

about a treasure. I won't know until it's found. But if I'm destined to find it, with your help, then so be it. I can't change the circumstances that have brought me to this point – the loss of my love, any of it. All I can do is try to maintain some control over my future. You talked about a partnership. Alright. If it turns out there *is* something valuable, let's consider that then."

There was a stunned silence around the two tables. Glexie looked appalled. I'd have to talk to her quietly that night, and trust her to go along with me meanwhile.

Blood was torn between satisfaction and suspicion, realising that in making my announcement so publicly I was trying to outmaneuver him. Still, he was the first to speak.

"Where?" was all he asked.

"Ah, now that's the tricky part. The directions I had were on a piece of paper that I presume is still on the *Emma*, drifting around out there somewhere. If she survived the storm."

"We've got charts," said Redbeard.

I shrugged. "What I had was more like a set of instructions. Landmarks to look out for, distances in whatever direction, that sort of thing. I don't know that I could translate it onto, or off of, a map."

"Give me – us, the information. We'll work it out," said Blood.

"I said I'd be co-operative, not bloody stupid. You want me to help you look for whatever it is, fair enough. That means I'm there, with you."

"In at the kill," suggested Blood, unsubtly.

"I can't imagine why a kill would be necessary. We find the right island, and the right place to look. I was given to understand the place was uninhabited."

The captain tugged at his beard, and nudged his lookout. "Mister McCallum, fetch the big chart of the whole Bay. We can start with an overview and narrow down from there."

I shook my head. "I told you, it's not that simple. I'm not from round here, remember. That sort of view isn't going to mean anything to me. Take me back to where you found us yesterday. Where you abandoned the *Emma*. I'll try to identify the route from there, as best as I can remember."

"Rather less than satisfactory," said Blood huffily.

"John B. was the one who committed it to memory, and we don't have him anymore, remember?" Redbeard shifted uncomfortably. So did Inigo, I noticed. "I've said that I'll do what I can. It's in my interest too. You've made that very plain."

The mate glared daggers at me, clearly implying his desire to apply such weapons more directly. I pressed on.

"If Black Sam's spirit really is looking after you, guiding your destiny or whatever, who knows? We might even find the *Emma* and my notes. But if we start from there I'm *some* chance, whereas stuck here I've got none."

Teef screeched, as if agreeing with my observation.

"There be sense in what ye say, Elizabeth."

Not all of his crew agreed with the captain's assessment, I knew that, but he still held sway. He'd made his decision.
"We take the cruiser out tomorrow, first thing. I know where it was that we first came across ye. Ye can cast yer eyes about and find yer way from there as best ye can."

"If you know what's good for you," added Bish, emphasizing his real leader's threat.

The mate nodded slowly, momentarily adding to the number of chins under his narrow beard. "I suggest you spend the night exercising your memory, madam. Recall everything you can of these directions you mentioned. If it proves to be a wild goose chase that you lead us on, remember that those birds are hunted for sport. Even a golden goose is not spared from the butcher's block if it fails to give up its bounty."

His brother looked askance at the book-keeper. He wasn't comfortable with the implication, but did recognise that it might help focus my attention. My sudden change of tack had caught everyone off-guard, and he hadn't had time to formulate a strategy of his own. I'd relied on that when I'd laid out my own proposal.

"An early breakfast, then," said Inigo, rostered to be the next cook. "Perhaps not the pancake stacks I'd had in mind."

He grinned, trying to ease the tension that Blood had fostered.

"Aye lad," agreed the captain. "Coffee an' oatmeal I think. The quicker the better."

The assembly broke up then. Glexie and I were escorted to our new quarters by Redbeard and a muttering Bill Wadsworth. We heard the sound of our door being locked outside. Only after we heard two sets of footsteps departing did my room-mate fold her arms and stare at me.

"I'm assuming you came up with a plan after all. Are you going to share it with me?"

As I sat on my bed and pulled my sweater off I sighed. "I'm really sorry, mate. I wouldn't dignify what I came up with by calling it a plan. But I suddenly realised just how dangerous Barry Lister is, and how important it was to put some sort of spoke in his wheels. I wish I could have talked it through with you, but I really was making it up as I went along."

Unbuttoning her coat and laying it on the bed as a makeshift quilt, Glexie nodded as she said, "You did well, then. You convinced me, and I *know* how you felt – feel – about John B."

That struck a nerve but I tried not to let it show. "Thank you. But it's really only a stay of execution. If you've any thoughts about what we do tomorrow and beyond, I'd love to hear them."

We undressed and climbed into our beds in silence, clicking off the little table lamp we'd been given.

"If we are lucky enough to find the *Emma* that at least might give us a means of getting away. We'd have to disable the *Ondine* so they couldn't follow us," mused Glexie in the darkness.

"Wouldn't be easy. If one of us could get onto the bridge we might be able to wreak merry hell on that control panel with a decent amount of some sort of liquid. Getting back off the bridge afterwards would be even more difficult, I suspect."

"I might be a better prospect of getting away with it. Give you a chance to get the lifeboat away while I keep them occupied," suggested my room-mate.

"Sounds like an offer of suicide to me, mate. I'm not sure Redbeard could, or even would, be able to protect you under those circumstances."

"Depends on what I offer him," came a soft voice in the darkness. "There are worse fates than staying with him. I might even be a good influence on him."

We couldn't see each other in the dark. I was glad. I didn't want her to see the tears that were suddenly welling up in my eyes.

I waited before I was sure my voice was under control before quietly continuing, "Of course, that's entirely contingent on finding the *Emma*, and after that storm she could be anywhere, on or under the water. We might happen onto some other boat, though, I suppose. Any other options?"

There was another long silence. I thought Glexie had fallen asleep, and wasn't far from doing that myself when suddenly she spoke again.

"Assuming you're right about John B., and I'm very happy to assume that you are, do you think he'd find some way here to Tepatamwa to look for us? He'd be wandering into the proverbial lion's den without knowing it."

"I've no idea how he'd manage it but yes, it would make sense for him to aim for where we knew we were aiming for in the first place. If there's any way of making it happen he'd find it. He'd studied Dorothy's chart. With his memory he could probably find the island. But you're right, he'll have no idea of what's here. More like a nest of vipers than a den of lions."

"Not all of them."

"No. But enough to be dangerous," I answered, mentally noting her defence of someone amongst the pirate crew.

"Do you think it would be wise if one of us found a way to stay behind tomorrow?"

"It's hard to imagine them letting us away with that," I said. "We're more easily watched and controlled together. I can't see them splitting the crew to leave someone here on guard duty, but we could try."

"Did you notice a radio or anything like it today? Any way of contacting the mainland? If I could slip whoever was guarding me…"

I shook my head, even though she couldn't see me. "I think any communications happen by phone. Ours have been locked away somewhere, I don't know where, and I've never seen Blood put his phone anywhere but in his pocket. I assume at least some of the others have devices – Redbeard has a computer that I saw him lock away in his cabin before I got to use the shower – but where, and how to get at them?"

"They're going to want you out there with them to lead the way to the treasure. I figure you'll have to get lost, or land somewhere and be disappointed. I'd be the one to stay here. Maybe, depending on who was guarding me, I might be able to get at something, somehow."

"A James Bond type secret container of knock-out drops would be handy."

 She laughed quietly. "Well, yes, but I was thinking more of a good whack on the head with something solid. I could manage that."

"Really?" I wasn't sure I could imagine her clobbering certain members of the crew.

"Oh, I mightn't like it, although in some cases I reckon I *would* enjoy it, but if it gets us rescued then I'll do it. Whoever I contacted would have to get here before the *Ondine* gets back, and be ready and waiting for them – you."

"It's worth a try. It's a long shot, but slightly better odds than chancing onto another boat, and being able to get onto it, and scupper any pursuit. Get some sleep, mate. We'll need it tomorrow. Oh, and Glexie? Thank you for even being willing to consider… well, sacrificing. Staying here longer term, I mean."

"Thanks. Maybe it wouldn't be such a big sacrifice. May be an adventure, hey? If I dream of any better plan, I'll tell you in the morning. G'night, hon," she said sleepily.

"Goodnight, mate. I'll do the same if I have any useful dreams. Sleep tight."

 A soft snore answered me. I couldn't quite manage the same. My brain was busy, trying to come up with plans, or at least devise ways of improving the desperate scheme we'd discussed.

 Eventually I did sleep, and I did dream. Nothing useful from a planning perspective, but I did dream of JB and I lying with our arms wrapped around each other. It may have been only a dream, but it was comforting.

.o0o.

27 CROSS CURRENTS

Sunday morning. I don't think I was particularly aware of that, having rather lost track of time over a few days. Miles away, on the mainland, John B. and Ariane were hearing the sound of church bells as they sat on the side of Perkins Cove waiting for their allies to arrive.

Avowed landlubber she may be, but Glexie's best friend and housemate was not going to wait ashore this time. Her new gun was tucked in an inside pocket of the black waterproof jacket she wore over a black-and-white striped t-shirt and black linen pants. (John B. had apparently teased her gently about looking 'nautical, in a French cartoon sort of way'.)

And arrive their benefactors soon did, Cowley's booming voice bellowing "Ahoy!" and "Hello!" to shatter any morning stillness the chimes hadn't broken.

Their "little boat" proved to be a bit grander than that: a flashy nine metre sports cruiser, made in Finland. With two V8 300 horsepower motors and an aerodynamic design, she could be seriously fast.

"Meet the *'Sense Of Adventure'*!" hailed Lanny, waving as the boat slid in to the side of the cove and eased to a halt.

"Nice name," my wizard called back.

"We call her *Addy* – it's shorter," replied Cowley with a big grin.

John B. and Ariane quickly climbed aboard. My beau patted the fiber-glass hull as he did so. "Good to meet you, *Addy*," he said quietly.

Lanny was as prepared for trouble as Ariane. Propped up beside his knee was a hunting rifle that looked well maintained and ready to be used quickly. Cowley turned out to share John B.'s distaste for guns. He believed that their over-availability was a great scourge of US society.

"I've heard it often enough. Guns don't people, people kill people. But ya know, I think it's too damned easy for any whacko to get themselves enough firepower to kill a whole mess o' people. And that happens far too damned often," he complained.

He'd get no argument from me. But in this instance even he was willing to admit that his partner's precaution might be a good idea.

Ariane's first action on boarding was to open their chart out on the big beech table that stood behind the navigator's roomy seat. All four of them sat around the table and examined the markings that should lead them to Tepatamwa.

"Ya sure the girls will be there?" mused Cowley.

"Not sure, no," admitted my beau. "But it's the only lead we've got. It's where we *were* going. I wish that we'll find them out there today."

"We-e-ell, if wishes were dollar bills, most everyone'd be a millionaire," warned Cowley. "But if it's all ya got, I understand ya gotta try. Gotta start somewhere."

Our legal advisor had enjoyed rather more experience of the wizard's strange talents than their new skipper.
"I think John B.'s wishes *are* ones that you can take to the bank," she said quietly.

With a last look at the chart Cowley restarted the two big engines and set off. *Addy* was in fact an ideal introduction to seafaring for the nervous Ariane. The boat's handling was nimble, her acceleration smooth and swift. There was no vibration, no jarring over waves even in fast turns. Soon hurtling across the Bay at a rapid forty knots, they would make much better time than we had in the humble steam-powered *Emma*.

*

Neither Glexie nor I had enjoyed any blinding flashes of inspiration during the night. The optimistic plan that we'd discussed before sleeping remained the best option that we could see, outside of our faith in our loved ones.

Over Inigo's coffee and oatmeal (very pleasantly spiced with nutmeg) with the whole crew we tried to put it into action.

"Couldn't I stay here on the island? I'm not going to be of any use to you out there anyway. I'd only be crowding your boat. You can leave a guard. Lock me in our room, even," offered Glexie.

Overnight she'd figured out a way of unlocking our small window, and was confident she could squeeze through it. More confident than I was when I considered her curves, but I wasn't going to argue.

But neither of the Lister brothers would hear of it. Blood wanted her where he could threaten her directly, although he didn't put it in those terms. His intent was clear enough in his eyes, though. Redbeard simply wanted her near him.

She gently put her hands on his arm and leaned close, whispering in his ear, "Please. I don't feel well. It's… it's a women's thing, you understand?"

Even that didn't work. I'm not sure the captain quite grasped what she was implying, but he did at least look sympathetic. Sympathetic, but not enough to change his mind.

"Ye can be made comfortable in the cabin, lass. I'll make sure there's somebody lookin' out fer ye all the time, makin' sure ye're alright. Even when we go ashore to unearth the treasure."

Clearly the man had faith in me. Or perhaps in Black Sam Bellamy.

That was Plan A scotched. We'd have to look out for the *Emma*, or some other possible means of escape, and hope we could manage to be in a position to take advantage of it.

At the captain's insistence the crew were dressed in close approximation of their buccaneer garb (except for Redbeard himself who was, as ever, in full costume) and were armed appropriately. Glexie and I had both been given grey striped canvas trousers and clean shirts – ruffled white linen for her, and a dark purple silk for me. We wore our own deck shoes over woolen socks.

The morning air was crisp but dry. Single file we made our way to the *Ondine*. Redbeard led, Blood at the rear. Glexie and I were in the middle, between the two Pirates Of Extreme Treachery. I was very conscious of the prospect of them living up to their sobriquet and resolved to keep as close a watch on them as I was sure they'd be keeping on us.

The cruiser looked immaculate under the floodlights of the camouflaged cave. Whatever repairs had been done the day before had been done well – there was no sign of any storm damage.

We all boarded and settled into the positions directed by Redbeard. Blood was at the helm, Inigo beside him in what I thought of as the co-pilot's chair. Bish and Bill were at the stern, one inside and one outside the rear door, both armed and watchful. Outside, Bill watched for unlikely pursuit and kept an eye on the hatch leading down to three small cabins below, normally kept for storing weapons and booty. Glexie had been installed in the cabin amidships, with Nook detailed to look after her. The cabin had its own ensuite in case she needed it – her claims of unwellness were being taken seriously by the captain.

That worthy was seated in the cabin beside me, tracing our route on a chart he had laid out on a teak tabletop that folded out from under a couch. I was surprised at the distance we'd travelled during that terrible storm.

Without the pirate ship 'shell' there was no need for the *Ondine* to move stealthily under the cover of fog. But fog there was. Not as dense as we'd experienced previously, but enough to have Blood travelling at a cautious speed in the reduced visibility.

"We be nearin' the spot where we first found ye, lass. Be there anythin' on this chart ye recognise as a landmark?"

I shook my head. "Nothing obvious, but like I said, it looks very different on paper. This fog isn't helping, of course," I added, looking out through the cockpit glass.

"Aye, I can understand that. Hmm… Mister Mate, cut engines. Let her drift for a few minutes. Come with me, Elizabeth."

Redbeard opened the ceiling hatch that I now realized was in a spot where a sunroof could have been originally designed. He pulled down the cleverly telescoped ladder and after handing me a sleeveless long black coat for warmth, bade me climb up.

Standing on the flat roof of the cabin, just below the level of where the pirate deck had been, certainly gave me a better view. A better view of nothing to see. At list the fog was thinning.

"Which way, can ye tell?"

I knew perfectly well that the correct way was back in the direction from which we'd come, but I had to obfuscate. The *Emma* hadn't quite been on that line when we were captured. I think we'd planned a slightly different route to Tepatamwa than the one that pirates regularly used. Would Redbeard or any of the others remember the bearing our lifeboat had been on at the time? I hoped not – there was no indication of it.

I thought of the chart, and considered options. Too obvious if I pointed us back towards the mainland. There were more small islands to the north-east, I remembered, so I pointed that way.

"Let's see… we were heading north-east doing about five knots, and I was going to have us bear north in about ten more minutes. There should have been a small island off to starboard soon after that – does that sound right?”

“Aye. Plausible at least. We’ll settle on the foredeck and see what appears.”

 Little rungs set in the forward port stanchion took us down to the foredeck, where we sat lightly holding the port side rail, keeping as clear as possible of Blood’s view. The parrot screeched and flapped its wings as if stretching. Beady white eyes seemed to scan the horizon.

“Ahead slow. North-east, five knots,” the captain called through the glass.

 Blood nodded, and got the cruiser in motion again. But in only a minute or two he suddenly brought her to a stop.

“What’s the trouble?” called Redbeard.

 His brother was staring at a screen, with a puzzled look on his face.

“Not sure. There’s something just ahead of us, under the surface. Something big.”

“Submerged rock? Don’t remember anythin’ of that sort on the chart…”

“No. It’s… moving.”

 Suddenly Teef launched himself from Redbeard’s shoulder, and squawking angrily shot out over the water. Screaming shrilly, the bird flew in circles not far off the bow, fluorescent green feathers flashing in the mist a few feet above a small patch of turbulence.

 The water erupted. Something like a huge grey-green snake burst up and through the ribbons of fog, towering into the sky. As it rose, a pair of great jaws snapped. As quickly as it had risen, the serpentine form turned in a graceful arc and plunged back down. A few apple green feathers drifted down to land in its wake.

Redbeard stared, mouth agape. "That worm just got my bird…"

.o0o.

28 IMPACT!

As speechless as the pirate beside me, I also stared through the shroud of mist into the water. It was my first experience of the sea serpent too.

It was Inigo slapping his hand on the cockpit window that brought us back to alertness.

"Whatever it is, it's circling us! Get inside, quick!" he cried.

That was a sensible suggestion, and we sprang up to comply. Still the model of chivalry, Redbeard insisted I lead the way back up onto the cabin roof and through the hatch. He slammed it shut behind us and jumped down off the ladder.

"What the hell was that thing?" demanded Blood, several shades paler than usual.

Redbeard tugged at his beard with one hand, grabbing at his now-vacant shoulder with the other.

"That were Cassie," he replied in a dazed voice. "She be a thing o' legend, or so I've always thought."

The mate tapped at the screen in front of him. "That 'legend' is circling around underneath us! What the hell does it…"

The unfinished question was answered by a resounding crash from below us as the stern of the *Ondine* was lifted a few feet out of the water. Bish threw open the aft door and Bill half dived, half fell into the cabin.

"Something just hit us from below!" shouted the gunman in blue, master of the obvious.

"Port side motor is gone!" cried Blood.

"Gone? What do ye mean, gone?" roared the captain.

"I mean that according to these instruments, we don't have a motor there anymore!"

"Fire up the other engine – get us out of here!" yelled Bish.

 The captain was reeling towards the cockpit, Inigo quickly vacating the seat for him. Redbeard thumbed the intercom down to the cabin below.

"Mister Lear – be ye and Glexie alright?"

"Aye cap'n. Shaken about, Glexie got thrown off the bed, but no damage. What's going on? I thought I saw something out the window – something big."

"We be under attack, I think, matey."

 There was a grinding, metallic sound from under the hull. It came over the intercom all too clearly. Redbeard and Blood both glared at the control panel in helpless frustration. Cassie's impact below, as well as shearing off the port motor, had damaged the propeller of its starboard partner. The *Ondine* wasn't going anywhere in a hurry.

"Mister Lear, can ye hear me?" the captain said quietly into the intercom.

"Aye sir."

"I be thinkin' that if it hits the undersides again, ye might be in the worst of all places down there. I want ye and the lass up here, with me – us."

"Are you kidding?" I said. "After what happened to Teef? You can't have them outside!"

 The captain ignored me. "Mister Brentford, stand by that door. I want it open and shut so fast that it's only a blur. Mister Lear, get a good hold o' the lass. Ye'll have to move and move fast."

"Aye sir. Ready on your command sir."

 Not taking his eye off the monitor, Redbeard said, "Wait for it… wait for it… it's goin' deeper, but slowly. Now, Nook – move, lad!"

 For such a huge man, Nook was quick. Even with a compliant woman held in one arm he was up and into our cabin in what seemed like seconds. It might have been twenty of them. Bish slammed the door shut behind them and they landed heavily on the couch beside me.

 We were all braced for another strike from underneath the boat. Redbeard continued to watch the screen intently.

"Beastie's not directly under us now. It's…" He paused for a moment, alternately staring at the monitor and out the window. "Out there!"

He jabbed his arm starboard. We all saw it at once. The great neck broke the surface again, perhaps forty feet off the bow. As the boat rocked, becalmed, the serpentine form was slowly circling us. We could look up through the clearing mist into a big crocodilian eye as the creature glided past.

"What's it up to?" breathed Glexie.

"Don't know, lass," admitted the captain. "Teasing us? Sizing us up afore it has another go?"

There was a look of fire and steel on Blood's face as he stared out at the reptile.
"No point in waiting like sitting ducks. We can send that thing back to whatever watery hell it came from," he growled.

"With what?" asked his brother. "Swords? A pistol? I don't reckon even Bill's rifle would have much effect on it."

"Explosives. We've got the firepower to blast it to pieces."

Redbeard stared, uncomprehending. "We don't *use* explosives…"

Bysshe Brentford suddenly laughed. "Oh my God, Blood – you were right! He's really never known!"

The captain now looked at him as blankly as he'd looked at the mate. "What be ye…?"

Blood snarled, "You bloody fool, Ed. How do you think we've cleaned up the times when it's looked like someone has recognised us? Or somehow worked out too much about us? Not everyone falls for your mad fantasy. Bish, get something effective. I don't know what this thing is, but it's time it became extinct!"

"Got plenty of plastique stored below. Ten second fuse. Maybe even five. Reckon if I throw with the wind behind me I can land it clear of us but blow that critter to kingdom come," said Brentford grimly.

"Risk to us?" asked Blood.

"I'll get the charge right. We might get rocked about a bit, but should be no major damage to us. But like I said – the stuff is stashed below," the POET said with a note of protest.

The mate pointed at Nook. "He was able to get up here safely, carrying the girl. Are you telling me you're not as quick as he is?"

The red-shirted pirate saluted. "Aye aye, sir," he said. He watched out the window and waited until Cassie's slow circuit had her off the prow, then opened the door and dashed out like a mongoose chasing a snake. Bill caught and closed the door.

We all watched anxiously, but the gigantic form didn't change pace, continuing its slow laps of us. If it saw Brentford's movement it gave no indication of it.

Redbeard turned his gaze back to his brother. "Just what have ye been doin'?" he asked quietly.

"Protecting our interests. My interests. When you first talked me out of the IRS and into your hare-brained scheme, I took a sabbatical and decided to enjoy a bit of harmless fun.   I also realised you were sitting on more money than I'd dreamed, and the idea of helping you to spend it appealed. But do you know, I soon realised just how lucrative this could be, so I made it permanent. You didn't need much encouragement, and I knew plenty of unscrupulous people to convert our plunder to cash."

 The IRS? He was a tax collector? Well, that wasn't such a big transition, I mused. And it was consistent with his talent for finances and administration.

"Ye've looked after the business well, lad, aye. I've always said so. Never begrudged ye any of yer own expenses…"

"And never told me any details of Bellamy's hoard, or where you've stashed the reserves I know you must have. Oh, you're ready enough to tip more money in for 'expenses' when required, so I know you've got it somewhere. But now I won't need it, or more importantly you, when I get hold of this blasted woman's treasure – oh yes, I know it's real. My sources confirmed it, each in their own way, before they died."

"This 'cleanin' up' ye spoke of? Did ye… kill people?"

"Of course, you dope. I just told you – this mad idea of yours turned out to be more lucrative than I'd imagined. But it could only remain so if we remained anonymous. If there was potential for anyone to identify us, they had to be eliminated."

 The captain was thunderstruck. I realised then why he'd been so shocked when John B. had seemingly leapt to his death. In a weird way, it had all been a game to the older Lister brother. He'd never expected or intended fatal consequences. His grasp on the reality of pirate life was even less firm than I'd thought.

"Did any of ye know?" the skipper asked his crew, plaintively.

Nook shook his head dumbly. Bill just laughed. Inigo reddened and wouldn't meet his captain's eye.

"I had – some idea," the young man said shamefully.

"But never the backbone to be of any help beyond your 'duty' as a look-out," sneered Blood.

"Nor to tell Redbeard, or anyone else. Told myself it was 'against the code' to rat on anyone," admitted Inigo.

The murderous book-keeper slapped the intercom. "Mister Brentford! Progress?"

Bish's voice crackled. "Almost done. Got three packages prepared, just in case. Just setting short fuses into them now. Buzz me when it's safe to come back up."

"I will," agreed his boss.

"But why is the beast circling us?" asked Glexie, who'd unconsciously taken the hand of the stunned captain who sat slumped on the couch beside her.

I suspected I knew the answer. Of course, at that point I had no idea that John B. had already encountered Cassie and apparently established some rapport with her. But somehow the whole bizarre situation had his finger-prints on it.

Blood was waiting for the great beast to be at the furthest forward part of its circuit before calling his henchman. Like most of us, he couldn't take his eyes off the long neck. Abruptly we realised that the creature's head was getting closer to the waterline.

"It's submerging! What's the blasted thing up to now?" called Bill.

"I can see that!" snapped the mate. "Ready to come at us from below again? Brentford, get up here now!" he snapped into the intercom.

"On my way," was the quick reply.

Cassie was gone from view. Inigo was watching the screen while everyone else peered out into the water.

"Submerged all right, and fast. I can't even be sure which way it's gone," he reported.

"No bad thing," said Bill nervously.

"Unless it's dived down to get a good run-up at us. Build momentum," I suggested, unable to resist adding to his discomfort. If my hunch was right, we'd be safe while I was on board. I hoped.

"Still can't see it," said Inigo. "But there is something else on the screen. Another vessel, and it's approaching fast from the south."

The aft door opened and Bysshe Brentford almost jumped into the cabin.

"Something coming from hard astern," he reported. "Too far yet for me to be sure, but could be a launch, or something a bit bigger."

By now we could all see the approaching vessel through the aft windows on either side of the door. There were still tendrils of fog hanging in the air, so the new arrival was slowing down as it neared us.

"Could be our ticket home," said Blood. "Let it get close, check on us. We can commandeer it. Weapons at the ready, men."

"Blood, brother, ye can't…"

"Shut up, Ed. If you make the slightest move, or sound, to give us away, the first thing you'll see is a bullet go through the brain of your pretty little trophy there. My next bullet will be for you. Elizabeth, you'll live long enough to deliver my treasure. By the time I'm finished you will be pleading to tell me where it is."

Nook started to get up from the couch. "No hurting girls!" he said angrily.

Casually Bill shot him in the leg, and the giant fell heavily.

"Want me to finish him?" the gunman asked.

"Not yet. My dear brother might be just as concerned to protect the life of his old friend as that of his new lady. Which gives me a thought. Bish, tie our erstwhile captain up. And the women."

Brentford pulled lines from a footlocker and quickly did as he was asked, first handing the gun in his pocket over to Blood, who kept the muzzle of it firmly against his brother's temple. Damn him, he was good with knots, as he made sure first Redbeard, then I wouldn't be able to so much as get to our feet.

"At least let me help him," said his next target, Glexie, pointing at Nook who was bleeding heavily from just below his knee.

The lead mutineer shrugged. I was impressed by her presence of mind. She tore the sleeve off her shirt and fashioned a makeshift tourniquet which she applied to the damaged leg. Then it was her turn to be trussed.

The mate turned to Inigo, who was in the co-pilot's seat. "I'll leave you free to move about, McCallum, because you may be useful. But place your sword on the floor, please. I don't want you getting any unlikely notions of heroism."

Judging by the immediate colouring of his face, I think the lookout may have been entertaining just such a thought. But confronted by the harsh reality of Blood's gun he had the sense to do as ordered.

A klaxon horn sounded behind us. A sleek sports cruiser bobbed in the water off our stern. Tinted glass on their cockpit meant that we couldn't make out anything of who was on board.

"Ahoy there! Are ya broken down there? Do ya need assistance?" boomed a voice across the water.

 I thought I recognised the voice, but just at that moment I couldn't place it. Well, I was under stress, and it was out of context, wasn't it?

"Can we help ya?" repeated the voice.

"Oh, I'm sure you can," replied Blood's quiet, malevolent voice.

.o0o.

29 WAR ON THE WATER

John B. knew nothing about the disguise of the pirate ship, but when he'd seen the name *Ondine* on our vessel's stern the alarm bells went off in his head. He'd seen too many coincidences to disregard any. He kept himself, Ariane and Lanny below the line of sight in their cockpit, warning Cowley to approach with extreme caution.

"Understood," the big skipper breathed before calling out to our motionless boat.

Bish had stepped out onto our transom, his deadly 'parcels' stuffed in the capacious pockets of his cargo pants along with the automatic pistol Blood had returned to him.

"Thanks!" he called. "We ran into something under the water. Did some damage down below, now we're stuck. Didn't realise our radio's not working either I'm afraid. Must have been when we got caught in that storm a few days ago."

"I got a fix on your position. I can call someone out to give ya a tow. Ya happy to stay on board?"

Hiding just inside the doorway Blood whispered instructions.

Bish spread his hands. "I've got some folks aboard who'd rather not be stranded out here. If you can come alongside I can throw a line to tether us. Transfer a couple of people over to you, if you've got space?"

"We-e-ell, I guess so. Wait there."

"Not like I've got a choice," answered Bish with disarming cheeriness.
He picked one of his lassos from a locker and prepared himself to throw it.

By now I'd recognised the voice, and my mind was racing. Looking out,

I still couldn't see anyone except the silhouette I knew to be Cowley.

As the new arrival eased closer to us, Cowley called out again. "Where are these folks ya want to hand over? I don't see anyone."

The sun that was backlighting our would-be rescuer was reflecting off the *Ondine*'s aft windows, so we weren't visible. Most of us were lying on the floor anyway.

Blood thought fast. The villainous mate prodded Glexie with his foot.

"You. With me. Bill, if you get a signal from me, or if our former captain makes any move to follow us, shoot him."

"Aye aye, sir," replied Wadsworth, with the vicious grin of someone who used to torture small animals in his youth.

Blood slashed Glexie's ties with the long knife he wore at his side. Then he grabbed her by the arm and yanked her to her feet. Redbeard started to squirm, heedless of the click of Bill's gun being readied to fire.

Glexie grabbed the captain's arm. "Please! Don't!"

"You should listen to her," instructed his brother.

He pulled his hostage away, and stayed so close behind her that the hammerlock he held on her wouldn't be visible to anyone on the other boat.

In his best jovial voice, he cried, "Ahoy, friend! Did I hear that you can get us back to Portland?" as he stepped out onto the transom.

As Blood shouted, Bish slung his lasso and neatly roped the signal light that protruded on a steel frame from the roof of Cowley's cabin. Although a small structure it was solid enough for the pirate to be able to pull the two vessels close.

From inside the cockpit of the *Sense Of Adventure*, Ariane recognised who'd just appeared at the rear of the other boat. She'd known John B. was suspicious of the other craft, but it hadn't occurred to her that her best friend might be aboard. Impulsively she stood up and called her house-mate's name.

Bedlam erupted.

Blood released his hammerlock on Glexie and threw his arm around her throat. Ariane drew a gun and tried to get a bead on the portly pirate. Bish pulled his own gun from his pocket and fired. A small pitch of one of the boats was all that saved the dark-haired girl, his bullet whanging off the stanchion beside her. It deflected onto the barrel of her gun, the impact jarring it from her unpracticed hand.

Not about to miss gunplay, Bill wedged open our cabin door and took aim at Cowley, still clearly visible in his cockpit. Inigo seized the moment to lunge for his sword. With one deft slash as he dived he was able to cut the line that tied my hands. But before he could do any more, Bill turned. He must have heard the movement. Sprawled on the floor, the lookout was an easy target. But even as the POET fired, Redbeard, still bound, flung himself forward, taking the bullet meant for his faithful swordsman.

My feet were still lashed but my hands were free. I made a desperate lunge and managed to grab Bill's gun arm. He slapped me hard with the back of his free hand, but I wasn't about to let go.

Simultaneously Lanny popped up from his cover and fired at Bish. Ariane was in his line of sight though, and his shot narrowly whistled past the red-shirted pirate who immediately ducked for the small shelter of a locker.

My momentum had carried Bill and I to the doorway. I still gripped his gun arm with both hands, and he'd got his free hand around my throat. Suddenly I yelped – Blood had reached out and grabbed a handful of my hair, without releasing his choke on Glexie.

"Throw down your weapons or they both die!" he roared.

Lanny paused, uncertain and unable to get a clear shot on the obvious leader of the cut-throats. Bish half-rose, taking aim at the rifleman. Quick-thinking Cowley tapped the throttle of his *Addy* for just a moment, banging the two boats together and upsetting everyone's balance as they bounced apart again.

There was a blur of long hair and purple flying between the boats. I don't know that John B. had played much rugby, but it was a perfectly executed tackle around Barry Lister's big legs. The pirate fell in an untidy heap, wrapped up with his assailant. He lost his grip on Glexie, but unfortunately still had my hair tangled in his hand, so I was pulled down with them. And when they rolled into the water of Casco Bay, so did I. Bloody hell, it was cold!

Both POETs tried to spot where we'd landed and pick off my Galahad. Aboard the *Sense Of Adventure* Ariane suddenly called out, "Hey, handsome!", and made a target of herself, pulling up her top and thrusting her breasts out impressively. As a distraction it worked brilliantly. Bill and Bish both looked up and momentarily stared. Lanny didn't miss twice, his shot hitting Bysshe Brentford amidships. The pirate doubled over and collapsed to his knees.

At the same moment Inigo, who hadn't been distracted by Ariane's display, brought his sword down in a silver arc that removed Bill's gun and the hand that held it, at the wrist. Cursing, the man in blue staggered and fell over the side, just as the two boats swung back together. The *Sense Of Adventure* weighed upwards of four tonnes, the *Ondine* probably five times that. The lean pirate was reduced to little more than a smear that slid unpleasantly below the surface.

Inigo kicked the severed hand contemptuously into the water after him, then went to support Glexie. He'd been beaten to that job though. Ariane had jumped between boats as they'd come together, and the two girls fell into each other's arms with great racking sobs.

The men on both vessels were peering into the water, trying to find where I'd landed with John B. and Blood.

The pirate had finally let go of my hair when we'd hit the water, but as I bobbed free I smacked my head on the hull of *Ondine*. Momentarily stunned and freezing, I had no better idea of where my hero and villain were than the watchers on the boats. Somewhere underwater, I presumed.

On the boarding platform of the pirate cruiser Bysshe had pulled himself up to his feet. Unnoticed by the others he was extracting one of his explosive parcels from a pocket. Probably guessing that his wound would be fatal, and even if it wasn't, his life of adventure was over, he must have determined to take everyone else out with him. But out of the cabin reeled the blood-soaked captain of the *Ondine*. Bill's bullet had gone through his upper arm and into his chest, miraculously not hitting anything instantly terminal.

The shock had stunned Redbeard though, and he'd lost a lot of blood. Revived by Nook, who was scarcely in better condition, the captain had looked out the door and spotted his former crewman's fumbling efforts to set a fuse. He doubtless felt like he was sprinting, but it was at least a determined stagger that propelled him out of the cabin. His right arm hanging uselessly, with his left hand he slapped the plastique from Brentford's grasp.

"No, ye scurvy knave!" he shouted, and with the aid of his own momentum headbutted Bish in the temple. They were both about to pitch into the bay, but Glexie had broken from Ariane's embrace and grabbed a handful of the captain's coattail – just enough to stop him from following the other man overboard.

The dying pirate landed a few feet from me, and sank like a stone. Then, about twenty feet forward of the boats two heads broke the surface, gasping for air. Both men's skin had a blue tinge already. Blood had his meaty hands around my beau's throat making breathing even more of a challenge. He must have already lost his knife underwater during the fight. John B. managed to get both feet up and slam them into Lister's ample belly. It broke the pirate's grip, and expelled much of the air he'd just managed to suck in as he was propelled a few feet back.

I was about to strike out swimming to help my darling wizard, when another female got there before me. Cassie was back.

The barrel-sized head shot up out of the water, jaws clamped around the shoulder and chest of the former mate. Blood screamed as he rose in the air, hoisted by the great serpentine neck. The scream disappeared in a gurgle as the waterhorse plunged back down below the surface. Neither she nor her victim reappeared.

I swam to JB's side. Neither of us said anything at first, ignoring the cold we just held each other while we were treading water. Then Cowley's anxious voice boomed out.

"Will ya get outta there, both of ya? Before that thing comes back!"

"It's okay. We're old friends. She's on our side," John B. said to me quietly.

"Tell me about it later. Let's reassure Cowley first, hey babe?"

"Fair enough. By the way, the colour looks good on you," he grinned, with a nod to the wet purple satin clinging to me.

John B. wasn't quite a dead weight, but I had to do a lot of the work in getting us back to where we could get a hold of the life preserver that Inigo had thrown out to us. We half climbed and were half hauled onto the *Ondine*. From there we all swiftly transferred onto *Addy* (as I was soon introduced to her), although before they departed Redbeard and Inigo disappeared first into the cabin and then below decks, emerging with two canvas bags packed with charts and personal belongings. I even glimpsed a fuzzy stuffed whale toy, which I later learned was Nook's (and had been a present from his captain).

Given the size of Nook, Cowley and Redbeard, it was a little squeezy for nine of us aboard the *Spirit Of Adventure*. Nobody complained though.

"It's not like the *Ondine* could go anywhere, after the job Cassie did on her," I observed.

"Aar, she'll not be goin' anywhere ever again," said Redbeard, less sadly than one might have expected that comment to sound. "Last thing I did was open up a couple of stopcocks on her. Memories on that boat I don't want to revisit. Restless ghosts…"

I looked back across and yes, sure enough, she was already lower in the water. She'd soon be sharing the same watery grave as her three late unlamented cold-hearted crewmen.

"Now lass, about yer treasure…"

Standing with hands on hips, Glexie glared at him. She'd been just about to console him on the loss of the boat.
"Really? Still? Are you truly mad? It's a hospital you need, not a box of somebody else's stuff. You *and* Nook."

The captain looked deflated. Single-minded as he could be, the prompting to consider his outsized friend struck home, especially given the source of the prompt. He looked over at the wounded giant who was sleeping, upright on a chair with his leg propped up on the table. Lanny's medicinal bottle of bourbon, kept for emergency use only, had been helpful.

In truth, Redbeard was just as in need of attention. There was a lot of blood soaked into his shirt and the coat he'd so far resisted removing, not least because he could scarcely move his right arm. He wasn't willing to have the coat cut off.

"Aye. O' course. Ye're right, fair lady."

Filling the awkward silence, Inigo asked, "How did you know where to find us?"

"Happy accident," grinned Cowley. "We were on our way to Teppy… Tepatamwa, and there ya were. We really did just stop to help a vessel in distress."

"To Tepatamwa?" repeated Redbeard. "How did you know we were…"

 The big man at the helm waved one hand airily.
"We-e-ell, that's where this treasure is supposed to be, isn't it?"

 I couldn't help myself. At the looks on Redbeard's and Inigo's faces, all I could do was laugh.

.oOo.

30 TREASURE

The pirates, or should I say ex-pirates, knew of a private medical clinic where, if enough money changed hands, no questions were asked about the origin of injuries.

Redbeard and Nook were patched up. Neither wound was life-threatening, although both had lost a lot of blood and the erstwhile captain was found to have been spared death by about one-and-a-half centimetres. At Ariane and Cowley's insistence, Glexie, John B. and I were all treated for the effects of shock. All five of us were ordered to rest.

Nonetheless, it was only a few days later that most of us were back on board the *Sense Of Adventure*, out on Casco Bay on our way back to Tepatamwa. The exception was Nook. The giant was comfortably ensconced on a motel bed with bags of pretzels, whoopie pies, and a television which had a 24-hour professional wrestling channel. I'd worried that I'd have to leave JB there with him – he admitted he was tempted.

Even Ariane was back out on the water, despite her last nerve-wracking experience in the unfamiliar environment of a boat.

We'd explained our destination on the northern part of the island. Redbeard and Inigo knew about the cliff we described. They'd seen it but paid no particular attention other than to recognise it as part of the island's useful natural defences. It certainly wasn't a place to land a boat.

Not to land a boat, but when we finally approached it, there was already a boat resting broadside to the cliff, her starboard hull bumping up against the rock face with the action of the waves.

Scuffed, battered, and with several inches of water slopping about her insides, it was the *Emma*. Our canvas bag full of towels and swimwear was even still there, albeit soaked through. This was where she'd eventually drifted to, driven by storm, captured by wind and currents.

I turned to JB and quietly asked, "Did you wish for that?"

He shrugged. "I wished that we'd find everything that we were looking for."

Once we were nearby, John B. jumped into the water. Ready to dive for the cave when we found it, he was already wearing boardshorts (a slightly morc faded purple than the long-sleeved t-shirt he had on, his token acknowledgement of the cold). He swam over to the lifeboat and attached a long line, the other end of which was secured to *Addy*. Cowley was happy to tow the battered craft back to Ogunquit with us.

Scanning the cliff from the navigator's chair, which Lanny had graciously vacated for me, I realised that one area of it protruded slightly from the generally flat surface. The slanting rays of the sun threw shadows that were the only way of spotting it. With two 'lobes' set quite high, the protrusion tapered down to a rough point about eight feet below. Yes. I didn't have to squint hard to see something like the shape of a heart outlined by the shadows.

A dark line running down almost the entire cliff indicated a deep crack. It passed through the left lobe of the 'heart'.

I pointed the feature out to Lanny.
"I don't know how visible that'll be from the water," I said. "Keep an eye on it, and let me know when I'm directly underneath it."

With that, I doffed the track pants and sweater that I'd been wearing. Having experienced the icy waters of Casco Bay only recently, I'd made sure that this time I was prepared. My beau's magic credit card had provided me with a good quality wetsuit. Nonetheless, I had to steel myself before I dived in. Similarly outfitted in skintight neoprene, Glexie followed suit, as I'd already invited her to. Redbeard sighed longingly.

"Yes, boss, I know you'd love to be diving for it as well," said Inigo sympathetically.

"Aye, matey. That too."

Inigo itched to be in the water as well, I think, but someone had to be in a position to come after us if there was any sign of trouble. He'd volunteered, but a little reluctantly.

There was no need for the diving equipment of Redbeard's earlier working life. As Wehmisemawa had indicated, the cave mouth wasn't far below the waterline, although deep enough to be invisible. There was a passage, filled with sea water. We resurfaced, inhaled big lungsful of air, and dived again. Using the waterproof torch Redbeard had provided, John B. cautiously led the way into the passage. He wasn't the strongest swimmer of the three of us, but was determined to face any potential risks first and rely on the two better swimmers to rescue him if required.

There were no risks. The passage very soon curved dramatically upward, and the three of us popped our heads up out of the water long before running out of breath became an issue. We found ourselves in a roughly spherical cavern. It was like a bubble inside the rock, maybe fifteen feet in diameter.

The torchlight created weird shadows from the irregular rock surface, but I saw one long dark horizontal shadow that I knew must have been cast by a ledge above us. It was about one-and-a-half body lengths above the waterline – a good climb for one of the muhkeahweesug, I mused. But not too challenging for my beau, who I knew had scaled far worse cliffs in the recent past.

Having held the torch to illuminate his ascent, I tossed it up to him on the ledge at his signal. I heard him whistle softly.

"There's room enough for us all up here, I reckon," he called quietly. A loud voice would have reverberated into a tangled noise in the small space.

Glexie was treading water, one hand resting on the rock wall.
"You go, hon," she said. "This is your moment, it's your treasure that's up there."

We both knew she didn't just mean whatever boxes or hoard that might be on the ledge. I clambered up the torchlit vertical path that my wizard provided for me, only as careful as my enthusiasm would allow.

The ledge sat at the front of a deep horizontal gash in the rock. I suspected the miniature cave may have been an offshoot of the long fissure visible on the cliff outside. The cleft was of a height and depth sufficient for two of the muhkeahweesug to have crawled in side by side on their bellies and been almost lost to view.

"Not sure that I can fit in there, pretty lady," John B. admitted. "Here, protect your wetsuit a bit with this. Best not to rip it and let the cold in, eh?"

He peeled off his purple shirt and handed it to me.

"You've been just waiting to see me in a wet t-shirt, haven't you?" I teased.

"Sure 'nough, ma'am," he replied in his cartoon Southern accent, a broad grin splitting his face.

I laughed, leaned forward and kissed him. I was glad of the material though, a torn wetsuit is pretty much useless and I'd quickly come to value this one's insulation. The rock surface was abrasive above and below as I wriggled in. I maneuvered the torch as best I could. I was a little more than hip-deep into the small cave when the light picked up one, then two oblong shapes. Wooden boxes, end-on to me.

Torch clutched firmly in my left hand, I inched further forward and grabbed one of the boxes with my right. When I pulled, the old wood started to split under my fingers. Something glittered in the beam of light.

Muttering, I propped the torch as best I could against a rock, and put a careful hand on each side of the nearest box. I tugged gently, and it slid towards me easily even though it was quite heavy. Using my elbows and knees, and with John B. gripping my hips then my waist, I backed out.

"Hold this please, babe," I said with a smile, handing him my find. "There's another one yet."

The second box was quickly retrieved, despite it weighing even more than the first. I didn't want to open them there and then. Well, actually I did, but I knew that it wasn't really practical. Nor was it quite fair on the rest of our 'expedition', I thought. The two containers were each the size and shape of an elongated shoe box. Together they fitted neatly inside John B.'s shirt, which we tied around them as securely as possible. He announced that he wouldn't be in the water long enough for the cold to be too much of a problem for him.

Very carefully we got the boxes down. I lay hanging over the ledge and handed the bundle to John B, clinging with one hand and toes to the vertical wall. Balancing it carefully, he descended a little way to where he could lean sideways and pass it on to Glexie, who'd climbed up just out of the water at a different point. Clutching the treasure tightly she dropped back off the wall. If we'd let go of them at any point they would have sunk like lead and may never have been found again.

John B. climbed down, with me close behind after handing the torch to him. The three of us bobbed in the water for a few moments. I suspect all of us wore smiles so bright you could have read by them.

"You better take this, hon," said Glexie, holding the heavy purple-wrapped parcel out to me.

"Thanks," I said, and was surprised when both she and my beau leaned to kiss me on the cheek as I took it.

John B. led the way back out with the torch. I followed, clutching Prince Henry's treasure, with our lovely tattooed lady swimming at my heels.

We were helped back aboard *Addy* with great enthusiasm, as you'd expect. The eight of us were soon clustered around the beech table behind Lanny's navigator's chair. I untied the purple t-shirt and gently slid the boxes out. Their wooden lids had been nailed in place, but the timber had softened with age and damp atmosphere, so offered little resistance when I pulled at the edges.

Nobody was disappointed, least of all me.

One box contained a mix of items. There were two gold goblets, studded with rubies and embossed with the St. Clair crest. Silver cutlery. A hunting knife with the same crest on the hilt together with an oval sapphire the size of the top joint of my thumb. A less opulent 'dress' dagger (called a *skean dubh* or 'black knife', JB tells me), set with a piece of polished jet. There were numerous loose gems, none of them small. None of the small quantity of jewellery was feminine. The locket that Wehmisemawa had given me was the closest thing to that. There were several gold chains with pendants, mostly in Celtic stylings. Some very masculine rings, gold with a variety of gems. We identified a few kilt pins and some silver buckles. One of the pins was set with a yellowish stone I recognised as a cairngorm – a distinctive and now rare Scottish stone. I'd been given one on a silver brooch when we were on Islay. This had been what first caught the light and glittered in the cave.

The other box had been the heavier one, and it held nothing but coins. Lots of them. Packed almost solid. We let them spill out across the tabletop. Mostly European coins, with a few others that John B. suggested might have been Persian. His history reading to the fore again, he identified currency from Scotland, England, Scandinavia and Spain, together with a few old Roman pieces. The majority however were Italian, or more precisely Venetian, from the 14th Century.

Now came the question of what to do with it all. I didn't ask it out loud – I figured I'd have been overwhelmed with answers. There were enough options already ringing in my head.

Instead, I insisted we pack it all away. Lanny provided a sturdy old ammunition box that held everything, and was far less likely to fall apart than the six-hundred-year-old wood.

"I'll inventory it all when I'm back in Portland," I announced. "First things first though. We have to get *Emma* back to Arnold Janesmann. Poor bloke's been remarkably patient with us."

Glexie smiled. She was Arnold's accountant. "He wasn't worried. The boat was well insured. I suspect he'd have been happy to take the money and start on a whole new project. Still, he'll have some restoration work to amuse himself with."

My beau quietly offered to help bankroll that with his Swiss-backed credit card. He expected there would be delays in any insurance claim, given that it had been arranged through Drake Professional Services.

We'd heard about the finding of Lachlan Drake's body. Both Ariane and Glexie had been routinely quizzed about their boss's movements, known associates, etcetera when they first returned to Ogunquit. Of course, they were as helpful as they could be, which was not at all. The only surviving person who could have been connected with the crime was Inigo McCallum, the murderers' lookout, and neither girl was interested in making his life any more difficult.

A contrite Redbeard also offered to anonymously help with repairing the *Emma*. Labour, money or both, as required.

In the end though, Arnold refused all assistance. His business was going well, he told us that afternoon when we returned his lifeboat to him. So well that he had the money and time to let his staff run the timber yard while he settled into his boatshed to enjoy the long and happy task of bringing *Emma* back to even better condition than she'd been in previously. Had some interesting ideas about improving the steam engine, too, if we wanted to hear them? He took my polite refusal with cheerful good grace, although I think he'd hoped Glexie might show some interest in helping him again. Her interests now seemed to be elsewhere.

After leaving Arnold's boatshed we went our separate ways. *Addy* was heading back to her berth in Ogunquit, where the fastidious Cowley would have the scuffs and bumps she'd sustained cleaned up. He and Lanny were delighted to have the company of the two girls for a little bit longer. Redbeard was correspondingly disappointed to be waving them farewell – he was staying in Portland.

He did brighten considerably at Glexie's cry of "See you in a few days!" – it had been directed to all of us, but in his mind the call was for an audience of one.

John B. and I had earlier reclaimed Yvette from the car park where we'd left her long before, remarkably not towed away despite the festoon of parking tickets she now wore. Another job for the magic credit card…

We dropped the former pirates at their hotel, letting them have the pleasure of recounting the story to Nook. He'd have been sorry he missed it. Then we headed for our own accommodation, several blocks away.

John B. lugged the ammunition box and its fabulous contents into our room, and put it on the floor under our little writing desk. I sat down on the end of the bed, landing (I must admit) like the proverbial sack of potatoes.

"Sorry babe," I said. "I know I should be skipping with delight right now, but honestly, after everything that's happened in the last little while, I'm just stuffed."

"The equivalent of a post-Christmas letdown," said JB as he sat beside me and put an arm around my shoulders. "Sweetheart, how about I take us to dinner tonight at that little French place we found? Would that lift your spirits? Especially if it included a good bottle of real champagne?"

I nestled into his embrace. "Sounds bloody lovely, babe."

My darling beau immediately got up and called the restaurant to make a booking. As he put the phone down he turned back to me.

"Dinner in two hours. Now, pretty lady, in the meantime, would you like a massage, or would you prefer to sit over here and start counting your doubloons?”

 My response was to get up off the bed and throw my arms around him as I whispered into his ear.
“I know what’s really valuable.”

 We were only a little late arriving for dinner.

.oOo.

31 LOOT

A letter from Peter Baron, a bartender who works the evening shift at the 'Aye Noah Place', to one of his former regular customers:

Dear Cliff

It was so lovely to receive your card, and I'm thrilled that you're intending to come back at the end of winter. I can't say I blame you for wanting to stay in Florida until then, although of course I'm terribly sorry it hasn't worked out for you there as you'd hoped.

There's been quite a bit of excitement here in our sleepy old part of Maine lately. That lawyer, Lachlan Drake, was murdered in the alleyway behind our very Club - can you imagine the shock? No-one's been arrested yet. We were all questioned, of course, but nobody saw anything. I was working that night and I hadn't even noticed Drake in the bar. Nothing on our expensive CCTV of course, it only shows the doorway and nobody came in or out that. All terribly mysterious!

Then Dean Parsons was found murdered near Popham Beach. You know - Sam McFerris' friend. That was quite gruesome, apparently. And again, no-one has been arrested. Not for the murder, anyway.

When the police went to Parsons' house over by the seaside looking for clues thy found a lot of stolen goods. Electrical goods, jewellery, all sorts of items.

Even a number of small things from our Club. Mc-
Ferris of course denied all knowledge of them and
said they must be Dean's, but apparently his finger-
prints were all over most of it.

There was a picture in the newspaper of him being
led away with a towel wrapped around his waist. It
seems that when they first went to arrest him he'd
tried to get away out the back of the house. In the
struggle he backed into an oil drum where he'd been
burning something - evidence I'd say, although I'm
not one to gossip - and his shorts had caught alight.
He's supposed to have screamed, "Not again!" before
the policemen beat out the flames. (I suspect they
enjoyed that more than he did, tee-hee!) The newspaper ran the picture under a heading, 'PANTS ON
FIRE'.

Even if he does talk his way out of the Receiving Stolen Goods charge, I don't think anyone here will be
believing any of Saxa's stories for a very long time.

I do hope the news of these unsolved murders doesn't
change your mind about coming back, my dear.
They seem to have been isolated incidents. If anything, the atmosphere is a little nicer here than
before. Some of the more unpleasant clientele have
stopped coming in - maybe it was the police presence,
or maybe they've just moved on.

Stay warm and safe, dear Cliff. I'm terribly excited at the prospect of seeing you again and I'll be
counting the weeks, oh alright months, until the end
of winter.

Love, Peter

.oOo.

32 SETTING COURSE FOR NEW HORIZONS

It was only a few days before we all got together again, but several people's lives had changed direction considerably in that time.

The demise of Lachlan Drake meant the demise of his business. His former staff would be financially secure for a while. The accountant and legal officer had made sure of that quite some time ago. But still, they were all suddenly unemployed. Jeremy had already grabbed his Separation Payment and gone west, intending to make his mark in Los Angeles. Neither Ariane nor Glexie had thought that far ahead though.

The former crew of the *Ondine* couldn't get out of their motel fast enough. Being stuck on the mainland gave them itchy feet right up to their armpits. Redbeard had simply walked out of his room and bought the first seaworthy vessel he could find that the three of them would be able to manage.

He was still financially secure thanks to Black Sam Bellamy. In fact, the captain had long since liquidated the vast assets he'd found, and had an account in the same Swiss bank as John B. He was quite possibly wealthier than my beau, not that they ever compared notes to my knowledge. Lacking the imagination to see past the story of the initial salvage, Blood had simply never guessed the truth.

I'm sure it was hard for Nook to put his considerable weight on that injured leg, even with a cast and crutches, but he was still determined to be back on Tepatamwa. There was work to be done, and even on one leg Nook could lift and carry more than two average men. Likewise, Redbeard himself was severely hampered by bandages and sling, but his organizational skills and creativity were undiminished, and he could still give orders.

He was a changed man, though. The betrayal by the POETs, and especially his brother, had hurt him deeply. Not just their betrayal of him, but

of the 'code' he'd thought they all lived by. He was torn – he'd completely immersed himself in the buccaneer life, but now some harsh reality was
intruding on his fantasy world. He had some sense of the impact of his
actions.

I'd already received a message at our hotel, letting me know John B.,
Glexie and I would be getting our phones back as soon as we all saw each
other again. Most of the other stolen goods had already long since passed
into the hands of the likes of Dean Parsons. Insurance would have eventually covered the majority of those losses, but Redbeard felt the weight of
an unknown number of lost lives on his shoulders. Neither Lister brother
had been well-endowed with conscience, but at least Edward was starting
to be aware of a moral compass.

I'd spent nearly a full day examining and listing every item in the White
Prince's legacy. I hadn't sought valuations yet, but I was pretty sure I'd
suddenly become Independently Wealthy. The 'independent' was the bit
that mattered to me. I love JB, and I want to be with him, but I'm much
happier for not feeling reliant on the magic credit card. In fact, I look
forward to setting up one of my own, now.

The next move for John B. and I would be to drive Yvette down to New
York, where I'd identified some reputable dealers and auctioneers. Not
the type who fenced stolen goods. The sort of people who would ask
pertinent questions about provenance and ownership – questions that, with
Ariane's help, I already had well-documented answers to.

We'd heard interesting things about Christmas time in the Big Apple, too.
It seemed like a good opportunity for a little break - just the two of us.

Not all of the boxes' contents would be being sold though. Not by me, at
any rate. I was determined that some of my windfall would be shared with
the people who'd helped me to acquire it.

I packaged up various items to present to people over the dinner we'd
planned. Cowley had recommended a place on the outskirts of town that
overlooked the Bay – the Green Swordfish. The view, he'd said, was

just about as good as the food, and that was superb. Ordinarily, I think we'd have struggled to book a large table on only a few days' notice, but Cowley and Lanny were regulars. I suspect a quiet wish from my wizard didn't go astray either.

As it turned out, the Misters Honeywell and French couldn't stay for dinner. ("Long-standing arrangement with Lanny's family. Can't argue with the in-laws," Cowley had quietly explained, disappointed.) They made sure to meet us all in the bar of the Green Swordfish beforehand though.

The two guys were thrilled when they unwrapped their package to find the two goblets.

"But it's your family heritage," Lanny had tried to protest.

"I have a family of choice who mean far more to me, my friend," I replied. "You two are a fabulous couple, and have an appreciation of history – these seemed appropriate."

"Ya got that right. On all counts," said Cowley, wrapping me in an enormous bearhug.

Texas Dorothy couldn't get to the restaurant, she said with regret, and had refused any gift other than to be told our story in more detail (another important reason for writing this all down – I'll be sending her the document soon). However, she was pleased to accept the offer of several chains on behalf of the Micmaq, doubtless to be used in their story-dancing. I even heard Mac barking his enthusiasm in the background.

When I'd mentioned the quantity of Venetian coins, Dorothy had gone unusually quiet for a moment. Just before ending our call, she said I might consider taking at least some of them back to Venice. There was a note of uncertainty in her voice as she recommended one particular museum there. "Ah don't reckon she'll be up fer payin' ya anythin' like top dollar, mind, but Ah do know she can give ya their history, if yer interested."

I wrote down the details.

Like the authoress, Redbeard was also reluctant to accept anything. He'd had enough treasure of his own, he now realised, and felt guilty about the trouble and distress he'd caused me. All of which was true, but I also recognised that he'd saved me from his brother's excesses on more than one occasion. As a nod to his piratical fascination, I'd hoped to find amongst the coin hoard some authentic 'pieces of eight'.

Unfortunately, my historically-inclined beau advised me that I was "about a hundred years too early". He explained that 'pieces of eight' were Spanish pesos, eight of which equaled a 'real', but that they hadn't been introduced until 1497, over a century after Prince Henry set out from his Orkneys home.

What I did have from Spain was a mix of silver maravedi, gold dobla and castellana. According to John B.'s reading, the relative values of these had changed wildly over many years, and this 'currency anarchy' was what prompted the change to pesos and reals. So, I settled for selecting a couple of impressive gold specimens.

Redbeard was delighted with them. There'd been nothing approaching their age in what he'd found of Black Sam's treasure. He wouldn't be selling them, he swore. Scribbling on a napkin he was soon designing a setting to turn the coins into a pair of earrings without damaging them, John B. watching with interest.

His two faithful crewmen were just as happy with their own 'rewards'. I'd found for Nook a ring, with a dark stone I thought matched his eyes. Knowing there was no prospect of it fitting on even his smallest finger, I'd looped one of the chains through it so he could wear it around his neck if he wished. For the expert swordsman I chose the black knife. Both the colour and the blade seemed ideal, and Inigo agreed.

I'm not quite sure what prompted me to pick out the cairngorm kilt pin for Ariane. It resembled the one from Islay that I loved. Perhaps there was something in me that recognised that we shared at least some similar tastes. Certainly, she seemed pleased with it.

The choice for her housemate was much easier. One of the pendants was a beautifully crafted piece of intertwined gold and silver. The design was a circle of stylized fish, or perhaps dolphins, set inside a thin band of Celtic knotwork. It was a perfect complement to the oceanic tattoo that adorned her arm, a fact immediately obvious at the Green Swordfish when she wore it as soon as she'd unwrapped it.

That had left one person. When I first offered JB his choice of anything amongst the White Prince's legacy he shook his head.
"I've got exactly what I want already. You. Alive, well, safe and happy."

But I was insistent. I wanted him to have something out of my family history, to keep as his own. He ran his fingers through the items spread out on the bed. First he selected a chain, from which he hung the Viking pendant he'd saved from Teef. After I looped that around his neck he picked up an amethyst, small but cut so as to capture its colour perfectly. "I reckon this would look good in a ring," he said. "Is there another like it?"

"No," I replied, then suddenly realised his meaning. "But there is a turquoise that caught my eye."

I found the stone I had in mind. They turned out to be almost the same size and shape as each other. Funny that. With old-fashioned formality we handed a stone to each other – JB bowed and I curtsied.

"Will y'all accept this as a token of mah affection, ma'am?"

"Why, goodness me – thank ya suh, Ah shall!" I replied, matching his cartoon drawl. "And will you accept this as a token of mine?"

"It would be my honour, pretty lady."

We didn't mention our small gems at the dinner, preferring to let everyone enjoy their own moments.

It wasn't a 'formal' occasion, but everyone had made efforts to look good.

We were an elegant group and attracted a few admiring looks from around
the restaurant as coats were hung up at the door and we all gathered at the
bar before being shepherded to our table, directly overlooking the waters
of Casco Bay.

The material of Glexie's strapless, sleeveless long dress reminded me of
the painting 'Waterlilies'. I wasn't the only person who thought it looked
superb, especially with the addition of her new pendant.

Ariane wore a beautiful black silk dress that bared one pale shoulder.
There was no white fabric in her ensemble, for a change, so her own complexion created the attractive contrast.

The same effect was achieved by Inigo's outfit, which included another
black satin shirt similar to the one he'd loaned me. Seeing the two of them
standing together chatting I mused that they might make a good couple, if
only one or the other was a different gender.

It was hard for a man of Nook's build to look dapper, but he was at least
smart. He wore a dark blue shirt and dark trousers that were well-tailored
to be comfortable without being baggy, even over the cast on his leg. I
suppose at his size most clothes had to be specially made to fit properly,
and Redbeard hadn't stinted at the expense.

Speaking of Redbeard, he was rather less eccentrically dressed than usual.
Long frock coat hanging in the foyer, he had an extravagant brown-and-
gold silk vest over a good white linen shirt and plain black trousers. He
still wore black leather boots, but they were only calf length, and weren't
adorned with silver buckles their whole length. He'd even trimmed his
beard, a little.

My beau was dressed very 'Islay'. I'd bought the purple silk shirt for him
there, and over it he wore the tartan waistcoat made from the plaid he'd
been presented with. I'd (just) convinced him that teaming it with the
trousers made from the same material would be overkill. Instead he wore
a newly acquired pair of black jeans. I did like the snug way they fitted
him.

As for me, I wore a green dress (well, 'sage' to be precise). Off the shoulder, a style JB loves and that I've also come to realise suits me. Long, but slit to above my knee. Of course, it was satin. I knew we weren't competing (I knew, I knew) but I thought my outfit stood up pretty well alongside Ariane and Glexie. Plenty of approving looks came my way anyway, most importantly from my beau.

During the course of our excellent meal Redbeard dropped a small bombshell. He was of the opinion that it was time for him to get away to somewhere different. Make a new start, somewhere well removed from recent history. The facilities on Tepatamwa could be disassembled and disposed of. The island would be left in something close to pristine condition

He still wanted to honour Black Sam Bellamy's legacy, but the thieving side of piracy had lost its appeal. He'd had the idea of building a new boat on the same lines as *Ondine* and setting her up somewhere as a tourist attraction. A small floating museum of buccaneer life. Day trips perhaps. Inigo and Nook had already made it clear that they wanted to stay on as his crew, wherever they wound up.

Deep in thought, Glexie mused, "I wonder if that would work in Hawaii. Would tourists want to 'sail with the pirates' there?"

"Hawaii? Good tourist dollars there, lass, aye. A long way away from Maine," the captain replied.

"I've got a property over there. Right on the water on the Big Island. I won it in a golf tournament," she said thoughtfully.

"So, ye think there might be a future for us, me darlin'?"

"A business future, bucko. Don't get your hopes up for anything more."

"Arr, but I was thinkin'…"

"Be very careful when you do that," warned Ariane. "It's got you into trouble before."

"Business future's better than no future, boss," said Nook, once again being smarter than he looked.

"I thought when we left there you said you were over Hawaii?" Ariane asked her best friend, more in amusement than criticism.

"Not half as much as I'm over New England!" Glexie exclaimed.

"And what about the homeless shelter?" the legal advisor continued, mildly.

"The what?" asked Inigo, who was struggling to keep up with where the conversation was headed.

The girls explained that when Glexie had won the ten-year lease on the beachfront property she'd given it over to construction of a shelter for the homeless, with the aid of Hiro Tanabe and his wife Shareta. Hiro was a wealthy Japanese Hawaiian businessman they'd befriended during the golf tournament, Shareta his beautiful Korean wife who'd narrowly lost to Glexie in the tournament final.

"Well," said Glexie thoughtfully, "it *is* a pretty substantial allotment. I don't mind setting up shop and living next door to the shelter. I'm sure Hiro and Shareta have got it running properly!"

Redbeard shifted in his chair awkwardly. "If it all turns out ta be a bit, er, squeezy, I might, er, have a few doubloons left ta help them poor unfortunates into a place not quite on the waterfront. Maybe a way of givin' back some of Blood's ill-gotten gains."

There was a good chance that there was more than enough left of what he'd found of Black Sam's haul to buy a very long lease on a handy bit of Hawaiian property, put up an appropriate building, pay some staff and feed twenty people well for a long time to come.

Ariane folded her arms and looked contemplative. "I suppose someone had better go along and make sure that everything is kept legal."

"You're over New England too?" asked John B., concern in his voice.

"Put it this way, my friend – there's nothing to keep me here." She reached out and squeezed his hand, both of them remembering their first meeting. "Never know what, or who, I might find in Hawaii."

"Might even find some new crew amongst 'em poor homeless folks," the newly reformed pirate captain mused.

"I used to be homeless," said Nook quietly.

"Just what I was thinkin', me old shipmate," his captain replied.

"That would be a good start to your new start," agreed my wizard, who'd been following the discussion with considerable interest. "If you're as good as your word on that, then I'll happily wish you – all of you – success in your new ventures and adventures."

"Dorothy is quite right. There's a story in this," I said, raising my glass. "And I think there are a lot of stories to come. Just so long as they don't involve anyone holding a sword at my or anyone else's throat," I added meaningfully.

 John B. looked fixedly at Lister and his crew, and said, "I reckon the odds of that are about the same as the odds of there being a mysterious sea serpent lurking off the Hawaiian coast."

 Redbeard looked over his shoulder for a moment, up into the far reaches of the bay where maybe Cassie was frolicking unseen in the waters around Tepatamwa Island. Then he clinked his glass against mine. "Aar, I'll drink ta that!" he said warmly.

"Boss, you'll drink to anything," observed Inigo with a laugh.

As all glasses were raised in the toast John B. quietly remarked to me, "It's funny – people used to say that about me, too. But maybe I'm not the man I used to be."

I looked at him, and thought of the name of the island where we'd fought so hard to be together. Tepatamwa. Love.

"Babe, I love the man you are."

.xXx.

– KISACYEMEWA –

The *Dubious Magic* Books:

THE WIZARD OF WARAMANGA

THE CARVINGS OF COBBEMARMOO

THE MAD MACHINES OF MUNDARA

THE WARRIORS OF WIWO'OLE

THE SPIRITS OF SRON DUBH

THE SAILORS OF SVALGSAY

THE TREASURE OF TEPATAMWA

Visit **renoirwords.com**

Next: Venice is very old, rich in history and tradition. It's also home to one of the world's great celebrations – Carnevale. Here, more than ever, John B. and Elizabeth learn that things are not always as they seem. Deceit and danger lurk in the shadows. Some of it is up close and personal, but some of it is ancient and may unleash dark forces that threaten far more than the city of canals.

THE MASKS OF MANOVALO - The Eighth Book of Dubious Magic